WORLD WEAVERS

SAM GAYTON

ANDERSEN PRESS

First published in 2023 by
Andersen Press Limited
20 Vauxhall Bridge Road, London SW1V 2SA, UK
Vijverlaan 48, 3062 HL Rotterdam, Nederland
www.andersenpress.co.uk

2 4 6 8 10 9 7 5 3 1

British Library Cataloguing in Publication Data available.

ISBN 978 1 83913 126 4

Printed and bound in Great Britain by Clays Ltd, Elcograf S.p.A.

For Buffy and for Ruth –
Not-So-Quiet Sisters

PART ONE

THE BOOK
OF SHADOW

Kid tracks the waythread west, until he crosses to a raggedy world.

Above him, twin suns burn like a pair of red unblinking eyes. There's not much left beneath their bloodshot gaze. The wind blows through the scorched grass and the dust devils upon the highways. The endless ashen slopes lie stubbled with the charred stumps of pine trees. The ranches are burned down and silent, their barns and houses all empty as skulls. People used to live here. Now there's only Kid.

He's been on this waythread's trail for a long, long time. Every step's an effort now. His boots are full of blisters and his shirt soaked with sweat. The thirst pounds in his head and rakes its nails down his throat. No water in this place, and Kid's own supply ran dry a few worlds back. Ever since then, he's been forced to pattern.

Dropping to his knees, he scoops up a handful of ground from beneath his boots. The rust-red dust is heaped with odd bits of coloured plastic trash. Curls and chunks and twists of it, like fossils of ancient plankton. Kid sits in the shade of a boulder and picks all them bits out carefully. Then he closes his eyes. He has to close his eyes before he can pattern. All world weavers do.

Kid takes hold of the tiny thing that he wears holstered

in the crook of his left arm, and slips it over the tip of his forefinger.

It looks just like a thimble. Exactly like a thimble.

As soon as it's on, Kid can see the dust in his hand. His mind holds the pattern of it, the way a loom holds thread. His thimbled fingertip twitches as he sets to work upon it, unravelling and reweaving its shape, thread by thread, turning its pattern from hot to cold, from dry to wet, from dust to water.

Kid opens his eyes again and sees it welling from his hand, clear and cold as a spring.

He drinks in deep gulps. Wetness runs down his chin. Then he rinses the dust from his mouth and turns his head and spits and it lands on a rock under the suns and sizzles like an egg in a pan. He patterns more handfuls, splashes the water over his suns-burned face. He wipes his wet hands in his hair and then he stands up and feels beads of it dribbling down his neck and soaking into his collar and drying almost instantly.

When Kid's done, he points the thimble at the ground, sweeping his finger back and forth as he feels around again for the waythread. It shimmers in and out of sight like a mirage in the heat, until finally Kid catches it again and pins it down beneath his boots. The waythread is a shining ribbon of silver, the width of a little finger and the colour and sheen of moonlit water. It runs through the dust like a rivulet, heading west, heading further than west, all the way beyond this world, and all the way to the Quiet sisters.

• • •

4

Later that afternoon the first shift comes on the wind. Kid stops walking and breathes it in. There's a smell of spring blossom and warm rain and wet grass. A scent not of this world but of the world that is to come, carried on a wind that weaves across two places and two patterns. The waythread is leading him out of this world and shifting him into the next. Perhaps this one will hold the sisters.

Pebbles slide down a slope behind him. Kid whirls around, the forefinger of his right hand quickly slipping on his thimble. He points his finger like a pistol and sweeps the hills with his eyes closed.

There's nothing. Just this world sliding further into ruin and dust. Must've been the breeze that moved them. But Kid's hand still tingles and his heart beats hard. If a breeze can cross over into this pattern then so can other things.

Further on, the waythread weaves around a vast scattering of boulders, all of them smooth and pink-speckled, like prehistoric eggs. As Kid passes by, some of those pink spots tremor and shed from the rock and flutter in the air like the ghosts of butterflies.

He kneels down and picks one of them up. They are blossom petals. From trees that did not bloom in this world. Kid nods. He smiles, even though smiling makes his cracked lips bleed. He's very close now.

He'll need to rest before the final shift. He hasn't slept or stopped in almost two days and he is beyond exhausted. His feet are blistered raw and his skin is scoured by the dust and burned by the suns and his head aches from the constant effort of tracking the waythread. He steps off it carefully and closes his eyes to watch its quicksilver gleam drain down into the dust again.

That evening he sits by his campfire and watches the flames of it stream upwards in orange ribbons tinged with green. When he needs more wood he weaves it out of the dust and tosses it inside the circle of stones. Above him the two suns slip away one after the other until night comes, starless and cold. All constellations here long since burned out like old lightbulbs. The fire is the only thing shining in all this vast and desolate world.

Sometimes blossom petals drift into light and vanish away again into the dark. Kid hunches up with his arms around his knees and shuffles closer to the flames. He slips on his thimble and from the rising smoke he weaves himself a blanket, thickening it in the air with his finger like candyfloss on a stick. He reaches out and pulls it around his shoulders and shivers until he's warm.

He badly needs to sleep but he's afraid. The dark is all around him, so deep it is like something he might fall into and drown. And not all of it is night-time dark. There is another darkness out here, as there is in all worlds gone raggedy. It is a darkness Kid can feel whenever he closes his eyes. A darkness that is bleeding through from the place beyond the pattern, until it clots like a scab into some horrendous thing, with teeth and a sucking mouth and dark pinhole eyes.

The blanket has warmed Kid but he is still shaking. His

fear is the kind of fear that grows deep down, like cancer in a bone. It burrows and it gnaws and he can't make it stop. He slips on his thimble and points a trembling finger at the darkness. At last his arm drops and Kid shakes his head. He needs rest. He needs to get his strength back for the last stretch of waythread. Can't be staring wide-eyed into the dark all night. Someone else'll have to do that for him.

With the thimble still on his forefinger, Kid looks around for something to pattern. Turns to the boulder nearest to him. It's rough and reddish and not too big. It'll do.

Closing his eyes, Kid gets to working. Begins to weave and quicken the stone. Until the boulder shudders and grunts and shakes off the blossom petals atop it. And all the while, beyond the firelight, the darkness blots and clots and thickens.

'Hello,' Kid says to the pattern he has made. 'I'm Kid.'

The rock sits up in the light of the fire and blinks its dark round eyes.

'I know!' it says happily. 'And I am your best friend.'

Kid is grinning. He's done it. Actually done it. Woven a living thing out of the stone. He wasn't sure if this world's pattern would let him, but it has. The rock is now this copper-coloured furry creature, with a long blunt face with little round ears on top of its head and a few short whiskers. It looks cute and kind of fierce and very, very friendly.

'What's your name?' he asks it.

His new friend stands up on hind legs. Tall as Kid's knees or thereabouts.

'My name,' it decides, 'is Crockett. Because you can't spell Crockett without rock in it, and you can't make a me unless you've got a rock too.'

Kid's grin is a grin with a chuckle now. 'That's smart. I like that.'

'And I like you. And I like your smile and your very nice teeth and I don't even care that they are a bit wonky.'

Kid laughs. He is not ashamed to admit that he is beyond pleased with how Crockett has turned out. In all honesty, he intended to pattern a dog, but somehow he has ended up with something much better. He watches his new friend comb through its reddish fur with little black paws and notice things about itself.

'My name is Crockett,' it says again. 'And I am a boy, I think?'

Kid shrugs beneath his blanket. 'That's up to you.'

'And I am three minutes old, and I am a best friend to a kid with no memory.'

'I've got a memory,' Kid says, a little more defensively than he meant to. 'It just . . . doesn't go back very far.'

'My memory only goes back to three minutes ago.' Crockett wrinkles up his nose and thinks some more. 'Although, I know some things from before that. Like words and how to speak them and what they mean.'

Kid nods. 'That's right. I wove that knowing into you. It comes from me.'

'It comes from you,' Crockett repeats. 'That is why I am not sure how I feel about some of the things that you have given me to know about. Like, what is my favourite song? Do I like Tuesdays?'

Kid looks away into the world beyond the fire. 'That's how it is with me too,' he says softly.

Crockett beams. 'We have so much in common! It is no wonder we are best friends. But Kid, why have you forgotten all about yourself? What world are you from? Who are your family? Where are they?'

'I don't think I've forgotten, Crockett. I think I'm like you. I think I've been made, not born.'

'Someone patterned you, the way you patterned me?'

Kid gives a shrug that says, *I reckon so*.

Crockett lets out an *ohhh* sound. Then looks around the campfire. 'If you're the someone that patterned me,' he says, 'then where's the someone that patterned you?'

Kid chuckles quietly. 'That, I'm not too sure of. You know as much as I do, Crockett.'

'I do?' Crockett tips his furry head from side to side as the knowledge Kid has woven there tumbles and slots into place. 'Oh! I do! You've been woven so you can fetch the Quiet sisters, from whichever world they are in?'

'Yes,' says Kid.

'And help them get back to their mother?'

'Yes,' says Kid.

'Because children need to be with their mothers?'

Kid considers this. 'Most do, yeah.'

Crockett does another *ohhhh*. 'Is this mother the one who wove you?'

'Could be.' Kid rubs at his jaw. His head is mostly gaps. No answers there, just spaces where answers ought to be. He prods at those holes, like a tongue at a gum after a tooth comes out.

Crockett puts his little hands on his hips and wrinkles up his nose. 'Well, it's all very secret.'

'Maybe it has to be. There's a war on, you know.' Kid waves a hand at the dark and ruined world around them, as if to say, *What else do you think did this?*

'The war,' says Crockett softly, remembering. 'Which side are we on?'

'The good side,' Kid says with certainty. 'The side that reunites missing children with their parents.'

'So you are like a spy? And the sisters are your mission?'

Kid nods. He likes that word. *Mission*. Something given to you, that you might not fully understand, but you know you have to do.

Beside him, Crockett stands up straight as a soldier. 'And it's my mission to help you with your mission, because helping is what best friends do! OK?'

Kid grins. 'OK.'

Crockett grins back, then he notices the little leather harness looped around his shoulder, and the ceramic dagger that Kid has patterned there in a scabbard.

'Is this for the baddies out in the dark that might come to kill you in your sleep?' he asks.

'They're not *in* the dark,' Kid tells him. 'They're *made* of dark. But yeah, I need you to guard me in case they come.'

Crockett looks at his knife dubiously. 'Can I not have a machine gun?' he asks. 'Or a bazooka?'

Kid shakes his head. 'Guns don't work that well against them.'

'Not even if it was a bazooka that fires laser-guided missiles and also can it please be made of cake?'

'Cake?' Kid shakes his head a second time. All kinds of weirdness are woven into this little critter.

'Yes,' Crockett confirms. 'Cake. Because once the laser missiles destroy the baddies, I would like to eat some and I think I should be allowed because, if you think about it, today is sort of my birthday.'

Kid shakes his head and grins despite everything. 'How are you making me smile right now?'

'That is the power of a best friend,' Crockett tells him solemnly. 'I can cheer you up no matter what. And your power is that you can make a gun that fires—'

Kid cuts him off. 'Not here, I can't. I can only weave what the world will let me. This isn't the sort of place where laser-missile gun-cakes can exist.'

'Oh.' Crockett lets out a sigh. 'Well, I will still not let them hurt you anyway. I will be guarding whilst you will be snoozing and if any baddies come they will be saying OUCH because my dagger will be poking them in the FACE.' Crockett shouts that last word beyond the fire's reach like a threat.

Kid's chuckle turns into a yawn that nearly topples him over. Now he has someone to watch over him, whatever was holding back his exhaustion breaks like a dam. He is so, so weary. Rest. He has to rest. Just for a little while. Just until he gets the strength to walk the final stretch of waythread. The last part is always the hardest. The most dangerous.

He snuggles up by the fire and wraps the blanket around his shoulders and slips the thimble over his finger, just in case. He sleeps without dreaming until he is woken by the undoers.

• • •

As Kid bolts up and throws off his blanket, the undoer is just shambling in to the light of the fire. It wears blue worn jeans and scuffed boots and a checked flannel shirt, the same as Kid is wearing. It looks like him in every aspect, apart from its face.

The undoer's face is not a face at all. Just two dark and lidless holes for eyes and a round lipless mouth with yellow inward teeth and no tongue. The mouth is hissing softly, like all undoer mouths do. It is the endless noise, like radio static, of this world's air and dust as it is sucked past those teeth and into the oblivion inside the undoer, where it is unravelled and annulled.

That is what undoers do. That is what they are. Emissaries of the darkness that hates all life, all pattern. Vessels for havoc.

On the far side of the fire stands Crockett, jabbing his tiny dagger at the undoer with two shaking paws. He is shouting, 'You will go away now, you bad baddie man!' But

Kid's little bestie is wrong in every way. The undoer will not go away, and it is not a man.

The undoer lunges for Crockett and it is fast but Kid is faster. He points his thimbled finger and shoots and the power lances from his hand, straight and sharp as a needle's jab. A quick mending stitch that weaves the undoer's mouth shut.

Even with the thimble to protect him, an icy cold shoots up Kid's arm and jolts his heart as he touches his power to the havoc inside the undoer. It falls backwards past the fire and reaches for Kid as it shrivels inwards. Then the dark hole in its chest drinks up its shape until it's gone.

Kid fumbles for the thimble that has fallen from his finger and into the folds of the blanket. He staggers to his feet, clutching his right arm. It feels like a frozen joint of meat. He hugs it to his chest to try and get some warmth back into it. He has no idea how much time has passed since he fell asleep but the suns have not yet risen and beyond the glow of the fire's embers the dark is absolute. Across from Kid, Crockett is standing on back legs, rigid with terror, his eyes wide and his little brown ears swivelling atop his head like radar dishes.

'How many more do you hear?' Kid says.

Crockett signals with his paw, and points south and east and north into the night. 'Lots,' he says back. His voice is very small.

Kid scrambles over to the fire and kicks out the embers and the sparks fly up from his boot heels like smithereens from beneath a hammer. Around him, the night is hissing faintly from a dozen unseen punctures. Won't be long before them holes start walking around for something to feed on.

Kid crouches behind a boulder with his right arm still numb and dangling and his thimble clutched tight in his left fist. He can hear the soft *pad pad pad* of boots across sand as more undoers shape and stand and walk in search of him. He swallows and tries to steady his breathing but the panic is like a hand over his mouth.

'Crockett!' he gasps, beckoning his friend to hide.

But Crockett doesn't move from beside the remnants of the fire. He stares at the dagger in his hand, and gives a small, heavy sigh.

Kid beckons at his bestie furiously. 'Crockett, what are you—'

'I am being a best friend,' Crockett says firmly. 'That's my mission. You do yours, Kid. You have to track the waythread. You must find the sisters.'

And before Kid can say or do anything, Crockett puts his dagger between his teeth and charges on all fours, yelling bizarre war cries of his own invention.

'I am on a mission of friendship!'

'Today is actually my birthday!'

'I am a laser-guided missile made of caaaaake!'

Kid rises from cover to run after his friend but Crockett has already leaped over the dying embers of the fire. He does a roly-poly into the dark on the far side, still yelling.

If Kid goes after him now, they're both dead. He crouches

14

back down and hides as Crockett – his poor, sweet friend Crockett – heads into the hissing darkness with nothing but a dagger and his courage.

Kid grits his teeth and closes his eyes tight so the tears can't squeeze out. Crockett's yells and the undoers' hissing both fade into the distance. Until at last Kid can't hear anything. Just silence settling back down upon the hills like a shroud. Sacrifices like that have to be honoured. They have to mean something. If Kid doesn't make it to the sisters now, Crockett lived and fought and died for nothing at all.

Staggering to his feet, holding back sobs, Kid gropes blindly for the waythread. Away from the embers the starless dark is deep and fathomless. Already he can hear more undoers opening up their mouths like a choir. He doesn't have long. Nor does this part of this world. Somewhere beneath the dust, the waythread is running like an underground river. Kid has to find it and pin it down and walk its last shifting stretch before the undoers reach him.

Something catches his boot. Kid stumbles and goes sprawling. His toe has snagged on something and pulled it up from the dirt in a shining, silver loop. The waythread, humming like a power line. Kid reaches out and grips it and yanks it upwards and its pale white glow illuminates the undoers all around him.

There are four that he can see. Each one a wretched and misshapen copy of Kid. With their matchstick limbs and coathanger shoulders. With their hollow chests like birdcages draped with chequered cloth. With their fingers pale and swollen and wriggling like grubs. With their empty pinprick eyes and open drainhole mouths.

Kid holds up his thimble, in the silence, in the dark, and the first undoer crumples up into a ball, like a paper bag. His arm goes numb to the elbow as it drops and shrivels to nothing. The others come hissing for him. Two of them fly backwards as Kid's power hits and the cold strikes him like a thunderclap. He staggers back, shuddering in some hideous dance, as the undoers thrash upon the floor and fade to stains in the dirt.

He turns and tries to run. Can't even open his eyes to see where the last undoer is. His eyelids have iced shut. His feet trip clumsily beneath him. He's so frozen he can barely breathe. The cold's like a hand on his throat. The fourth undoer is behind him, hissing like a viper.

Kid stumbles in blind terror. Flails out for the waythread as he falls. Scrapes his side and tears his shirt but is too cold to feel a thing. He scrabbles forward on hands and knees and reaches out, grips the waythread. It quivers, taut as a tightrope, as he hauls himself on. A little bit further. Just a little bit more.

Around him the pattern starts shifting. Leaves rustle. The smell of blossom and peaches. Warmth upon his skin that burns with cold fire. The waythread is crackling and shuddering as he passes from the fringe of this world to the next. A pale sun glows in the sky like an afterimage behind Kid's eyelids. Yellow sunlight flickers on and off like a faulty bulb.

Thin hands clutch him by his boot. Kid twists and kicks and pulls out his foot just as the undoer crams the whole shoe into its mouth. There's a crackle like dry leaves burning as the boot disappears into havoc. Kid drags himself by the hands across the waythread a little more. *Just cross, just cross, just make it across.* The thought shrieks out over and over like a klaxon. The worlds are shifting over him, back and forth like tides. Sunlight stutters back to darkness. Sand spikes into grass that crumbles back to sand. Trees sprout and wither and vanish and suddenly conjure again. The last undoer crouches over him, hissing.

It rolls Kid over and he throws a weak punch with his free hand and the side of the undoer's face crumples inwards like a plastic sheet and then inflates itself out again. It pins him down and kneels like a supplicant and lowers its plughole mouth to drain his pattern away.

Then the hands holding Kid are gone. The undoer rears back and is thrown sideways, bleeding havoc from the stumps of its arms. And Kid sees Crockett, there in his left eye and not there in his right, flickering like a candle flame in and out of sight. Caked in dust and riddled with bloody wounds. Darkness dripping like gore from the blade of his dagger. And before the undoer can reshape itself, Kid reaches out and hauls his bestie across two worlds and two patterns and hugs him tight as the worlds shift a final time.

The waythread is gone. There are trees around them and clouds. There is only one sun in the sky. There are no undoers.

Kid collapses onto wet grass, shuddering. His bestie beside him. They made it. They crossed over.

'Hooray,' Crockett says weakly. 'We are both not dead.'

They are in an orchard. Peaches the colour of setting suns hang above them in the branches. The trees are all in blossom and scenting the wind, and the wind moves the fat peaches hanging on their stems. Kid stares up at them, caked in dust from another world. Crockett is slumped beside him and likewise embalmed. Both his eyes are closed as if he has turned back into a stone.

'Kid?' says Crockett in a very small voice. 'I am leaking a little bit from fighting those undoers.'

Crockett's eyes flutter open. His breathing is very shallow. Kid tries to stand and can't. His strength has all run out of him like water from cupped hands. Crockett has so many wounds and they won't stop bleeding and the blossom falls petal by petal over him and over Kid.

Then Crockett looks left and Kid sees her at the exact same time. Through the gaps between the trees, they watch the girl picking. Walking through the rows, arms outstretched towards the boughs. Peaches piled deep in a wide wicker basket that she balances on one hip. She is singing very badly. Some song about a shotgun. All Kid can do is shiver weakly. The girl almost trips over his legs before she notices them.

'Good gosh,' she says in surprise. She backs away and cups her free hand to her mouth and hollers. 'Matilda? Matilda?'

From somewhere nearby another girl hollers back: 'Hush, I'm hauling water.'

'Well bring us some, would you?'

'What for?'

'Come see.' The girl takes off her cap, which is blue like her nails and has the word CHOREDOM written on it. She looks at Kid. 'What's your name, stranger?'

'Kid,' he says through chattering teeth. 'And this—' He doubles up, coughing. Whenever he blinks he sees men with terrible faces crowding behind his eyelids.

'Kid? That a nickname? I'm Celeste, but most people call me Hush. Our surname's Quiet, me and my sister. Only we're not. "You hush, Celeste Quiet." See how I got it? My sister that you heard just now is Matilda. Woe befall anyone that tries nicknaming her. Sometimes I call her Mattie but that's mostly just to goad her . . . I'm talking too much, ain't I? We all got flaws, and talking's mine. What colour waythread you track here, anyway?'

'Silvery-white. Like moonlight.' Kid lets his eyelids close again and this time the blackness behind them doesn't hold any monsters.

The Quiet sisters. He found them.

Everything will be all right now.

Another girl a little older and shorter than Hush stomps into view, hauling a tin bucket full to the brim. Must be Matilda. Broad freckled arms, rolled-up sleeves and dungarees. Twin braids swinging like fists in a prizefight. Water slops onto her boots as she comes to a standstill. She regards Kid

19

and Crockett, each in turn, and neither has the strength to do anything except be regarded.

'Havoc.' Matilda says the word like it's a curse. She fumbles in her pocket for her thimble. 'Stay back, Hush. You hear me?'

Hush just sighs. 'Aint like their eyes are pinholes, Mattie. It's just a boy and his, umm . . . his chinchilla, maybe?'

'Actually I am a best friend,' Crockett corrects in a whisper.

'A talking chinchilla,' says Hush in delight. 'And will you just look at that cute little sword.'

'Havoc,' says Matilda again. 'Is he thimbled?'

'Guessing he was but it fell off.' Hush peers around the grass until she finds it and holds it up. The little gleaming thing that Kid made Crockett and crossed a world with. 'Here it is.'

'Give it.' Matilda comes over and snatches the thimble and breathes out with visible relief. Then she peers down at Kid and Crockett. 'How in the worlds did they get here? All the waythreads are meant to be hid.'

Hush pokes her tongue into the gap between her teeth as she shrugs. 'Why're you asking me? Ask the guests.'

'Guests ain't the word for what they are, Hush—'

'Please help Crockett,' Kid rasps. It takes all of his strength to say.

Hush turns from squabbling with her sister and puts down the peach basket and squints at Kid and Crockett and

20

her eyes go even wider. 'Love and Mercy, Matilda. I thought they was just in need of a wash. The creetie's hurt pretty bad. Looks like undoers. I didn't see it for the dirt and the damn blossom—'

'Please,' Kid rasps. Crockett's breathing is very fast and very shallow. They have to mend him. They have to help.

'We ain't going near your creetie,' Matilda says. 'Why in all the worlds would you give a thing like that a sword?'

'I have been chopping off hands,' Crockett says very faintly.

Matilda's eyes go wide. 'I'm fetching Gram.' She points a finger. There's blue varnish on her nails, too, all shiny but chipped. 'Hush, you do not go near these two. I mean it. Stay right where you are. I ain't having you murdered and leaving me with all the housework.'

Matilda turns and barges her way through the trees. As soon as she is gone, Hush goes and gets the bucket and brings it over and kneels down by Kid and Crockett. There is sweat on her nose and at the base of her throat and she smells of chores and wet cut grass. Her eyes are muddy-coloured and her face is freckle-spattered and she is all joints and knuckles and she is greyhound-thin. She starts washing the dust off Crockett and her expression turns very grim and then she forces a smile and sits back and just takes hold of Crockett's tiny paw.

'You're going to be OK,' she says softly, like she's ashamed of the lie.

'You can't spell Crockett without rock in it,' Crockett whispers. Then he goes still as stone and dies and Kid sobs tears that wash clean lines down his face.

• • •

For three days, Kid fights a fever in a bed in the Quiets' house. His body shivers and burns and his head swirls with terrible dreams. Burning yellow eyes and trails of silver blood. Gloved hands sprouting up like weeds and reaching for his throat.

He is dimly aware of the cool cloths pressed to his forehead. Of the smouldering leaves that uncurl smoke from a tin dish by his bed. Hot broth gets fed to him in sips. A faint voice sings distant songs.

When he wakes, Kid is alone in a dimly lit room. A lamp glows on the cabinet beside his bed. The burning leaves in the tin dish have crumbled to ash and the air smells faintly of their peppery medicinal smoke. He sits up on elbows and looks at the whitewashed walls and thick wool curtains. His clothes are clean and dry and mended and folded neat as parcels on the seat of a battered cane chair.

That's all there is to look at. He closes his eyes to see what he can feel in the pattern. But there's nothing, because his thimble is gone. It's not on his finger. It's not on the cabinet. It's not over with his clothes, in the leather holster that straps around the sleeve of his shirt. It's not anywhere.

Can't weave without a thimble. Kid falls back onto the

pillow and lies there thinking for a long time. Around him, he listens to the sounds of the house. He must be on the upper floor because below him he hears kitchen noise. The groan and splash of taps, the clank of a tub, the scraping of plates.

It all sounds normal and safe. No raggedyness here, no undoers, no war. So why does he feel scared all of a sudden? Why is fear spreading through him like venom from a sting?

Because they took his thimble.

Because he's powerless and all alone.

And suddenly Kid remembers not being alone.

He remembers Crockett.

'Aw, Crockett,' Kid whispers. Tears are leaking out of his shut eyes. 'Aw, please no.'

He travelled through a world of dust and nightmares to find these sisters. He fought undoers in the dark. He watched his loyal little bestie turn still as a stone. All for his mission. All to find these sisters.

Below him a door slams and a trio of footsteps come up creaking stairs. Kid closes his eyes on instinct. He doesn't want them to know he's awake. When you've been scared your whole life, it's hard to shake the habit.

A key turns in the door and it opens a crack.

'Kid.' It's Hush. 'You awake yet?'

Kid says nothing. Just thinks: *So I'm locked in here, like a prisoner.*

Hush comes in, carrying water slopping in a pan. She clonks it not too gently upon the bedside cabinet with the lamp and the burned leaves and proceeds to dab at Kid's head with a wet cloth. The water is cool and beads of it dribble into his eyes. Would it be more convincing to lie still or fidget? Kid opts for fidgeting and turns his head away.

Matilda's voice comes from by the door frame. 'Wring out the rag, Hush.'

'I know.'

'She knows, Matilda,' says an older lady's voice. This must be the Gram they mentioned before. All three of them have the same rough and stomping accent.

'Don't lean over him like that,' Matilda tells her sister. 'I won't have a clean shot if he goes for you.'

There's a splosh as Hush sends the cloth into the basin. 'You could wash him for once, you know, Mattie.' Her voice is a raised whisper. 'But no, all you want to do is snipe and hold the shotgun.'

'I'm the only one with the guts here to shoot it.'

Gram's voice cracks like a whip. 'Let be. The pair of you.'

Kid just lies there, his breathing deep and slow. But in his chest his heart is hammering. He imagines a shotgun, its dark barrel pointing at him and Matilda's finger resting by the trigger. She couldn't be more scared of Kid if he had pinholes for eyes.

The sisters aren't lost here, he realises. They're not trapped, either.

They're hiding.

And they don't want to be found.

Hush takes up the cloth again and twists out the water over the basin. 'Mattie, why're you so paranoid?'

Matilda's voice is dripping with disapproval. 'Because you're so stupid.'

'Quit calling me that.'

'Quit saying stupid things then.'

'I'm not. He ain't dangerous.'

'Havoc's sake, Hush. You need to see things how they are, not how you want them to be. You said it yourself, he tracked a white waythread here. White's the colour of cowards and lies—'

'And purity, and new beginnings too. Besides, he said silvery-white. Silver means value.'

'And also betrayal.'

Gram thumps the doorframe with something. Maybe her fist, maybe her forehead. Kid gets the sense that she's near-impossible to enrage, whilst Matilda and Hush strike him as kids who enjoy a challenge.

'Enough now,' Gram says evenly. 'Neither of you is expert enough to be commenting on the colour of this kid's waythread. None of us are. Now maybe he ain't dangerous. But until we know for sure, a little caution won't hurt.'

'We're way past caution,' Matilda says. 'We never should've taken him in the first place. There's barely enough world for the three of us as it is. He can't be here. You both know it. I'm just saying it.'

'What would you have us do, Mattie?' says Hush. 'We ain't killers.'

'I ain't saying kill him. I'm saying we hand him to the McCluskeys. Let them figure him out.'

'The McCluskeys?' Hush hisses inwards like an angry cat. 'They'll slave him to them awful eyestones, more like.'

'So what if they do? Bad stuff happens when there's a war on.'

Gram's voice is like flint: brittle and full of spark. 'You unharden your heart, Matilda. He's a child, not a soldier.'

'If he's a child, how'd he find us?' Matilda says back. 'You said this place was well hid.'

'It is.'

'So how come a kid got in?'

'I don't know,' Gram admits grimly.

'You don't know, I don't know, Hush don't know. That's what I'm trying to say. We don't know anything about him. He might look like a kid, he might call himself Kid, but that don't mean he is one.' Matilda's voice darkens as she adds, 'They can look like anything, you know.'

Hush stands up with the bowl and they all leave, still bickering, locking the door behind them. Kid lies there with eyes shut for the longest time. Matilda and Gram's conversation dust devils round his mind. Power and enslavement and sacrifice and war. *There's barely enough world for the three of us as it is. They can look like anything, you know.*

Tracking the waythread, Kid thought he only had to find the sisters. But bringing them back with him might be even more challenging. Maybe they'll come if he says he was sent

26

by their mother. But what if they won't? What if they are too scared, or too suspicious? And who is this 'Gram', too? What if she hears Kid out and just decides 'no'?

Kid sits up on his elbows, knowing what he has to do. First, he needs to get his thimble back. Then he has to get the sisters out of here, whether they like it or not. That's the mission he was made for. The mission he was sent for. The mission that Crockett died for.

Quiet as he can, Kid pulls the bedsheets aside. He swings both legs off the mattress and touches the tips of his toes to the floorboards. Slowly eases himself up to standing. His legs are wobbly as a newborn foal's.

He puts on his shirt and mended jeans. Leaves his one remaining boot where it is. Barefoot will be better for now. His plan needs stealth. After he gets his thimble and crosses over to a new world, he can pattern a new pair.

He slides across the floorboards, careful not to make them creak. Reaching the window, he parts the curtains. There's dust on the sill and a yellow twist of flypaper tacked to the frame. Kid stares at the dead bugs gummed to it.

His one advantage right now is that Gram and the sisters think they have him trapped. He needs to act quickly, before they have a chance to think otherwise.

Kid opens the window. It rolls up with a quiet rumble. Outside it is evening and the sky is turning starry and the cool lilac air is squirming with bugs. Then he notices the horizon with a sudden lurch of vertigo. His hands actually grip hold of the window like he's about to topple through it.

Ahead the sky curves into a sheer drop. The orchard rolls steeply downwards too, like a rollercoaster track, until the whole world falls away out of sight.

Kid stares and stares again. No wonder Matilda said there wasn't room for him here. This world is so small, it's only got two places in it. Walk through the orchard and you'll end up at this house. Walk out of the house and you'll come to the orchard. The terrain is looped to fold back upon itself.

Knowing unfurls in Kid's mind like a flower in the sun. He's in a pocket world. That's the name for places like this. Pocket worlds: little hidden folds of space and time, all sewn up small and tight. Places you can hide like coins down the back of a couch.

Kid nods to himself. This is good. It means two things. Firstly, the waythread leading out of here will be much shorter than the one that led him in. Mere steps. Crossing out of a pocket world is easy. It's finding it in the first place that takes so long.

Secondly, it isn't just him that can't pattern. Pocket worlds are as fragile and tiny as silk purses. Try to alter them too much and they're prone to tearing. He doubts Gram will risk using her thimble here. If she wants to stop him leaving with the sisters, she'll have to do it without weaving.

Kid breathes out. He actually has a chance to pull this off. If he's quick. If he acts now. There's just the vaguest sense of unease about it all, though. Coming here, he thought he was mounting a rescue. This feels more like a kidnapping.

'No,' Kid mutters to himself. 'You're taking these girls to be with their mother. How can that be wrong?'

The silence after he speaks puts a lump in his throat. It wasn't so long ago that he had a bestie to answer him. What would Crockett be saying now? Something cake-related, no doubt. But he'd also tell Kid to remember his mission. What he was woven for. The reason he was made. What is the purpose of Kid, if it isn't to do this?

He slides out on all fours onto the roof beneath his window. The tiles are covered with moss that's dry and crumbly under his fingers. He goes very slowly and makes no noise. He reaches the gutter and swings his feet down onto the downpipe and onto one of the brackets holding it to the wall. Slowly he edges off the roof and onto the pipe. He listens out for any creaks. His muscles are trembling already from the effort and his head is swimming. He is in no fit shape to be doing this. But surprise is his one advantage and if he waits any longer, he'll lose it.

Below him inside the house, Hush is in the kitchen, dragging mugs up from a bowl of suds and clonking them steadily down on the side. Kid can tell it is her because she is whistling, loud and tuneless as a kettle. That girl does not have a way with melody. He predicts her next clonk and drops to the ground and rolls onto the grass.

He stands up in the backyard. Everything is moonlit. There's a stoop with stacked wood under it, and steps that lead up to the kitchen. Further back in the garden he can see a small stone well and an old push cart and a tall shed no wider than its door that is probably an outhouse. Behind the yard is the orchard of peach trees in their rows. If Kid walks through them for long enough, he'll arrive full-circle at the house's front door.

No waythreads. Without a thimble, they're all hidden from him. He crouches by the stoop's wooden steps and peers up at the back door. It is open except for a screen on hinges that keeps out the bugs. Moths and gnats are wheeling out of the darkness and throwing themselves against the mesh. A shadow moves across the kitchen. He shrinks back. It's Hush. She is wearing rolled-up jeans and a grey jumper too short in the arms and a butter yellow cap backwards on her head with ALL MY NEEDS ARE MET BY TOAST written on it. Kid watches her cleaning suds off the washed mugs and hang them back on their hooks. Whistling through the gap in her front teeth all the while.

Hush goes into the pantry by the side of the kitchen and Kid sees his chance. He skips soundlessly up the steps and opens the mesh door and eases it shut. He looks around the kitchen. It's bright and warm and lined with wooden cupboards and pots hanging off hooks. The nearest weapon is a small knife on the draining board with a wet wooden handle. Kid grabs it. As Hush comes out the pantry carrying a big candy tin, he slips one hand around the back of her neck and presses the point of the knife to her throat so she'll know what it is. She stops whistling and clutches the tin and yips like a dog that's had its tail stood on. Kid locks eyes with her. They are freckly as her face. Dark brown. Quick. They dart to the sideboard he took the knife from.

'Don't scream, I don't want to hurt you,' he tells her. 'Give me your thimble right now.'

Hush just blinks at Kid. 'You're up,' she says in surprise.

'Hush?' Matilda's voice comes through from the other room. 'You OK?'

'Tell her you're fine,' Kid whispers. 'Give me your thimble.'

'I'm fine,' Hush yells. 'I'm with Kid.'

For a moment he is too shocked to do anything. Hush looks apologetic.

'I did warn you,' she says. 'Talking's my flaw.'

Matilda appears in the doorway that leads to the rest of the house. She's carrying a strange sort of shotgun. There's a hive-shaped thing under the barrel and it seems to be humming.

'Hurt my sister and you're dead,' she informs Kid coolly.

He spins around with the knife still at Hush's throat and backs away snarling. Of course, he's not going to hurt either sister. But he won't pull this off unless they think that he will.

'Put the gun down,' he says. 'Now.'

Matilda's look of murder drops off her face at once. She gives Kid a sideways grin. 'I take it you're new to all this?'

He ignores her jibe. 'You've got ten seconds to hand over my thimble. I just want a waythread out of here, that's all.'

Matilda just sniggers. A bad feeling starts chewing

31

through Kid's gut. Something's not right here. Up in the bedroom they were afraid of him. Now suddenly they're not. Before he can decide what to do, Gram appears behind Matilda. Kid catches a glimpse of her craggy face and iron-coloured hair cut short like his.

'Love and Mercy, Matilda, put that down,' she says. 'Do not let one of those things loose in the house.'

Matilda pats the shotgun. 'It's only a stunnerbee, Gram.'

'It's a whole heap of trouble, is what it is.'

'Fine then.' Matilda holds the gun up like a club. 'I'll just whack him.'

'You won't,' says Hush sharply. 'His head is messed up enough as it is.'

'Oh, Hush! You save yourself then.'

'Save myself indeed. It's only a potato peeler.'

Kid's eyes flick from Matilda to the blade he holds to her sister's neck. It is just as Hush described. Not a knife at all.

Then Hush drops the tin of candy she's holding and the hard metal corner of it falls on Kid's bare toes. He yelps as she shoves him sideways out of the screen door. It slams open and shut as Kid trips down the steps and falls. In the space of a heartbeat his whole plan has unravelled. They'll likely just end him here, in the backyard dirt, like a dog.

'You cut, Hush?' Matilda comes into view and checks her sister's neck. It is blotchy red and a dark little bruise is already forming in the v-shape of the peeler from where Kid pressed it in.

'I told you we couldn't trust him,' Matilda says. 'But why would they send an idiot?'

Then she elbows open the screen door and shoots Kid in the chest.

• • •

Kid is keeled over in the dirt, chin touching his collarbone. Can't move. Can't speak neither. Is this what being dead is like? He reckoned it would be quieter.

'You shouldn't have shot him, Mattie.'

'Well, he shouldn't have hurt you.'

'Oh, please. You've been itching to fire that gun at him ever since he got here.'

Quickly Kid realises that he is very much alive. It wasn't a metal bullet Matilda shot him with, it was something living, something that stung him. Its stinger is lodged in Kid's chest now, about the size and shape of a rose thorn. The bug it came from is in his lap, curled up and dead. A vivid violet bee with iridescent wings that shimmer and shift like petrol on water. Its venom has turned him into a kid-sized raggy doll.

And over by the door, the sisters squabble and squabble.

'Weren't no need to do that, Mattie. He said he didn't want to hurt me.'

'Love and Mercy, Hush, you're stupider than I thought.'

'Stupider isn't a word, stupid,' says Hush.

'Yes it is.'

'Well, it don't sound like one.'

'That's you all over. Just going on the sound of things rather than how they actually work. He was pretending he didn't want to hurt you. Like he was pretending to be asleep. The sneaky little—'

'Curse and there'll be extra chores,' Gram warns, and Matilda goes quiet.

Feet clunk down the steps. Gram's coming over to Kid. She squats with a grunt and her knees make a pop like wood does when it burns. She is wearing a crumpled fleece shirt with the sleeves rolled up. Kid notices her left arm ends in a smooth nub at the wrist. For the first time he properly sees her face. Sort of strict and sort of impish. Sharp nose, stern eyes, round steel-rimmed glasses. Wrinkles threading over her face like cracks beneath porcelain glaze. The sort of old lady that might be fifty or a hundred.

Gram tips his chin up with one finger. Her nails are painted the same blue as the sisters'. 'Not much of a kidnapper, are you?' she says.

Kid tries to tell her he's not a kidnapper, but nothing comes out but dribble. Gram flicks the stinger from his side. He feels a tingle that spreads and becomes a cold burning as the venom releases its grip on him.

'Once the stunnerbee sting's worn off,' she informs him, 'we're gonna ask you some questions. And you're gonna answer them. If I reckon you're lying, Matilda'll shoot you. You try anything funny, Matilda'll shoot you. Any profanities, Matilda'll shoot you. You understand your situation?'

Kid finds that he can nod.

'Good,' Gram says. 'So let's start.'

'Hold it!' Hush says, skipping off to the kitchen. 'I was about to fix some coffee. You take sugar, Kid?'

'Uh,' is all Kid can manage.

Gram chuckles. 'Coffee? Not two moments ago he had a knife to your throat, Hush.'

'For the millionth, billionth time it was only a potato peeler. Ain't no need to give me that look, Mattie. We want him to talk, don't we? Coffee helps talking.'

Hush heads into the kitchen and starts banging around. Matilda stares with a look of incomprehension through the mesh door at her sister. The boiling kettle seems to soundtrack her mood.

By the time Hush comes back out, Kid can raise his arms and flex his fingers and he can wince from the pins and needles that shoot through him whenever he moves. Hush hands him a tin mug with something hot and black and thick in it that resembles road tar.

'Thanksh,' Kid slurs, taking the mug clumsily in both hands.

Hush laughs goofily. 'Thashh OK.'

Kid slugs the coffee back and gives an almighty shudder and spits into the empty mug to rid his mouth of the bitterness. He doesn't remember drinking coffee before and doesn't intend to do so ever again. Stuff tastes like burned mud. But it gives his mind a jolt like a kick from a mule, and seems to shake a bit more of the venom out of his system.

35

'All right then,' Gram says, finishing her own coffee and setting it down on the step.

But Hush darts back into the kitchen, shouting, 'Hold it, hold it, one second.' She re-emerges with a plate of fried potatoes and buttered greens, topped with a thick blob of sour cream and pink pickled shreds of cabbage and a drizzle of pepper sauce.

Kid's hunger opens up in him as sudden as a sinkhole. He needs to eat that food.

Matilda presses her fingers to the top of her nose, like she has a migraine coming on. 'This is meant to be an interrogation,' she growls. 'Gram, tell her.'

But Hush is already laying the food down by Kid and he gives Gram an imploring look like a puppy, until she rolls her eyes and nods. Kid drags himself forward and takes the plate with a grateful gasp. He wolfs down fried potatoes with his bare hands, kneeling in the dirt with no regard for cutlery or his clothes. It is the most delicious thing Kid has eaten in all his remembered life. Real, grown food. Not patterned, like the stuff he wove for himself whilst tracking through the desert. He wonders where they got it all. No fields of potatoes or cabbage in this world.

'Are we ready now?' Matilda is biting the end of one of her plaits like she is trying not to scream at Kid. 'Hush, do you maybe want to give him a back rub before we start?'

Gram's voice is tight. 'Matilda, let be.'

'His toenails look like they could do with a cut, too—'

'Please, child. I'm hushing you more than Hush, lately.'

36

'Actually,' Kid says, feeling his face flush, 'I need to, um, avail myself first. Please.'

'Avail yourself?' Matilda says.

'He means . . .' Hush says, and mouths the word.

So Matilda marches him to the outhouse at a distance of ten paces, muttering curses and vowing all the time to shoot Kid if he isn't quick about his business. He opens the wonky door into that cramped and smelly little space and yanks the lightswitch string and a bright naked bulb stutters on above him and all the moths up by the roof start flapping around it in mayhem. He closes the door and squats and uses that time to work out what to tell these sisters and their grandma.

Matilda raps on the door. 'You better be finishing in there.'

When Kid comes back out, Hush and Gram have brought a chair from the house and put it in the yard facing the stoop. He sits on it obediently and looks at them looking at him.

'So,' Gram says eventually. 'Let's start with your name.'

Kid wonders how to answer that. Sees Matilda's trigger finger twitch and just blurts out the truth.

'I have no idea what my name is,' he says. 'I don't think she gave me one.'

The Quiets share glances. It's clear they weren't expecting this answer.

'Do I get to shoot him for that?' Matilda asks, but Gram holds up her hand.

'Let him explain,' she says.

Kid takes a deep breath and tells them his story. His whole remembered life. What little of it there is to tell. Crossing into the orchard. The battle against the undoers. Patterning Crockett. The desert world with the twin suns. The silvery waythread he tracked there. All the numberless, nameless, featureless wastelands he followed it through. He keeps on explaining for as long as he can, telling everything and anything he knows. Until he finally mentions who he thinks it was that wove him, and sent him on this mission, to bring them back home.

'I think it was your mother,' he says.

The sisters react in the exact opposite fashion. Hush goes silent for the first time since Kid met her. She even stops drumming her fingers on the stoop's wooden rail.

Whereas Matilda goes off like a bomb.

'LIAR,' she says, swinging the shotgun up at Kid. Just before she pulls the trigger, Gram grabs the barrel and shoves it back downwards. There's a *pthhp* and a buzz as a stunnerbee fires into the dirt, and then a crunch as Gram's boot smashes down on it before the bee can sting anyone.

'Enough, Matilda. Let me deal with this. I said enough!' Gram's mouth is pressed into a thin grim line. She scuffles with Matilda for a few moments more, until Matilda roars a curse and finally backs off.

Kid gets the feeling that Gram saved his life just then. Matilda's eyes have a murderous glaze to them still. She bares her teeth and shakes her head, her plaits taking wild swings at the air. She spits on the floor in front of Kid, then walks back into the house, barging past Hush and snorting like a bull in a rage. A door slams, and then another, hard enough to make the whole world shake. Until finally there's just Hush and Gram, breathing heavily, holding the stunnerbee shotgun one-handed.

'Probably best if you don't mention Ma again,' Hush tells him, very quietly, looking at her feet.

'Love and Mercy.' Gram looks up and lets out a big shuddering breath. 'Hush, get on inside. Go on now. Go.'

Her tone makes it clear that she will brook no further disobedience. Hush gets the message. She stands and gathers up Kid's coffee mug and plate, and heads back up the stoop and through the screen door. Gram holds off speaking until Hush clonks the crockery in the sink and heads upstairs.

For a long time, there's just the quiet of the orchard trees around them, and the faint hum of the shotgun as the stunnerbees inside it calm themselves back down.

'They'll be eavesdropping,' Gram says, nodding up at the house where the sisters are. 'So just to advise you again, not to mention who you just mentioned.'

Kid's happy to take that advice, though he doesn't understand it. He doesn't understand anything here. It's nothing like how he thought it would be.

'I'm sorry,' he says desolately. 'I never thought that . . . When I was coming here I just . . . I assumed that they would want to go back to . . . to her.'

Gram shakes her head and holds her stump up against

her forehead like she's coming down with a fever. 'Of course they want to go back to her. That ain't the problem.'

Kid knows he should keep quiet, but he's so bewildered, he can't help it. 'But if they want to—'

'I'm gonna reiterate the advice Hush gave you,' Gram snaps. 'You are ignorant as an ickle baby right now. You are dumber than a box of rocks. In this world, it'd behoove you not to speak for a while, do you hear? You got a whole lot of listening and learning to do before we'll abide your talking again.'

Kid winces. That was a real tongue lashing. Gram huffs wearily and takes off her glasses and cleans the lenses on her shirt, one-handed. Then she puts them back on and fixes Kid with a long stare of stern appraisal. He realises that she's deciding right now what she's going to do with him. It feels like someone being in a class, awaiting the results of some test. Kid doesn't even want to think about the consequences of flunking.

'Ain't no neat way of solving this,' she says at last. She's speaking both to Matilda and Hush, in the house, and to Kid, out there in the yard.

'If we send him back the way he came, he won't last five minutes. Not without a thimble. We could give him to the McCluskeys, but we know what they'd do. I ain't sending anyone to be slavestoned, and that's final. So the only option we've got is letting him stay with us, for the time being at least.

'Doesn't mean I trust him and doesn't mean I don't. It means I don't see anything else to do with him. I know it's

40

a big risk. But here, we can at least contain that risk a little. And maybe we can figure out who really sent him, too. And whether we're still as well hid as I thought we were.

'That's my decision and it ain't changing. Kid stays. For now. Whilst he's here with us, I'll have certain expectations. No violence, no scheming, no worldweaving of any kind. No cursing, neither. Maybe Kid can be a good influence on the girls in that regard. And no contacting the other worlds either. Especially not the McCluskeys. We don't want them catching wind of Kid, OK?'

Gram's voice booms out loud across the whole wide world. Laying down the law. Putting a truce in place. For a fight that Kid somehow started, with his stupid actions and foolish words.

'You reckon you can abide by them rules, Kid?' Gram asks him.

When he nods, she gives him a hard stare that says *You better*, then turns and climbs the stoop and opens the screen door. 'You want more coffee?'

Kid gets up off the chair with his legs all pins and needles and tells her, 'No thanks.'

'You sure?' she says, going over to the stove and putting the kettle on to boil. 'This might take a while.'

Kid steps inside the bright warmth of the kitchen. 'What might?'

'Helping you not to say anything stupid,' Gram says, spooning grounds in a pot. 'Though I can't guarantee that, of course. But I'll tell you why it's absolutely impossible that

41

Hush and Matilda's mother sent you here. If you want to know, that is?'

Kid nods. He does. It's in him like a hunger.

'Good,' says Gram. 'Come through, then.'

Gram brews her coffee and pours it and brings Kid through into a wide open space that takes up almost the entire lower floor of the house. There are timbered walls and leather couches and shaggy rugs over bare floorboards. A so-so oil painting hangs above the woodstove, of Gram and the sisters in the orchard, sun high over them, standing on their own shadows. The artist hasn't quite got Matilda right somehow. Maybe he's toned down her scowl or something.

Apart from the painting, there are a few lamps glowing with a honeycomb light and some shelves beneath the stairs, stacked with stuff that speaks of boredom. Brass-countered games and dice bags and clumsy, half-finished whittlings: dogs and too-shallow spoons. Each thing a relic of a day with nothing to do. The three of them have been holed up in this pocket world for a long time.

Gram sits down at a formica table. Pats the chair opposite for Kid to join her. Above him he hears the sound of one of the sisters brushing their teeth.

'So.' Gram cracks the knuckles of her one hand. 'Let me tell you a little about this power we have. This worldweaving. Though none of us understand it like we must've done, once.' She pulls out a silver chain from under her shirt, and gazes at the thing that dangles on the end of its clasp. Like

Kid's, it resembles a thimble. And yet, even an arm's reach away, Kid knows that it was made for a higher form of sewing. He swears he can feel the power in it. Humming like a bee inside Matilda's shotgun.

'No one left now who knows how to make these,' Gram says, gazing at the thimble. 'I couldn't begin to tell you how they work. Same way I can't really explain why magnets stick or fires burn or cars move. All I know is how to use the thing. You have to keep it on your fingertip. You have to close your eyes. You can't weave a thimble itself, nor anyone else's.'

Kid nods. He knows those rules. And there are others too, like how whatever you weave has to still fit within the pattern of the world that you're in.

'You can't weave bazookas made of cake,' he murmurs sadly to himself.

Gram gives Kid a curious glance. 'No,' she agrees. 'Not unless you're in a world with lollipop trees and chocolate rivers. But that doesn't mean you can't make miracles with them. Take you, for example. Someone spun you into life, using not much more than their mind and their thimble. That's a thing that a god in a story would do, ain't it?

'Maybe that's where it all started to go wrong. We started to reckon ourselves gods. We wove ourselves new worlds and then we spun our tightropes between the worlds – waythreads, like the one you crossed. Joined them all up into a republic of wonders. A place fit for gods to live in.'

Gram trails off, her eyes shiny with sorrow and remembering.

'There were worlds where rainbows were rivers, where moons sang lullabies, where you could drink up the sunbeams until you were glowing with their light. I stood on the jewelled cliffs on Cassilda as the seven suns rose. I watched the clouds break like waves upon the sky's rim on Demhe. But all that's gone to havoc now. Eaten away by undoers.'

Kid shudders and in his mind he sees those pinhole eyes with nothing in them at all but death and loathing. He remembers the horror of those hissing black mouths, the endless empty inside them that could never be filled. He remembers one of those holes above him, trying to drink him up like he was a water trough.

'I can see you know all about undoers,' Gram says.

Kid swallows and nods. Looking at Gram's missing left hand, he reckons she knows all about them too.

'They come from a place that lies beyond all patterns,' she says. 'A place that's dark. And the undoers are made of that dark. We call that darkness "havoc".

'You see, Kid, when you boil it all down, there are two types of stuff. There are things that are of the "pattern" – this table and this coffee, and everything in this pocket world, and every world beyond it. And people, of course, whether born or woven. What else are we but patterns, too? Knitted synapses and woven muscle? Bone threaded to sinew, cells stitched on cells? Double helixes spiralling endlessly until they spin out a person?

'But undoers are the second type of thing. They're made of stuff that's the exact opposite of pattern.'

44

'Havoc,' says Kid. He thinks back to the void inside those pinhole eyes, those lipless sucking mouths, and he shudders.

'Havoc and pattern,' Gram explains. 'Chaos and order. Meaning and void. Being opposites, the two can't abide one another. Think Hush and Matilda, and then some. That's why undoers, as creatures made of havoc, seek to kill and destroy all pattern.'

Kid puts his fingers up to his neck, like the gloved hand is still there. Then he frowns and thinks. 'But if undoers are made of havoc, how come they got form? Isn't that a pattern of sorts? The ones hunting me had my shape, at least on the outside, they did.'

Gram nods. 'That contradiction is what torments them. To exist here, they have to take form, which is anathema to them.' She sees his blank look and gives a bashful shrug. 'Anathema means hateful. I used to be a tutor, before the war.'

The war. Kid wonders something. 'So the war is pattern against havoc?' he asks. 'World weavers against undoers?'

Gram's chuckle is like a boot stomping through dry leaves. 'Oh, no, Kid. You can't war with undoers. Ain't no army of them – chaos ain't that organised. No. Maybe you could argue that undoers started the war, but they certainly ain't the ones fighting it. We world weavers are doing that just fine all on our own.'

Kid is shocked at that. 'We're fighting ourselves? Over what?'

'Over the power itself,' Gram says.

Kid doesn't understand. Gram sees it in his face.

'I can explain,' she tells him. 'But in a roundabout way. You see, I grew up in a place called Dustbowl. Tiny world, only fifty miles wide. Growing up there, undoers were still rare, and pinprick-small. Every now and then, you'd find one in a dark corner, hissing like a puncture, trying to suck up enough of the pattern to build itself a body with. Weren't too hard to sew those undoers shut. But over time the holes grew bigger, and there were more of them. And we knew the reason why. All of us did. We could feel it.

'It was the thimbles. Every time we changed Dustbowl's pattern, we weakened it a little: tipped it further towards havoc. We knew that. But did it stop us patterning? Did it heck. We were world weavers, weren't we? What were we supposed to do, give up being gods?

' "You betcha," said the wisest of us. But it weren't so easy convincing everyone to start learning how to grow true food and build proper houses and all sorts of other tiresome stuff. Not when they could just use their thimbles.

'And so we kept patterning, even though we knew it was wrong. You'd be surprised how easy it was. All we had to do was stop thinking about it. That's it. We convinced ourselves that undoers had always been this big, and this common. We shrugged and said that, when the time came, we'd just pattern new worlds and cross over. And we kept patterning. Patterning and patterning. All sorts of stuff, whatever we wanted. I remember one time, me and my friends wove ourselves birds big enough to ride. Then we flew up into the sky and made the clouds around us bouncy, so we could jump on them like they were trampolines. Deep down, I remember thinking: *This can't be good for Dustbowl.* But what was I supposed to do? Be the one shmuck stood on the ground, watching my friends somersaulting in the sky? And so I stopped thinking about it, same as everybody else.

'Over years, slowly at first, then quicker and quicker, Dustbowl got worn out. Once a world gets raggedy, it breeds undoers, the way bad meat breeds maggots.'

'It was like that in the world I crossed over from,' Kid tells her. 'The undoers came because of me. And they looked like me. Because I was patterning.'

Gram nods grimly. 'Most probably that world was Dustbowl, since that's where we crossed here from. You tracked us through the mountains?'

'No mountains there any more,' Kid says. 'They've all worn away to hills.'

Gram lets out a sad sigh. 'Same story all over now. Everything's wearing out. Kindness and charity quickest of all. Weavers who still have well-patterned worlds suddenly ain't so keen to share them. They hide their waythreads. Some, like the McCluskeys you've heard us talk of, even cut them. To keep people out. And what do you reckon the weavers who found themselves worldless do?'

Kid winces. 'Let me guess. They fight to get in?'

'You got it.' Gram sips her coffee and smiles bitterly at Kid. 'Ain't a righteous side and a wicked side to it, just everybody looking out for their own. Of course, all the fighting has just led to more havoc. That's fighting for you.

Three years we've been hiding here, and the worlds-war has been raging closer to four, by my count. Ain't many left to fight it. We've lost so much. The few of us who are left are just trying to hold on to what we still have.'

'Is that why you think I've come?' Kid asks. 'To steal what you've got here? Because I couldn't care less about this world. I just want Matilda and Hush. To reunite them with—'

'That's what you say,' Gram says, cutting him off before he can say the word 'mother'. 'I even think you might believe it, too. But it's not possible. It just ain't. There's no one left out there that loves these girls. No one. Do you get me?'

And Kid gets it. It finally hits him. Like a punch in the gut. Hush and Matilda's mother couldn't have woven him. Because Hush and Matilda don't have a mother. Not any more. Only each other, and Gram.

• • •

After their talk, Gram fetches Kid a spare pair of Matilda's old boots, then hands him a toothbrush and a tiny tube of minty paste and a chunk off a brick of soap and a towel for washing and a comb for his hair. Then she takes him back up to his room and locks him in. He tries to sleep but he just can't. He lies down on the bed and ties his thoughts in knots. He paces about and sits around, whilst the questions come, one after the other.

Who was it that wove him, if not the mother?

If not the mother, who?

And why would anyone else want to find these sisters so badly?

He just can't make sense of it. It's all so confusing. He still feels, down in his gut, that Hush and Matilda's mother has played some part in his creation, in his mission, in everything. But how can that be, if she died in the war?

One thing's for certain. Gram's not telling him the whole truth. She's hiding things. He knows it. And there's nothing Kid can do about it. He's got no thimble, no power, no leverage, nothing.

He lies on the bed, brooding. About everything Gram told him. About everything that she's hiding.

• • •

Morning in the pocket world comes sudden as a light switching on. Kid is half-dozing and watching the darkness outside his window, when the moon spins like a coin in the sky and suddenly becomes the sun. No sunrise in this place. Pocket worlds don't have enough of a horizon for the sun to come up over.

Kid gets up and dresses and squeezes his feet into Matilda's old boots. To his surprise, they fit perfect. He tries his door, fully expecting it to be locked. It opens up. He steps out into the hallway and freezes. A dark green bee the size of his thumb is on the wall opposite his door, its furry body gently throbbing, feelers tasting the air.

49

Kid is about to slam his door shut when he spots the note left by his feet.

It's called a beady-eye, the note says. *It's watching you. Don't piss it (or me) off.*

The note isn't signed but Kid knows who it is from. He imagines the three of them discussing it last night. Hush saying: *You can't keep him locked in there forever.* Matilda answering: *Well if he comes out, he's gotta be supervised.*

He reminds himself of Gram's rules. No scheming, no violence, no patterning, no cursing. Then he heads towards the stairs, the beady-eye crawling silently after him.

A little way down the hallway are two wooden doors with signs pinned to them. One of the signs says *Do Not Come In, Ever* in the same handwriting as the note on his door. Matilda's room then. The other door is covered with flyers for gigs featuring a band Kid has never heard of, called Bang! Bang! One Dollar! There's also a notice that says I DEMAND KNOCKING AND IN MOST INSTANCES CHOCOLATE.

Below, there is an addition that says, I MEAN IT, MATILDA.

And then a third one adds, in a new colour, YOU TOO, KID.

Behind him, the beady-eye's wings flicker once and the tip of its stinger pulses.

'OK, I get it,' Kid tells it. Chocolate or no chocolate, he is not to go into Hush's room. He carries on past the doors to the sisters' bedrooms and down the stairs and the beady-eye flies after him with a low and leisurely hum.

The sisters are outside and both doing chores. Maybe paying penance for last night's cursing. Matilda is halfway up the side of the house on a ladder, mucking out the gutters. Kid can see her boots at the top of one of the front windows. Hush's bad singing drifts in from the backyard, mingled with the sound of sweeping. When Kid goes into the kitchen and looks out, she waves at him like he's her best friend. Her cap is navy blue with a green frog on it, sitting on a lily and saying WELCOME TO MY PAD.

They left Kid some breakfast. A pan of mush on the stove with a spoon and a bowl. There is coffee in a mug too, which Kid doesn't touch. He takes the food back into the living room and sits and he eats and the beady-eye watches him whilst perched on a lampshade.

The mush is pretty good. Kid wonders again where it all comes from. Other worlds, surely. Ones that grow oats or coffee, the way this one grows peaches. There must be dozens of waythreads to all kinds of places squirrelled away around here. If only he had his thimble, he'd be able to see them . . .

This doesn't bode well. Not even the end of breakfast and Kid is already scheming of escape. Frustration rises up in him, black and bitter as coffee. Isn't his scheming justified? Do they really expect him to just wait here, obedient as a dog? Until when, exactly? Until Matilda suggests some guilt-free way to get rid of him? He pushes his bowl away and sits clenching his fists, like his anger is something he can strangle.

He goes (and the beady-eye follows) to sit in surly silence in the yard. No one comes to check on him. They all look too busy. Up the ladder, Matilda has finished with the gutters and is beating nails into Kid's windowframe with a hammer. Hush and Gram are doing washing by the well, treading dirt out of big buckets of shirts and suds.

'Pocket worlds,' Kid mutters in disgust. If they were somewhere bigger, he could pattern those clothes clean in a fingersnap.

Gram scrubs and Hush sings and Matilda's hammer bangs harder to drown her out. Kid skulks round the yard and makes a pile of pebbles and starts throwing them at the outhouse door. After a time, he devises a game in which he scores points by hitting various knots in the wood.

That's how the morning goes, until the Quiets stop and go inside the house, and Hush yells out to him: 'LUUUNCH!'

Kid ignores her. And the gnats biting his arms. He just sits and throws his pebbles until he breaks his high score.

When the Quiets come back out, Hush sits down next to him with a half-finished plate of toast. The beady-eye gives a loud buzz, just to remind Kid not to try anything. Hush ignores it and with her chin on her knees, shows him all her nails that she's just reapplied with the same old blue.

'Pretty, don't you think? It's called Blue Ruin. It's Gram's. She brought a whole box of varnishes here, back when we first came. Still has about fifty little bottles kept under her bed. Funny, ain't it? The stuff people just can't leave behind.

On the waythread outta Dustbowl, I remember seeing this one man with . . . havoc, it must've been a dozen pairs of shoes. He had them all tied to his belt, swinging by the laces like a skirt. Me and Matilda still giggle about that.'

She laughs, stretching it out as long as it'll go, like she's waiting for Kid to join in with her. He doesn't. He shrugs and shifts his body away from her but she keeps chattering on regardless.

She says, 'You ever had your nails painted, Kid? I can do them, if you like? You ain't allowed Blue Ruin. Long story, but that colour's just for me and Mattie and Gram. But look – you could have another one though, if you like? There's one called Pineapple Sunset that would really suit your eyes.'

She says, 'You know I ain't gonna stop talking. Like I told you, it's my flaw.'

She hums under her breath for a bit then says, 'Quiet by name, not by nature.'

'Don't you get a hint?' Kid snaps finally. 'Do I have to be rude or something?'

That does silence her. He feels bad immediately.

'Sorry,' he tells her.

Hush shrugs. 'Gram's world makes everyone tetchy.'

'I'm not surprised, all those chores you do by hand. If you could pattern, you could do them like *that*.' He snaps his fingers.

Hush laughs at that. 'I wish. I'm a scant.'

Kid frowns. 'Can't what?'

'No, I said I'm a *scant*. Means I don't have much skill

53

with a thimble. Matilda's nearly as bad as I am, though she'd never admit it. She'd just say her skill was rusty on account of us not being able to use it here.'

That surprises Kid. He hasn't ever considered that some people might be better world weavers than others.

'How comes it varies?' he asks. 'The power, I mean?'

Hush shrugs again. 'Just does. Same as any other talent. Like how some voices can sing whilst others can't. I ain't bothered though. I got words. Them, I can spin and spin. That's my power – filling up silence.'

Kid smiles wryly and Hush grins and for a long time she sits there looking at her toes and wiggling them in her sandals so the sun flashes off the varnish.

'Although now and then a little silence can be nice,' she says.

Kid feels his skin prickle, like Hush's words hold some sort of electric charge. He wonders if she can see the goosebumps on his forearms. He tries hiding them with his hands.

'So what happens next, do you think?' Kid says eventually. 'According to Matilda, I can't stay. According to Gram, I can't leave.'

'There's a lot to figure out,' Hush says.

'I know it,' Kid says. 'I don't even know what day it is.'

'Tuesday,' she tells him.

Kid thinks about Crockett, and what they'd talked about back in Dustbowl, back when the future had been an unmapped land that they were going to explore together. 'So this is what Tuesdays are like,' he mutters.

54

Hush stares. 'Oh wow,' she says. 'Whoever wove you really just sketched you out. Didn't even name you, let alone tell you how boring Tuesdays are. They didn't want you to know anything, did they?'

Kid stays quiet. Hush keeps on talking anyway.

'I mean, I sort of knew that,' she says quietly. 'As soon as you told us that Ma made you. You really believed it, didn't you? Did Gram tell you that Ma is even more of a scant than me? I've seen her weave a kettle hot, or mend a cracked plate, but weaving something as amazing as you? Forget it. Not even with thimbles on all of her fingers and toes.'

Kid tries not to blush at her calling him amazing, and focuses instead on how Hush talks about her mother. *She is a scant. I've seen her weave.* Not in past tense, but in present. Like her ma's still alive somehow. Maybe part of grieving is denial, and Hush can't bear to admit that her Ma is gone.

'You don't think,' he wonders aloud, 'that she might have changed? Maybe gotten more powerful? Before she . . . before you lost her?'

Hush grins, her eyes shining. 'Oh, but Ma couldn't have been more powerful.'

'But you just said she was a scant?'

'I don't mean at worldweaving, Kid. There are other ways to be mighty, you know. We got all sorts of other powers, ones that don't need thimbles. Slower, surer ways to weave the world around us. I'm talking about kindness. I'm talking about love. That's what Ma was strong in.'

Hush is crying now. Tears are rolling down her nose. She

wipes at them with the heel of her hand as Kid starts to murmur that he's sorry.

'No, no. It's OK.' She smiles at him through her tears. 'I love talking about her. Even though it makes me sad. I ain't like my sister. Three years since we came here, and she's not said Ma's name once.'

Hush sniffs and slaps her hands together in satisfaction and changes the subject in an abrupt but somehow expert fashion. She really is good at filling up silence, Kid thinks.

'I think you're going to be my new hobby,' she tells him.

'Hobby?'

'Oh, sure. Have to have something to do here. Else you go stir crazy. And I'm going to help you find out who you are, Kid. All the stuff you like. We'll make a list. Put "Stuff Kid Likes" at the top. And underneath that, we can put "potato peelers", and "throwing rocks at toilets".'

Kid grins and Hush laughs and he joins in. Glances sideways as he does so, like it's something he doesn't want her to notice him doing. Her cap today has a pug on it and the words SORRY, MY HEART IS TAKEN. He likes almost everything about her. He likes the sunburn on the bridge of her nose.

There are no more stones to throw or jokes to make but they still sit together. Hush turns back to her half-finished plate of toast and eats the last two slices. After a while she goes and fetches the little yellow bottle called Sunset Pineapple and begins painting Kid's fingers and toes.

• • •

The days go by. Kid doesn't forget about his mission, not exactly. It's just that other things get in the way. Hush most of all. As good as her word, she really does start up a list called STUFF KID LIKES. He spends a lot of time helping her fill it in. To his surprise, after a few days coffee evens ends up on there. Especially after Hush teaches him to sneak a handful of candy from the tin, to fix the taste.

'That's the trick to living here,' she tells him. 'Cover up the bitterness and convince yourself life is sweet.'

For Kid, that's easier said than done. Even when having fun with Hush – self portraits and board games and making peachpit catapults – his mission is always in the back of his mind, maddening as an itch. And then there are the questions: about who wove him, about the war, about Kid's own future.

Gram, whenever he asks her stuff, is as cagey as ever. One evening at the table, she tells him to find out who he is first, before coming and bothering her with questions. He has to bite his tongue to keep from pointing out that if he knew a bit more about what was going on beyond the pocket world, he might actually be able to work out where he'd come from, and why. But of course, Gram knows this.

It's like she's playing for time – but why, and for how much longer? More questions to add to the pile. Questions upon questions. All building up in Kid like steam inside a kettle. Sometimes they shriek so loud, they are all he can hear.

He does his best to ignore them. Along with Hush, the chores are a help. So much work for such a little world. Floors to sweep and plates to scrub. Linen to wash and dry and fold. And it all has to be done without thimbles. Kid spends all Wednesday and Thursday in the orchard, picking peaches that Hush informs him are called July Flames. She walks him from tree to tree, teaching him how to sort ripe from rotten. The beady-eye goes with them, lazily buzzing from branch to leaf. Hush chats all the while. She is a runaway train of talk. All sorts of opinions on just about everything, though mostly on just herself and her sister.

'Well, what else am I gonna gab about?' she tells Kid as they walk the rows. 'It's either Mattie or peach trees.'

By Wednesday afternoon, he knows the sisters better than he knows himself. Turns out Hush has her own list of things she likes, and it's a long one.

'My favourite colour is blue and my best day is Saturday and I like music and toast and tormenting Matilda until she goes kaboom,' she tells him.

'What does Matilda like?' Kids asks. 'Apart from shotguns.'

Hush considers this. 'Pranks. And cursing. And murder-ballads. Her favourite one is "Janey's Lying Still". Also she likes creeping up behind me and making me jump. She's really good at that, on account of the fact she ain't got a shadow.'

'No shadow?' Kid squints when he hears this. And now that he thinks about it, he realises what it was that struck him as odd in the painting of the sisters and Gram. Matilda had a shadow in that picture. But Hush is right. Now she doesn't. Ever. Not even when the sun's as bright as can be. 'What happened to it?'

'I tell people she had it murdered because she thought it was out to get her.'

Kid grins. The story doesn't even strike him as unlikely.

'And she likes her coffee with two sugars, and a board game called *Triumvirate*, and . . .' Hush reveals the next piece of information with great relish, 'Matilda loves writing love letters to boys from the other worlds we know of.'

Hush doesn't pass comment on her own feelings towards those boys. Kid wonders about asking her but doesn't trust his face not to blush. So he remembers the posters on her bedroom door, and asks her about her favourite music, instead.

'I prefer making my own,' Hush says. 'I'm in a one-person band called Bang! Bang! One Dollar. I am lead singer and also play the saucepan lid. We have released eighteen albums. The rap segments on our last release were particularly innovative.'

'I see,' Kid says. 'I think.'

'Do you play any instruments, Kid? My band is currently looking for a guitarist, just so you know.'

Kid shrugs. 'Don't know. I could give it a go, I guess.'

'Guitar is easy. You just hit the strings loud.'

'Who do you play for though?'

He asks her this then stands back to let her talk train pick up speed again. And sure enough, a little later, that's how he learns about another family of world weavers called the McCluskeys. According to Hush, there are lots of them and they own a big world called Garrison, which they've closed off to all outsiders. Hush reckons Matilda is in love with the second-eldest McCluskey boy, whose name is Nate.

'They've been sending each other little notes for years now,' Hush explains as they lug back the big wicker basket, filled with peaches. 'Don't ask me how they send them, Gram said not to tell you about it. Obviously, it's like a waythread, you've figured that much out, but don't try and find it because it's hidden and we can't cross over it ourselves because – well, I ain't gonna say.'

'Matilda hasn't been able to write to Nate since I came here,' Kid realises, remembering that Gram suspended all contact with the McCluskeys on the night of his botched escape. 'No wonder she hates me.'

'Ah, that's her own silly fault. If Gram trusted her not to tell the McCluskeys about you, she'd let Mattie keep sending her love notes. Nate probably thinks she's gone cold on him. I bet he's a blubbering wreck. A few weeks back he sent her a seed and when Mattie planted it, it grew into a singing rose. But then she plucked all its petals off and threw away the stem before I could get close to hear what he'd taught it to sing. I don't know where she gets these notions.'

'What notions?' Kid asks.

'That love's a secret, and something to be ashamed of. If I loved someone, I'd tell them so they'd know.'

'Me too.' Kid turns back to the peaches, his cheeks as flushed as the July Flames.

A little further on, they come to the tree where Crockett died. The reddish boulder that Kid wove him from is still there in the grass like a gravestone. If Kid squints real hard, sometimes he swears he can see the curled up shape of his bestie, locked away like a fossil in the rock. He's come out here a few times, in the evenings before the sun spins around into the moon, and tried chatting to Crockett as if his friend could still listen. It isn't the same though. The silence is too empty.

'Maybe when you get your thimble back,' Hush says softly, 'you could try weaving him back to life.'

Kid looks uneasy. 'I don't know. He wouldn't be the same.'

Hush considers this. 'Why not? Same rock, ain't it? And he's still in your mind, right?'

Kid shrugs. 'I guess so.'

'There we go then.' Hush taps the side of her head. 'As long as someone's in there, they're not gone. Not truly.'

Kid isn't sure, but he isn't going to argue with her. It feels like Hush isn't just talking about Crockett. Like she's trying to comfort her own grief, as well as his.

They carry their haul of fruit over to the stoop. Hush swans off to the outhouse as Matilda comes out from the kitchen. Kid sneaks a look at her feet. Hush is right. No shadow. Now that he's seen it, he wonders how he ever didn't see it.

Matilda glares at him and sits on the back steps with a short stubby knife and a wide white pan. Taking up the peaches that Kid and Hush have gathered one by one, she shucks out their stones with a quick stab and flick. She's faintly smiling as she does so, maybe imagining that she's gutting her enemies.

'Need any help?' Kid asks her.

The blade flashes in Matilda's grip. 'You think I trust you with one of these?'

So Kid sits away from her and pits with his fingers. It's messy but fun. The inside of the peaches are almost molten and he shucks out the stones until his shirt is soaked to the elbows and the pan beneath Matilda is swimming with juice.

'By the way,' Kid says, trying to make his tone as casual as possible, 'I wanted to say I'm sorry you can't write to Nate right now.'

Matilda pauses with her knife halfway in a peach. Kid can see her cheeks turning sunburn red.

'Never mind,' he says. 'I just . . . Never mind.'

Talking isn't Matilda's thing, he realises. Maybe she'd be happier if it was. It strikes Kid that she's got a lot bottled up: her love for Nate and her hate for Kid and her grief for her Ma. No wonder she is always on the edge of going kaboom, as Hush put it.

• • •

It is late afternoon by the time the peaches are ready for Gram in the kitchen. There, they get boiled and sieved into jam, or pressed in a squeezer for juice, or cut up and turned into cobbler. Gram says whatever they don't eat gets sent for trading with the families hiding in other pocket worlds.

'How many of them are there?' Kid asks.

Gram stirs the pot of peaches she has spent the past hour reducing down to syrupy gold. 'Hideyfolk? Not as many as there used to be. And I thought you were holding off on the questions until you knew your own self better?'

Matilda sticks her head through the screen door briefly. 'He's a liar. He lied. That's what liars do.'

'Don't start,' Gram tells her.

Matilda stomps off, muttering words under her breath that sound like they could very well be curses and Gram's knuckles go white around the spoon she is stirring and then she sighs very loudly and deeply. Kid has seen them do this a lot: come to the brink of some monumental bust-up and then pull back at the very last moment.

'She really hates me, huh?' he says in the awkward silence.

Gram stews the peaches for so long, he doesn't think he'll get an answer. Technically it is a question. It's only when he goes to the sink to make a start on the pans that she finally speaks.

'She'll get used to you. And you to her.'

• • •

Gram is right. Kid does. Give it enough days, and you can acclimatise to almost anything. Morning coffee, the beady-eye, the chores, Matilda's sniping. But not Hush, though.

He never gets used to her, or her infinite hatwear, or the fragile unspoken thing he feels them weaving together invisibly in the space between their hearts.

That Friday night, they sit down to play a new board game of Hush's own invention – or rather, they sit down to try to understand it. Hush has written down the rules in a handmade booklet that's eighteen pages long. They get to page six before Matilda throws a hissy fit and pushes her chair from the table.

'Why can't we just play Triumvirate?' She points to the game over on the shelf. 'We know how to play that. And it's actually good.'

'I made this up especially for Kid,' Hush explains. '*Triumvirate* only has three players.'

Matilda scowls at Kid. 'I know. That's what's good about it.'

'Matilda,' Gram says warningly, although even she looks worn out by the complexity of the new game.

'It's OK,' says Kid. 'You guys play *Triumvirate*. I'll sit here and finish reading the rules to *Horsey-Horsey Hee-Haw-Hey*.'

'Even the name is too long,' says Matilda.

And the jibes carry on until Hush throws one of the game's whittled wooden horses at Matilda's head and Matilda rips up all the stable cards and they all get sent to bed.

• • •

When Kid wakes on Saturday morning, the orchard branches have been stripped bare. Winter has swept in during the night like a thief, and taken every leaf and every peach in the pocket world. Kid stands in the kitchen behind the screen door, hugging his arms to his chest and shivering. He wishes he could pattern himself a jumper and some slippers. Gram walks in behind him, stretches and cracks her knuckles one-handed and gets the kettle going for the morning's mush and coffee.

'It'll warm up soon enough,' she says when she glances over and sees Kid hopping on the cold floor. 'Winter don't last long here. Seasons in pocket worlds are patterned real short and real sudden, and to a strict schedule too. Friday night is when I timetabled autumn and winter. Get all that cold and gloom over and done with, nice and quick whilst we sleep.' She spoons out the coffee and taps the spoon on the side of the tin and squints at the clock ticking above the cabinets. 'Things ought to be brightening up any second now.'

And sure enough, suddenly the sunbeams brighten and a breeze full of a sweet pollen smell rolls into the kitchen through the screen door. It's Saturday morning, and spring is here. Kid shakes his head in amazement.

Gram chuckles. 'There we go. I guess that means technically, you've been here a whole year. Though I don't like to count in pocket world time. Makes me even more ancient.' She puts the kettle on the stove and hollers up through the ceiling. 'GIRLS! ANY NECESSITIES? SPRING'S HERE AND I'M HEADING OUT!'

There's a thump that shakes the kitchen ceiling and then feet clonk down the stairs three at a time. Hush skids into the kitchen in her socks and says breathlessly, 'Drumsticks. And a kazoo.' And when Gram raises her eyebrows, she says, 'For Kid to try out. He's maybe joining Bang! Bang! One Dollar.'

'Ah.' Gram doesn't quite manage to hide a wince. 'I thought Bang! Bang! split up after that last album?'

Hush boggles at her Gram. 'After *Chores, Snores and Encores*? Are you kidding? The reviews said it was a masterpiece.'

'It was certainly something, all right.' Gram pulls a thick notepad from a shelf and heads swiftly for the front door. 'But drumsticks and kazoos ain't necessities, are they?'

'Guess not,' Hush grumbles.

'You can use pencils for drumsticks. We need pencils. Is Matilda still asleep?'

Hush nods. 'Cuddling her shotgun like it's a teddy.'

'You snooze, you lose. How about you, Kid? Got any requests? Things you need, not things you want, mind.'

Kid gives Gram a look that says, *Huh?*

'For the trees,' says Gram. And when Kid still looks puzzled, she elaborates further. 'For what the trees should grow this summer. Come with, if you ain't made up your mind yet.'

So Kid follows Gram out of the front door and into the bare-branched rows, where the trees are already beginning to bud in the spring sun. The wet mulch of last week's leaves goes squelch beneath their boots and the wind gusts and blusters and the crisp air tingles on Kid's bare arms. Glittery backed beetles have emerged from who knows where, and are scurrying over the ground, chewing it all to compost. Pocket world ecosystems must be intricate as wristwatches.

Gram stops by the first tree and flicks through the notepad one-handed with practised skill, like someone performing a card trick. She mutters under her breath. Kid hears the odd word. *Nails. Soap. Oats. Bread for Hush's toast.* Then she tots it all up quickly and gives a satisfied nod.

'We don't just grow peaches here,' she says to Kid. Then her hand goes to the chain at her neck and she turns to the first tree and closes her eyes and patterns it. Kid doesn't have a thimble, so he can't feel her doing it, but he still knows she is weaving. A slight shiver runs up the trunk of the tree and right to the tips of all its branches and then Gram moves on to the next tree.

'What did you do?' Kid asks.

'See for yourself.' Gram closes her eyes and does it again and moves on. She's halfway down one row now and as Kid turns back to the first tree she worked on, his jaw drops a little. Amongst the green uncurling leaves, tiny slivers of cutlery are starting to sprout. Knives and forks and spoons, their metal glinting in the sun, each one already as long as Kid's little finger.

'Don't pick them yet,' Gram calls. 'Wait for them to ripen.'

Kid hurries back to her, past trees bearing all manner of strange fruit: slowly inflating paper bags of ground coffee, bars of soap the size of sweets, glass jars ballooning like bubbles, slices of bread expanding like white foam.

'But I thought patterning was bad for worlds,' he says.

'It is.' Gram closes her eyes and patterns the next tree to grow white cotton socks. 'Which is why I only weave when I absolutely have to. Some summers – which are every week here, remember – I leave the trees be. Let them grow peaches. But most times, we're needing oats, and sugar, and milk, and bread, and everything else besides. Like socks – Kid, you wouldn't believe how many socks them girls wear holes in. It's like they're keeping score. Probably they are. They got all sorts of games.'

Kid squints. Three years, Hush said they've been here. Gram has been patterning all that time without even a hint of havoc? It makes no sense. He thought pocket worlds were supposed to be too delicate to tolerate any use of the power.

Gram chuckles when he tells her that. 'That's what I thought, too. But it seems like you can pattern here without causing havoc. I've got my theories. Maybe if worldweaving is necessary, then it doesn't wear out the world as much. Maybe if you weave in little bursts, a world's pattern can mend. Or perhaps, if patterning becomes routine enough – if it becomes part of the pattern of things itself . . . But who knows? We world weavers know all about making patterns, don't we? But almost nothing about caring for them.'

As she talks, Gram keeps working, and Kid follows her, watching what she patterns the trees to grow. Little hessian pouches with oats in them, or brass tacks. Dangling pillars of salt crystals that hang off the branches in little pink stalactites. Pencils that uncurl like runner beans, still all green and bendy. Candies in little twists of wrapper.

Kid raises his eyebrows. 'So candy's a necessity, is it?'

'You've tasted our coffee,' Gram says with a grimace. 'Candy's a necessity.' She leans backwards to stretch out her back and wipes her brow with her stump. 'Time for a breather. And I reckon this is as good a time and place as any.'

Kid cocks his head. 'For what?'

He stands there, silent, waiting for Gram to answer. She looks down at her missing hand for a long time before she does.

'Hush and Matilda's ma,' she says wearily. 'She ain't dead.'

Kid knew it. He just knew that Gram was hiding something from him. Now the way that Hush talks about her ma makes complete sense. She's alive. Of course she is. Kid's always known that whoever wove him and sent him here loves Hush and Matilda like only a parent could.

He wonders what question to ask first.

Eventually, he settles on: 'Why did you lie?'

'I didn't lie,' Gram says tartly. 'I told you that no one outside of this pocket world loves these girls any more. Which is true. If you took that to mean that Hush and Matilda's ma got killed, then that's your assumption.'

Kid doesn't understand. He is just so confused. 'So you're telling me the mother's alive, but she doesn't love them?'

'Not any more, no.'

Kid snorts and makes a face. That's so absurd that he

can't even fathom it. Mothers don't just stop loving their kids. Love doesn't work like that. It doesn't just go away. When he tells Gram that, she looks very sad and very old and very tired.

'You're right,' she says. 'It didn't go away. It got taken. To Carcosa.'

Carcosa. That word brings a memory back to Kid, quick like a thunder flash, sudden like a knife stab. He steps backwards, suddenly trembling. In his mind black stars are shining above a silent city of yellow stone, where shadows hang like tattered flags, and people have gems instead of eyes.

'Carcosa,' he whispers. 'I've been there. Carcosa's where I was woven.'

'Well now.' Gram presses her mouth into a thin, grim line. 'That's what I was afraid of, Kid.'

And there in the orchard, she tells him why.

It started, for me at least, in Dustbowl. On Deeker Street. I remember losing my purse in the market there.

Pickpocketed, I thought. Ah well. It happens. Let be. Go home.

So I left the market, went back down the emptying streets. It was almost curfew, but I lived nearby on the corner of Scrub and Ninth. You see, by then, my homestead had been burned by undoers, and I had moved into the city that our most powerful world weavers had patterned at the centre of Dustbowl. Cities were the only places you could be safe by then. I suppose really that it was more of a fortress. Very high walls.

And behind them, so many people! As well as all the survivors of Dustbowl, there were folk from dozens of other worlds that had been destroyed by havoc.

It was crowded and ugly. Squat brown buildings with domed roofs. When I first saw the city, from a distance, it looked like the backs of toads all huddled together. But like everything on Dustbowl, our city had a beauty to it. It was rough and it was harsh, but it was full of good people all helping each other survive.

I lived in a little flat, with one bedroom and an office, and a balcony above the communal garden where I could sit and mark students' work.

I don't remember much about that evening after I came back from the market, apart from seeing my very old neighbour, Hogan, in the garden with his easel and oil paints. His beady-eye was buzzing around him anxiously – everyone had them, you understand, as protection from undoers – but Hogan swatted the thing aside and poured himself a wine and started to paint.

Risky of him, to stay outside like that, in the dark. Even within the city. But then Hogan was from an older time. And his paintings were wonderful. There weren't many artists left in Dustbowl. Soldiers? Plenty. Builders of walls and breeders of beady-eyes? Sure. But not many like Hogan. He was quite famous because of it. The whole city loved him. He was proof, you see, that there was still beauty in our world, if you had the eyes to see it. Hogan helped us believe we were living for something, instead of just living.

We talked a little, Hogan and me. City chitchat. News of

undoers thickening again at Dustbowl's western edge. Yet another uprising on yet another world. Gossip about the delegation from one of the most ancient and powerful worlds, Carcosa, who were visiting the city to negotiate some sort of refugee exchange with Dustbowl's own congress. We talked about this and that, and then I told Hogan not to stay out late, and I locked my doors and barred my windows and went to bed with my own beady-eye beside me. The book I was reading that night had no page 278. A printing error, of course. Annoyed, I put it down and went to sleep.

In the morning my cat, Sprocket, wasn't in her basket. I worried a little. But not too much. Even with the threat of undoers, cats in Dustbowl were like cats in any other world: they came and went as they pleased.

The rest of my morning went by normally. I washed and made myself coffee. Discovered I was out of milk. Could've sworn I had bought some at Deeker Street. In fact I knew I had. But I convinced myself that maybe I hadn't, because of my purse getting stolen.

I sat down at my breakfast table to mark a student's test. Realised he hadn't submitted it, even though I remembered him doing so. Now I was really starting to worry. My purse, last night's book, the milk, now this work. Was I going mad?

I recall thinking: blame Sprocket. That cat was always swiping things. I went out onto the balcony to look down into the garden, fully expecting to see torn up pages of mathematics strewn across the lavender beds.

I didn't see Sprocket. Nor any work from my student. But

beneath me, in the garden, old Hogan was still in his painter's overalls, standing in front of his easel. A dozen finished pictures lay discarded around him. Hearing me open the balcony, he turned around. His teeth were dark with too much wine, and his eyes were red-rimmed. I had never seen him look so frightened or upset.

'Hogan!' I said, using my strict teacher voice. 'Surely you ain't been painting out here all night?'

He answered me back: 'Not all night. I went in and tried to sleep, thinking that might help. But it made no difference. I can't any more. It's all gone.'

I didn't understand him at first. Not until I saw his paintings. They were average. Do you understand? Hogan, the greatest artist in all Dustbowl. Even a shopping list by Hogan was worth putting in a frame. But these pictures he had worked all night on, every one of them was the work of an amateur.

That was when it began to dawn on me that something really wrong was happening. And happening to all of us.

I talked to Hogan some more. He said he did not know how to paint any more. It just wasn't in his mind. One moment it had been there, and then his talent was gone. Cut away. Snipped out of his head, as if with a pair of scissors.

The worlds-war, you see, had already begun the day before. It was going on around us even as Hogan and I spoke.

It turns out the weavers from Carcosa didn't want to take in refugees – just pieces of them.

You can't imagine those first few days . . . The things we all

73

lost. The Carcosans hacked through our city with the grace of a butcher. Cutting away at any and everything: roof tiles, newborns, road signs. People's voices, their little fingers, their bravery, their laughs. They cut the colour blue from me, I don't see it any more, just grey. They took Sprocket and my bedroom wallpaper and all the lavender on my balcony. And page 278 of my book, of course, and the milk I bought at Deeker. And maybe my purse. Although it really might have been a pickpocket.

I got off lightly compared to some. Like Cora Quiet, the woman who lived three streets away. She was mother of two kids. A Carcosan took the love she had for them. Cut it from her heart. After that she didn't love them any more. Couldn't love them. Wasn't able to. Her own daughters.

That's how I came to care for them. It was just too painful otherwise. Cora tracked a waythread out of Dustbowl and went to a world called Yonder. Said she was going to wait there, until the war was over and she could get back what they'd stolen. So that's some small mercy, I suppose. They took her love but not her hope.

What do the Carcosans do with all those . . . those parts? That's what you're wondering, right, Kid? I didn't know for a long time. Dustbowl sent off an army to Carcosa, to get back what'd been taken. Never saw any of those soldiers again. People that looked like them came back, but they were Carcosans, with the stolen faces of our warrior weavers patterned over their own, like masks. And this time, they cut us up so much that Dustbowl went teetering into havoc.

Now you see why Matilda's so paranoid. Carcosans can look like anything. The only way to spot them is to watch for the tattoo that they all carry somewhere upon them. A yellow eye that blinks open when one Carcosan meets another. We call that the Yellow Sign.

As Dustbowl fell, I took Hush and Matilda and ran. We made it out of the city, more or less. That's when I lost my left hand, and Matilda lost her shadow. A Carcosan took a fancy to it, and cut it off her feet as she fled.

We tried to make it into Yonder, the world where Cora was waiting, but by then we were too late. All the waythreads there had been cut, to stop the Carcosans. So we had nowhere else to go, except to hide out here. In my little pocket world. I was supposed to retire here. I was going to sit and grow old and watch the peach blossoms fall, and Hogan was going to visit and paint me and my orchard. But none of that happened. Instead, this place became our shelter. Our hidey.

After we got here, we managed to make contact with survivors in other hideys. That's when we learned the truth. About what the Carcosans do with all those . . . pieces.

They trade them, Kid. In Carcosa, at enormous pattern markets. Someone can buy Cora's love for her two children, and have that feeling stitched into their own heart. It's all in Carcosa. My hand. Hogan's talent. They wear us, Kid. They wear what they took from us like it's fashion.

After Gram's story is finished, Kid is silent. He can't find any words to say. The horror of what he's just been told churns and rolls in him until he feels sick. Around him the spring wind blows and clinks the cutlery on the orchard's branches.

'You OK, Kid?' Gram asks him softly.

He swallows and nods his head. 'Why wouldn't you tell me about this before?'

'Didn't want to remind you about Carcosans, just in case you used to be one. Some of them cut up their own heads, you see. To try and get folk to trust them to let them into their hideys.'

Kid's eyes go wide. 'But I do remember Carcosa. What if I am one of them?'

Gram just smiles at him fondly. She leans forward and pats his arm. 'I've been watching you. Seen you with Hush. If you came here as a Carcosan, you ain't here as one any more. Are you?'

Kid looks at her and shakes his head. Whatever he is, he knows it's not that.

Gram chuckles in an all-knowing teacher kind of way. 'Those slow, sure powers,' she says, half to herself. 'Knew I was right to trust in them.'

By this point, Gram has worked just over half the rows, and Kid can see the front door of the house ahead of them as they come full circle through the trees. It's there, right in the heart of the orchard, one row from Crockett's gravestone, that Kid first spots the smoke. Black and rising, far to the east. Which is impossible. There's no east here in the pocket world, no north, no south, no west. Just the orchard and the house.

And now smoke.

Gram sees it too. She frowns and rubs her glasses like the smoke is a smudge on the lenses. But it's there. Puffing towards them in a dark plume.

'What is it?' Kid mutters. 'Gram?'

She's gone very still, very silent, very pale. Fixes Kid with a look he's never seen before. A look like a curse. She takes a step away from him. Then another and another. Then she turns to the house, yelling out for Matilda and Hush.

Kid doesn't understand what's going on. He goes to follow Gram but the beady-eye buzzes into his path, more furious than he's ever seen it. He backs away, terrified, holding up his hands. A sound is building up from where the smoke is coming from. A grinding, growling rhythm that Kid starts to feel coming up through the soles of his boots. Then a few rows over, the trees start to shudder and topple as a train roars into view: a slick black beast of shrieking steam and dervishing wheels, pulling three gilded carriages behind it.

How did it get here? How could it cross? Kid has no idea. The train comes on regardless, ploughing through the orchard, smashing the trees to kindling, just missing Crockett's rock. Its pistons clang out iron thunder, its chimney spouts brimstone. The grass beneath it is quicksilvering as someone patterns fresh rails under the wheels.

The locomotive screeches as it slows and shudders to a halt, hissing out white clouds of smoke and wobbling faintly in its own heat. A man steps down from the front carriage in a cream linen suit. A silk handkerchief pokes out from the pocket of his blazer, dark buttons flash at his cuffs and down his waistcoat, and a thimble glints on the end of his left forefinger. The man is waving a little paper fan beneath his chin. On the side of his neck, just below his ear, is a small glowing mark in the shape of an eye. It shines on his skin like it has been tattooed with light instead of ink. And Kid knows it is the Yellow Sign, and that this man is from Carcosa, just like he is.

The Carcosan walks past the train wheels, through the wafting smoke, and stands there, waving his fan and watching Kid cower in the grass.

'Where are my girls?' he asks in a voice like warm silk.

Kid looks up at the man from Carcosa. His face is perfect as a painting. Porcelain skin, short blond hair pomaded and parted down the middle, and a black moustache that looks like it has been drawn on with two neat swipes of a fountain pen. His left cheek has a single dimple that sinks in as he smiles. And yet to Kid something seems fake about it all. As if the man's clothes are just a costume and his face is a mask. Most probably it is. Probably this man's eyes, his lips, his cheeks, were all someone else's once. Until he cut them out and made them his.

'My girls,' he says to Kid again. 'Where are they?' Then he gives a theatrical sigh and looks towards the house.

Shouts are coming from inside, high and panicked and hard to make out.

'Ah,' says the Carcosan. 'That sounds like my Mattie.'

As he steps forward, the beady-eye attacks. It was hiding around the other side of a tree trunk, and now it buzzes out at full speed. Wings a blur, stinger pulsing. The man from Carcosa just points his thimbled finger and blinks once, and the bug comes apart like a handful of confetti. All of its pieces twirl and flutter in the air and rest on his arm. The beady-eye has been patterned into a dozen tiny blue butterflies that line up obediently on his sleeve.

As Kid watches, the Carcosan pulls a skewer from the air, drawing it out like a splinter from a thumb. He impales the blue butterflies upon it, one by one, and then he starts licking them off with his tongue like they're made of candy.

Over at the house, the screen door opens. It's Gram. She comes back out and stands on the stoop and folds her arms. Does it in such a way that everyone can see the thimble that she's wearing.

'Not a step further,' she says. 'You cross back out of here.'

The Carcosan loses interest in Kid immediately. He patterns a hat on his head and tips it at Gram and then throws the hat away like it's trash. When he smiles, his mouth is stained blue with crushed butterfly wings.

'Morning, madam. My name is James Décollage Rapture. Can I tempt you with a candied butterfly?'

Gram looks at him stonily. Rapture tosses the skewer away and whips out his pocket handkerchief. He passes it over his face once and all trace of blue is gone from his lips.

'A fine, fine pocket world you have here, madam.'

Behind her glasses, Gram's eyes narrow. 'Sure used to be.'

'Ah.' The Carcosan looks around at his train and the upturned orchard and makes an *oops!* face. 'I'll tidy all that up before I leave, you have my word.'

'No need. You can just go.'

'Go?' Rapture patterns a tear on his cheek and wipes it away with one finger. 'Hospitality these days is not what it was. Very well then. I'll be happy to leave you be, here in your charming pocket world. But I will be bringing my two beloved daughters back to Carcosa with me, of course.'

There's silence. For a long time. Rapture enjoys the looks on Kid and Gram's faces before he continues.

'I mean, they aren't strictly my daughters. But I am utterly devoted to them. Even though we've never met. It's quite a sublime feeling, a mother's love for her children. I'm very lucky to own it. Cost me dearly at the pattern markets.'

It all connects together in Kid's head. This man has bought Cora Quiet's love for Hush and Matilda at Carcosa's pattern markets, and sewn that part of their mother into his own heart. He thinks: *I was woven by a mother who was also not a mother*.

'You people . . .' Gram breathes, loathing in her voice. 'You're monsters.'

'Oh certainly,' agrees Rapture. 'Most of the time, that's entirely true. But you can rest assured – I'm not going to hurt our girls. I love them just as much as you do, see. Just as much as Cora did. She's in me, now. That part of her. And she misses them. Which means I miss them. Very, very much. That's why I went to great, great lengths to find them. You know what they say about a mother's love – it won't be stopped.'

Gram steps back, shaking her head, as if she might be able to unsee and unhear the horror of this man. Then she seems to force herself to stay put. She chuckles, like she's impressed.

'So where does the kid come into all this?' she asks. 'I'm presuming his coming here wasn't just coincidence?'

She's stalling him. Buying time with talking. Rapture either doesn't know it or doesn't care. Maybe he's spent so long getting here, that's he determined to enjoy every moment of it.

'Well, madam.' Rapture taps the side of his head twice. 'This is where I excelled myself. You see, as soon I started loving my darling girls, I thought I would just see a waythread leading straight to them. But that didn't happen. Couldn't track them at all. And tracking is what I do.

'It caused me no end of heartache. I still don't quite understand why I can't. But then, I've never been a parent before. This is all new to me.

'I searched a hundred worlds for a trace of my daughters. You've hidden this pocket world very well, I must say. At times it felt like scouring a beach for one particular grain of sand. In the end, I found something. A little girl's shadow.'

'Matilda's,' whispers Gram, and Kid remembers what Hush told him, back in the orchard.

'Matilda's,' repeats Rapture, his voice strangely tender. 'A Carcosan cut her shadow off her heels as she was fleeing Dustbowl. And off it went to our pattern markets. Where I tracked it down. Took me a long, long time to find. We have thousands of shadows for sale in Carcosa. There was a fashion in the city, for a time, to paste them on to walls like wallpaper and force them to dance. But I had a much better use for Matilda's shadow: I had it spun into Kid here.'

The words fall like sledgehammers, cracking everything wide open. A shadow? That's just – no. How can he be a shadow? The same way Crockett was a rock, Kid tells himself. The same way anything can be anything, given a thimble and enough talent. And suddenly Kid is remembering all the moments he has felt like no one, like an outline waiting to be filled in. Isn't that just what someone patterned from a shadow would feel?

But how can he be made from Matilda's shadow? He's nothing like her.

'Of course you're nothing like her,' Rapture says, and Kid realises he must have said that last thought out loud. 'Our shadows aren't our twins, are they? They're more like . . . dance partners. Alike us in some ways, and opposite in others. And what is it they do, more than anything else?'

'They follow,' whispers Kid, and Rapture bows like he's being applauded.

'You became my little hunting hound, Kid. Understand?

You tracked after Matilda, whilst I tracked you. Although, it didn't work smoothly at first. You kept developing a conscience. Refused to follow the waythread which only you could see. Most frustrating. I had to make some alterations to your pattern. Take out some unnecessary memories.'

Rapture's thimbelled finger twirls lazily in Kid's direction, and Kid feels the edge of the Carcosan's power, poised and ready and scalpel-sharp. Terror wells up in him, like blood from a cut. He cowers back against a tree, suddenly understanding. Rapture cut out his memories so that Kid would do what he wanted him to do.

'Now, then.' Rapture grins and takes a step closer to the house. 'This has been just delightful. But I think it's time I took my little princesses and went off on my way, don't you?'

Gram doesn't answer.

She's done talking.

She whips up her hand and points her thimble at Rapture and starts to weave.

Gram points and patterns fast. But Rapture is faster. Around Kid, the world flickers and alters like someone flipping through a sketchbook of nightmares. The orchard trees have pink tentacles for branches that coil around Rapture and crush him but then suddenly their suckers swell up and become bubbles that rise away and pop. Then the air around Gram turns to a poisonous green mist and the last Kid sees is her gagging and clawing her throat. But a moment later, she strides out from it wearing a gas mask and

83

melts the sun over Rapture's head. Golden fire waterfalls over him and then arcs like lightning back into the sky and becomes a sun again.

The duel goes on, shifting from reality to reality, as Gram and Rapture each try to weave themselves as winners. Kid cowers to one side. Without a thimble, his power is useless. All he can do is watch as the pocket world warps and thins and darkens, its pattern growing more and more ragged with each reweaving. Black spots start to pinprick in the air, hissing loud as wasp hives as they drink up the sky, sucking it into havoc. Then one of them appears like a gunshot in Gram's thigh and she cries out and staggers to one side. Her thimble falls off her forefinger and the pattern she was weaving – a world that slopes forward, so that Rapture's train steamrollers over him from behind – loses shape and dissolves.

As Rapture steps forward to end the duel, Kid finds his courage at last. He has no power but he still has his fists, and he clenches them and launches himself at the Carcosan with a yell. Rapture turns and simply weaves a tree in Kid's way so that he runs head first into its trunk.

Pain lights up in Kid's skull like fireworks and he falls backwards, holding his scraped face and groaning. But he's bought Gram a vital second, and she uses that time to escape. Kid sees her roll sideways onto a waythread, and vanish through the side of the house like a ghost. Rapture aims his power at her, but he's too late. She's crossed out of the pocket world.

Rapture lets her go. He turns back to the house, pointing his finger from room to room as he searches the pattern for Hush and Matilda. He's running out of time to find them. The world is tilting like a shipwreck as it slides down into havoc. Undoers are thickening everywhere, their bodies flickering into being like candle flames in the gloom. Rapture strides over to Kid and grabs him by the collar and hauls him to his feet.

'Where are my girls?' Rapture's perfect face is inches from Kid's. His cologne smells like peppermint but his breath is rotten and putrid. He takes a thimble from his suit pocket and jams it onto Kid's forefinger and shakes him like a rag doll: 'FIND THEM.'

Suddenly Kid is a worldweaver again. He blinks and sees the world's pattern, shredding behind his eyelids. Everything is tipping sideways into raggedy oblivion. Waythreads sprout from his feet like neon roots. Red lines that lead to the undoers, and glowing green ones that promise Kid safety, all fraying and snapping one by one as the pocket world disintegrates. But the silver-white thread joining him and the sisters together shines bright as a moonlit path. Heading west. There is no west here in this world, but that is where the silver waythread leads. Because the Quiet sisters are gone. That's why Gram was stalling. That's why she talked and then fought and maybe died – so Hush and Matilda could get their thimbles and run.

Rapture must realise this, because he turns and drags Kid by his shirt back through the ruined orchard and towards the waiting train. Kid struggles and stumbles in the Carcosan's iron grip, as around him the pocket world dies. The sun burns down like a campfire and the trees winnow to sticks and the air whistles away through the mouths of the undoers.

The first of them opens its pinhole eyes and raises its pale crescent head. It only vaguely resembles a person: arms long and slack as skipping ropes and a slumped body like a guttering candle. It oozes towards the train. Rapture aims his forefinger and the undoer shuts its mouth and its body bursts apart like a rotted peach and moulders away to nothing. Kid gasps as cold courses down from the Carcosan's hand and into him like an electric current. That same heart-stopping chill Kid felt when he ended the undoers that chased him here.

Rapture snorts a white plume of air and slings Kid onto the first carriage like he's a piece of luggage and then steps aboard himself. Whoever is driving the train backs it slowly out of the pocket world on the waythread it crossed here on. Before they shift into another place, Kid closes his eyes and searches all the ruination and suddenly his mind fixes upon a red waythread that is unlike all the others: this one is a rusty brown and is a colour that he knows.

His mind follows it to where the waythread ends at a place still as stone, and with all his pent-up power, Kid weaves just before they cross. This second time it takes only an instant to rouse his bestie, as if Crockett had been sleeping all that time. The world around him gives a dying spasm, and then the train is in a place where the sun still shines and the wind still blows and the pattern still holds.

Kid gets up off the carriage corridor's plush black carpet and closes his eyes to feel for Crockett. Did his bestie make it across?

But Rapture has felt him patterning and turns to slam a fist into his belly. Kid falls back down, face first, gasping breaths in sips. Rapture turns him over with his boot. Kid has woven a pistol from the air around his fingers. Rapture turns it into a water pistol. Kid fills the water pistol with acid. Rapture patterns the acid into lemonade. Then he kicks the toy gun from Kid's hand and leans down and seizes Kid around the neck. Kid bucks and struggles but Rapture just grips harder and smiles. His front teeth are all perfect but the ones at the back are rotten and black.

'So,' he says softly. 'The grandma got them out, did she? Where to? Which way is that silver waythread telling you to go, Kid?'

The waythread ribbons west, out of this world to somewhere else, somewhere far away and elsewhere. But Kid swallows and sucks in a breath and shakes his head as much as Rapture's hand allows.

'I don't see it any more,' he lies. 'They must have been stranded back in the pocket world. They must be dead now.'

Rapture laughs delightedly. Then his smile falls off his face, guillotine-quick.

'Now, I don't blame you for forgetting this,' he says. 'But you don't ever lie to James Décollage Rapture.'

As he speaks, Rapture is drawing a little black box from his inside blazer pocket and opening it up. Two round and glittering opals the size of coins are sitting on the cushioned velvet and Rapture tips the box sideways so that the opals plop onto Kid's chest. At once the gems start moving, crawling like glitter-backed bugs, up his shirt and over Rapture's hand and across Kid's cheeks, towards his eyes. He can hear the opals making tiny little noises, burbling to each other in anticipation, in excitement, as they reach Kid's eyelids, and wriggle and burrow beneath them.

• • •

After Kid tells him everything he wants to know, Rapture prises the opals off Kid's eyes with the blade of his switchknife. There's a sucking pop as they come loose, followed by their tiny disappointed screams. They only fed for a little while, so there isn't too much blood. Rapture takes out his yellow silk handkerchief and wipes away the blood so Kid can see and then he flicks the handkerchief once and it is clean again.

'There now,' he says. 'Wasn't so hard, was it?'

Kid lies on his back, head lolling on the carpet, looking up at the carriage's dark wood panelled ceiling and ornate brass lamps shaped like the necks of swans. He is still hypnotised by what he saw when the opal stones were over his eyes. Those colours – he'd do anything to see those colours again. They made everything glitter. Painted the world something beautiful. And whilst he was seeing them, nothing else mattered.

Rapture stands and pockets away the gems. 'Catelin?'

Down the corridor comes the sound of footsteps, and a thin lady appears. She is wearing jeans and a once-white vest with a bright green cap and a red bandana, and her entire body is etched with purple tattoos. Some of the tattoos are moving in simple animated loops. Cats winking and comets sparkling and skeletons dancing. As she draws nearer, Kid sees two emeralds glittering where her eyes ought to be.

'They escaped?' Catelin asks.

'Not far,' Rapture replies. 'Westward, two or three worlds away. Four at the most.'

Catelin stands there, expressionless, emotionless, jewelled eyes sparkling. 'You can track them now?'

'No,' snaps Rapture, and something in his tone tells Kid that he is embarrassed by this, that a parent ought to be able to find their own daughters. 'I think it must be Cora. The bit of her that's in me, it doesn't want me finding them.'

'You're relying on the boy then?' says Catelin.

Rapture gives Kid a look of grudging admiration. 'He attacked me. Then lied to me. Had to slavestone him to get the truth.'

'That's a problem.' Catelin rubs at a tattooed tiger prowling around and around her neck. 'Kid can't track waythreads with slavestones over his eyes.'

'There is another way he'll help me,' Rapture says softly, taking out his handkerchief and wiping it over his face.

'Take him into my cabin, Catelin. Keep the train heading westward until I'm done with him.'

Catelin leans over and hauls Kid up by the armpits. He puts up no resistance at all. Just thinks those colours, those colours, those colours . . .

Catelin drags him down the corridor to one of the doors that lead off of it. The door is glass-fronted and its insides are obscured by ruffled pink curtains. Catelin shoulders it open and heaves Kid inside like he's a sack. He lands on a rug made from the flayed skin of a purple tiger and sits up and looks around.

He is in a cabin with an unmade bed with yellow silk sheets and a dark wooden wardrobe and a dresser with a golden mirror surrounded by bottles of face tincture and jars of hair pomade. Kid's gaze slips over all of it without interest. He is thinking about the slavestones. He is thinking about those colours they showed him and he feels an ache behind his eyes to see them again.

'Was it real?' he asks, before Catelin closes the door. 'What I just saw?'

Catelin pauses and cocks her head as she understands. 'Through the slavestones? Naw.' She sighs, and it is a sigh that holds both utter contentment and unfathomable sadness. 'Not that it matters when you've got them on. You'll do anything, won't you, to keep seeing those colours? That's why you told Rapture what he wanted to know, about these sisters we're hunting. And that's why I do everything he tells me, too.'

Kid looks away, shamefaced. It isn't just that he told Rapture, told him everything, but that he did it eagerly too.

'Don't blame yourself,' Catelin says, her emeralds glittering like they're full of tears. 'That's what being slavestoned will do to you.' Her voice goes quiet. 'Why d'you think I'm helping him?'

Catelin's talking to him kindly now, but suddenly Kid realises that this lady will do anything Rapture tells her to. No matter how loathsome or cruel. He stares at her gemstone eyes in pity and in fear and – despite everything she's told him – in envy too. Because right now, Catelin's seeing those colours, those hypnotic wondrous colours . . .

Maybe she sees the longing in him, because as she turns away, she says, 'Take my advice, and its advice from someone who knows: don't you put them stones on again. You'll want to. But don't. If you put them on for too long, they . . . they eat away your eyes. If I take these gems off, I won't see the colours, or any colours ever again. Not that it matters. After Rapture gets his girls, he's taking me to Carcosa, to sing in their suicide opera.'

Catelin leaves and the train lets out a shriek and the carriage judders. The slats of light through the cabin's barred windows slide slowly away and then back again as they start to move. Heading west, towards this world's edge. Hunting down the sisters.

'Psst.'

Kid sits up. The sound came from the wood panelled wall at the far end of the carriage. There's a brass air vent there about the size of a letterbox and peering behind that grill are a small pair of shiny black eyes lined with reddish fur.

'Crockett!' Kid almost shouts out the name, then claps a hand over his mouth and looks back to the door. He crouches down and tries to keep a lid on his joy. His friend. His little woven bestie. He's back. Hush really was right. If you hold someone in your head and in your heart, they're never truly gone.

'I am a teeny bit confused as to what is going on,' Crockett confides through the grill. 'But I am guessing that you need me to poke someone with my dagger again?'

Kid can't speak past the lump in his throat, so he just nods. It is good to see his friend again. After everything he's just gone through, Kid could stare forever at Crockett's adorably squished face inside the air vent. His world has gone to havoc and horror, but if Kid just focuses on Crockett's cheeks, plump as peaches, things don't seem so bad.

'Keep quiet,' Kid tells him.

'I will be very sneaky.' Crockett tries to nod, which gets his nose covered in dust, and makes him sneeze. 'Oops.'

Kid scrambles to his feet and whirls around as the door opens. In saunters Rapture. Kid stands in front of the air vent and tries his best to look casual. Rapture stares at him and Kid stares back, unable to keep the hatred from his stare. Rapture sees it and smiles like it pleases him.

'You reckon I'm a monster,' he says.

Kid shrugs and doesn't deny it.

Rapture laughs and claps him. 'The kid's learning! Why,

it was only a little while ago that you thought you could get away with lying to me. This is better, much better.'

As he talks, Rapture patterns himself an armchair from the air and sits back in it with his legs stretched out and his boots crossed.

'You probably think you won't help me. Don't you? But you will. You did before.'

Rapture sits, lazily waving his thimbled finger. He patterns tears under his eyes. Weaves a gold oval picture frame with a photograph of Hush and Matilda smiling in it. Clasps his hands around it and falls to his knees, begging.

'Please,' he chokes. 'Please. You have to help me. You have to help me find them. I'm just a father who loves his daughters. I'm just a father who wants to bring them home.'

Kid stares at the Carcosan, feeling both contempt and rising dread. 'What are you doing?'

'Practising,' says Rapture. 'I want to make a good impression when you meet me again.'

Kid feels the cut in his mind, cold and sharp and precise as a scalpel. Rapture just took something from him. A memory. Kid doesn't even know what it was any more. He just knows it's gone. He throws up his own power but the Carcosan is too strong. Whatever defences Kid weaves, Rapture tears them down. He takes and he takes, and Kid can't stop forgetting. Little things, then big things, then everything, all cut away. What was Hush's band called? Didn't she have a sister? Where are they now? Aboard this train, or somewhere else? Why has a little furry creature just launched itself from its hiding place, yelling and waving a tiny sword? How has that sword just become a bunch of flowers? And who is this man in front of Kid now, kneeling down and crying, holding out a gold-framed picture of his two beloved girls?

PART
TWO

THE BOOK
OF HUSH

Hush is in the kitchen sneaking candies from the tin when Gram runs up the stoop and says one word that ends the world.

'Carcosans!'

That's all it takes to undo everything the last three years has woven around their lives. All that safety and sameness is suddenly gone.

'You hear me?' Gram seizes Hush by the shoulders and pushes her away from the screen door. 'Carcosans are crossing. They'll be here any moment.'

Hush's mouth is still too full of candy to say anything back. She spits the sweets back into their wrappers and twists them up and pops them in the back pocket of her jeans. Fear's buzzing through her like a sugar rush. And in her ears comes a rumbling, louder and louder, as something rollicks towards the house at speed.

'Where's your sister?' Gram pulls out her thimble on its chain and bites it between her teeth and jams her finger in and undoes the clasp. 'Go get Matilda. Just like we planned, OK?' She snaps her fingers in front of Hush's eyes. 'Celeste!'

Hush blinks and nods. It's all happening too fast. Gram goes to the door with her thimble humming on her finger and peers through the screen. Outside, smoke is rising and the orchard trees are toppling and a black train is shuddering to a halt in front of Kid.

Kid.

Hush liked him. She trusted him. She defended him to Matilda. She painted his nails and snuck him sweets and made a four-player board game so he could join in. She was going to teach him how to play kazoo super loud and super bad. All for him to bring Carcosans here?

She thought he was her friend.

'I'LL KILL HIM!' Matilda hurricanes into the kitchen, slamming a fresh hive into the bottom of her shotgun. Her hair's not yet plaited and it's dark and frizzy as a stormcloud. She barges past Hush and beelines for the screen door until Gram hauls her back by the dungarees.

'You be still, Matilda Quiet!' she thunders in the voice she nearly never uses. The one that makes it seem like she's their teacher instead of their Gram. It's a tone that still works on Hush, but Matilda seems immune to it.

'I WON'T,' she yells back. 'I WAS RIGHT, WE NEVER SHOULDA TRUSTED HIM—'

Gram curses. Strongly. She hasn't ever even said a borderline one before. Not in three full years. Matilda's so surprised that she actually shuts up. For the first time Hush sees how frightened her sister looks. The stunnerbee shotgun is shaking in her white-knuckled grip.

'You swore you wouldn't do this,' Gram says at them, teeth bared and clenched like each word she speaks is an agony. 'You swore to me that if they came – when they came – and I told you to go, you'd go.'

Hush and Matilda glance sideways at each other. Both remembering. They did promise. Not the regular, flimsy kind that breaks after a few hours at best. *I'll never annoy you again. I won't tell anyone about Nate's singing rose.* Not a promise like that.

'We knew this could happen,' Gram says. 'We planned for it. You're ready, ain't you? You got your thimbles? Show me your hands. Look at them fingers.'

Hush and Matilda look down at their shellacked nails. Blue Ruin. The same colour they've had to paint them for the last three years, just in case today came. Gram holds out the bottle that she keeps, always, like a totem, in her shirt pocket. She presses it into Matilda's hands.

'Put some patterns between you and here,' Gram reminds them. 'Once you reckon you're safe enough, give Nate the varnish using the gobetween and look for that blue waythread. You get me?'

Hush and Matilda don't say a thing. Tears are rolling down Hush's nose and onto the kitchen tiles and Matilda is swiping at her own eyes like she's furious at them for crying.

'You get me?' Gram says again, using the teacher voice again.

'We get you, Gram,' Hush manages to say.

Gram takes a long look at both of them. Sees how scared

they are. Her expression softens and she turns her teacher voice off like a switch.

'Hey, now. It's OK. Hush, Matilda, it'll be OK. Maybe this ain't my end, you hear me? If I can, I'll get away. I'll meet you in Garrison if I'm able.'

She comes forward and tips both their heads forward and kisses them. Just holds them and kisses them again, and once more. The three of them cling to each other for a few more seconds, knowing that seconds are all they have left.

'Gram, I – I love you,' Hush manages to say before starting to sob. 'But I'm so scared.'

'That's good.' Gram kisses them one last time. 'Fear'll keep you alive. Fear, and Matilda's shotgun. But only for a time. Sooner or later, you'll need them slow, sure powers. You know the ones I mean. I don't know what'll happen to you out there, but I know you'll need love and kindness to make it.'

She squeezes them once, then straightens her steel-rimmed glasses and takes a long, shuddering breath.

'Make sure this Nate is good to you,' she says to Matilda.

'You make sure of that, too,' she says to Hush.

'You're sisters,' she reminds them both. 'Don't ever forget that you're sisters.'

Then she turns and walks out onto the stoop with her thimblefinger readied.

Hush's heart feels like it's being torn from her chest like a stone from a peach, but she takes Matilda's hand and turns away from Gram. Because they promised. And because her sacrifice has to mean something.

Outside the house, someone's talking. It ain't Gram and it ain't Kid, which means it has to be a Carcosan.

They have to go. They have to go *now*.

Hush lets Matilda pull her into the living room. She tries to focus on the plan. The one meant to save them from Carcosans. She runs to the painting that Hogan did, to where the gobetween is hidden. Where he lives, when he's not carrying messages between the patterns. Matilda hooks her fingers under the frame and pulls and it swings upwards like a hatch. In his nest inside the chimney, the gobetween stirs. He pokes his head from his shell and unfurls his eyes on stalks.

'Lettuh?' he says in his burbly little voice.

To Hush, the gobetween looks like a swamp monster's ice cream that's fallen upside-down onto the floor. His body is a slimy green ball, stuffed into a pinecone-shaped shell. His silvery trails are all over the chimney bricks.

'Lettuh?' he says again.

Matilda snatches up a pen and a scrap of paper. 'Just a quick one, Gobi.' That's what she calls him, which is just typical of her. Can't abide a nickname for herself, but happy to give them to anyone and everyone else.

'Little quicky lovey dovey,' chirps Gobi.

'Very little and very quicky,' Hush hisses at her sister. 'Gram said to do that after we run.'

'Well I've started now, Hush.'

'So hurry.'

'I *am* hurrying!' Matilda finishes scribbling her message to Nate McCluskey. Signs her name. Flickers her eyes briefly at Hush, then scowls and adds a bunch of kisses to the end, like it's something she has to do instead of wants to do. Then she rolls up the miniature note and hands it to Gobi.

'Lettuh!' he says, with it gripped in his eyestalks.

'And a present,' Matilda says, giving him the blue nail varnish.

'Woooo,' says Gobi, taking the bottle too and spiralling back into his shell. When Matilda picks it up and peers inside, it's already empty. Patterns and worlds and waythreads away, Gobi will be emerging from another shell identical to this one, carrying the letter and the varnish.

'He's crossed over,' she says, putting the shell in her pocket and taking out her thimble. 'Come on. Our turn now.'

Hush gulps as she puts her own thimble on. The little bucket-shaped thing sits tight on the end of her finger. Her heart beats fast. Her free hand seeks out Matilda's. She grips it tight and Matilda actually lets her.

Together they close their eyes and raise their thimbles and search. For a long time, all Hush sees is darkness. Panic's rising up in her like water. It's in her belly, in her chest, in her throat. Three years since she's used her power, and it was scant even back then. What if it's wasted away, like a muscle would?

At last a waythread bleeds up into Hush's mind, dark as a vein of sap. A way out of the pocket world. Safety somewhere in that reddish-green colour, but all kinds of danger too.

'You see it?' she hears Matilda whisper.

'I see it,' Hush says, and then they run.

They skip across worlds and waythreads like stones over water, both eyes shut and holding hands, trying to put as many patterns between themselves and the pocket world, to go as far as they can, as fast as they can, for as long as they can.

Places flicker and then they're gone again, sudden and shocking as flashes of thunder. First they're slipping over black ice beneath a night sky. An aurora moves above them in violet ribbons and a cruel wind makes Hush gasp. Then they hop on a darker green waythread and the frozen world fractals and shatters. All its shards melt and then bubble into a glowing mushroom jungle. Gilled caps tower above their heads and the air is thick with spores that shine like sparks from a fire. Every step spongey and squelching, until they stumble sideways onto an emerald route, and the mushrooms balloon and burst one by one, and Hush finds herself atop a narrow jewelled bridge that arcs like a rainbow over a golden sea of sunlit cloud.

'You ain't talking,' Matilda pants. 'Usually you'd be talking.'

'Don't feel like talking,' Hush pants back. 'Too busy focusing.'

'Fine by me.'

They're running under red skies through a city of crumbling pyramids and wild flying horses. They stumble onto a stretch of white sand beside a midnight ocean that swims with things that look like galaxies, their spiralled arms trailing down to the depths in starry forevers. Hush's head is starting to pound now, just like her heart.

'When,' she gasps, 'do we stop running?'

'Oh,' Matilda gasps. 'So we *are* talking.'

'Shut up. When though?'

'Love and Mercy, how do I know? I'm doing this first time, same as you.'

'No need – to get – short with me – Mattie.'

The pale sand shifts and scatters into the next world. The ground here is the consistency of oatmeal. Hush slips, comes off the waythread, and pulls Matilda down with her. They fall into an ankle-deep swamp that's like a giant serving of Gram's black bean soup. All sorts of stuff is swimming in it: broken nubs of plastic and rusted grids of metal and rotted chunks of wood. Car tyres and shredded bags and twists of old pipe. It's lukewarm and slimy and it stinks awful bad.

'Urrrrgh!' Matilda leaps up, scowling, hands and knees dripping with muck. 'Havoc's sake, Hush, I thought you said you were focusing?'

'I was.' Hush struggles to her feet too. 'But then we started talking.'

'*You* started talking.'

'We both started talking, it takes two to talk.'

Matilda glares. 'This is such a mature way to apologise for pulling us off the waythread. Tell me you still have your thimble on?'

Hush does, but she hopes they're not crossing any time soon. Part of the reason she fell was that she couldn't go on any longer. Her head is pounding from the effort of all that wayfaring. Matilda must feel the same because she opens her eyes and looks around, glaring at the world they've come to.

Nothing in it but the lumpy black stew and hot clammy white mist and the odd island of a rusted car wreck.

Off in the distance, something spurts into the swamp from on high and then stops, like a giant tap turning on and off. Hush peers up through the mist. That's not sky up there. It's some sort of ceiling. Matilda closes her eyes and manages to pattern a gust of wind and the mist clears just enough for them to see it clear for a moment. The top of the world is covered in plumbing: huge rusted pipes, all squirmed together like guts, their open mouths pointed downwards.

'Great,' Matilda says, 'we're in a slurry bowl.'

Slurry bowls are basically outhouses. Worlds where other worlds can dump all their rubbish and waste. As they stand there, another pipe to their left groans and rattles and gushes out more muck and trash. There's a lot of metal in that one. The sound of it reminds Hush of pulling out the cutlery drawer in the kitchen too far and scattering spoons and forks and knives everywhere.

'You've really landed us in it,' Matilda grumbles.

'I slipped,' Hush snaps. 'I'm sorry, OK?'

'You sound it. You sound it.'

'Stop going by how things sound, Mattie. Aint you always telling me that?'

Matilda's reply contains words that would've gotten her a whole week's worth of chores back in the pocket world. But here she can say them as loud as she wants. Because this world doesn't have Gram in it. They both go quiet, thinking that same thought. Somewhere, another pipe groans and gushes.

'She might beat them,' Hush says after a while. 'She might. She's good with a thimble.' She notices the way Matilda's looking at her, and blushes and hangs her head. 'You're gonna tell me to see things how they are, and not how I want them to be, right?'

Matilda just grunts and with some effort, she patterns their boots so that they're rubber and up to the knees. Not wanting to be outdone, Hush takes some split pieces of plastic from the slurry by her feet and just about manages to weave them into nosepegs. Scants are usually too weak to pattern things from the air, but they can sometimes convince stuff that's already there to shift itself around a bit.

'Where my be?' says a muffled voice in Matilda's dungarees.

'Thank havoc, that was quick.' Matilda pulls out Gobi's shell from her front pocket just as the gobetween emerges. Gripped in his eyestalks is a small note from Nate that's rolled up like a cigarette. A message carried between two shells and two patterns and two worlds. Matilda snatches it and pulls it open and scans it quick.

'Oh deary,' Gobi says, eyes swivelling around. 'Mucky poop.'

'We are well aware, Gobi,' Hush snaps. 'We are well aware. What does Nate say, Mattie? Did he get the varnish okay?'

She peers at the writing but Matilda turns on her heel so Hush can't read. 'Course he has.' She scans the letter some more. 'Says to meet him at a place called Travlin.'

'Travlin?' It isn't a world Hush has ever heard of. 'But why can't we just cross straight into Garrison?'

'Because the McCluskeys are smart, that's why. Remember what happened when we just let someone into our world without checking if they were really who they said they were?'

'Yeah, yeah,' Hush grumbles. 'I get it. The McCluskeys are clever and careful and I'm stupid and careless.'

'Your words, not mine. Let's just meet Nate where we're supposed to meet him.' Matilda flicks at the letter. 'At this Travlin, wherever and whatever that is. Ain't like we exactly have a choice, is it?'

'Fine.' Hush huffs and turns away and closes her eyes, feeling the endless pattern of the slurry bowl as it tangles around her feet. Crossing out of the pocket world, all they needed to do was put some patterns between them and the Carcosans. Almost any route with a hint of green, the colour of crossing and safety and life, would do. Now they have to find one specific waythread, Blue Ruin in colour.

'Let's get searching then,' Matilda says, scribbling on the back of the note. 'I'll tell Nate that we're coming.'

'Natty-Cakes,' chirps Gobi as he shrinks back inside his shell with Matilda's quick reply. 'Tilly-Boo.'

Hush blinks. 'Tilly-Boo? Did – did Gobi just call you Tilly-Boo?'

Matilda gives her a molten stare. 'What? No. Shut up.'

'He did!' Hush giggles. 'Does Nate call you that?'

'I said shut up.'

'Let me read that letter!' She makes a grab for it, but Matilda scrunches it into a ball and chucks it into the swamp.

'Tilly-Boo!' Hush claps her hands with delight. 'It really must be true love if you've let him nickname you.'

'It ain't true love.'

'You sure about that, Tilly-Boo?'

'I'm warning you, Hush. Shut up or I will stunnerbee you.'

Hush sobers up. Because she can see that's not a threat, it's a promise. Matilda's looking at her the same way she looked at Kid. *Just give me one more reason*, her eyes are saying. And all of a sudden Hush isn't laughing no more. Now she's scared. It's not just undoers and Carcosans and falling trash and who knows what else that she needs to look out for. There's danger right here and right now, between her and Matilda. Stacked up like kindling, waiting for a spark.

She closes her eyes and starts searching for the waythread. It'll be some sort of miracle if they can find it before they kill each other.

• • •

They wade through the slurry bowl with their eyes closed, fossicking around for the way to Nate McCluskey. Finding waythreads ain't the problem. Hush just has to focus to see them, sprouting in every direction and glowing in every colour. It's like closing her eyes turns the slurry bowl into one giant serving of multi-coloured noodles. Her thimblefinger snags up route after route from the muck. Most get sent straight back, but any blue ones get checked against Hush's varnished fingernails. Gram made them reapply it every week for three years. Always in the same hue. Always Blue Ruin. Setting down a pattern. Because in a pattern, there's power. Flowing between their fingertips and that bottle in Nate's hands, like an electric current. Woven and rewoven every Tuesday for three years. By now the connection will be so strong that even two scants ought to be able to see it as a waythread.

They just got to find it. How hard can that be?

A long time passes. Enough time for Hush to get hungry again. Not quite hungry enough to try patterning the muck into bread, but still. Her belly's rumbling. She tries drowning it out with talk.

'What sort of food they got in Garrison?'

Bent-backed over to her left, Matilda gives a grunt that says *How am I supposed to know?*

'Well, I reckoned Nate would've told you or something,' Hush says.

Matilda scowls and pretends like she has to go check some waythreads further away. Which she doesn't need to do, because they all connect to her boots anyway.

'I reckon it's too faint,' Hush whines. 'It's only Saturday. Tuesday's when it'll be really—'

'Tuesday is a long way away, Hush. We are two scants, and we're alone, and there may be Carcosans tracking us. We need to get to Nate *now*.'

Hush looks sideways slyly. 'You looking forward to finally seeing him?'

'No.'

'Are you scared you won't like how he looks? Because I don't reckon that matters if it's true love. Although if his laugh is really annoying, or he picks his nose and eats it, then I reckon that might be a problem—'

'Shut up, Hush.'

'Aw, come on, Mattie.' Hush stands up and clicks her neck. 'Why're you always pretending like you don't like him?'

'I don't like him. You went sweet on a Carcosan spy, so I hardly reckon you're in the position to tell me anything about *true love*.' Matilda does air quotes with her fingers for those last two words.

Hush squints at her sister. 'You think I was sweet on Kid?'

'Of course you were sweet on him. I never got asked to be in Bang! Bang! One Dollar!, did I?'

It's surprising to hear the hurt in Matilda's voice, throbbing under her anger like a bassline under a song.

'I didn't think you wanted to be in my band,' Hush says softly.

'I didn't.' Matilda chews on her lip a while. 'Just didn't want anyone else being in it with you, either. Especially not him.'

Hush laughs. 'You know that's part of why I enjoyed hanging out with him, don't you? Because it annoyed you.'

Matilda tuts and rolls her eyes, but there's a sly smile on her face too. 'Even talking about him is fouling up my temper. Let's talk about something else. And let's keep looking.'

Matilda's right. No use thinking about Kid any more. When you're searching for a waythread, it helps to keep your thoughts fixed on where you're headed.

'What's it gonna be like?' Hush asks. 'When we finally get there?'

'To Garrison?' Matilda shrugs. 'Safe.'

'Such an amazingly insightful answer.'

'It's the only answer that matters. Carcosans can't get in.'

'You don't know that for sure.'

'I do. The McCluskeys don't trust anyone. Don't let no one cross.'

'They're letting us.'

Matilda hesitates for a moment, caught between telling and not telling Hush something. Finally she caves to temptation. 'And why do you think that is? Because I sent Nate McCluskey sweetheart letters twice a week for three years.'

Hush gawps. It isn't often she's lost for words. Matilda stands there, enjoying the moment.

'It was all just an act? Mattie, I thought you liked him. As in, like-like.'

'I kept telling you I didn't, though?'

'Yeah, but that's what you would say.'

'Look, we needed somewhere to go, in case something like this happened and we had to leave the pocket world. Nate is our ticket into Garrison.'

'You tricked him! Poor Nate.'

'Poor us. We're the worldless ones, ain't we?'

'What are you gonna do when you meet him?' Hush asks. 'Fake being his sweetheart?'

Matilda shrugs. 'Ain't that what most girls do with boys? It'll be easy.'

Hush reaches new levels of dumbfoundedness. 'Did Gram know about this?' She shakes her head at her mistake. 'Does . . . Does Gram know about this.'

'That I faked the sweetheart stuff? Well, not exactly. But she'd approve.' Matilda sees Hush's expression and shrugs. 'What? She would. Ain't she a big believer in them "slower, surer powers"?'

But Hush shakes her head again. Love and kindness aren't things to lie about. They're not tools to use to get what you want.

'Stop looking so shocked, Hush. And don't look so hurt, either. I would've told you, but I couldn't.'

'Why not?'

'Why not tell the biggest blabbermouth in all the worlds?' Matilda makes a face like *Oh gosh, gee, I don't know.*

Hush looks down at the swamp and blushes. That's fair enough. Talking's her flaw. She knows it. Everyone does. She probably would've let it slip somehow. She gave letters to Gobi too, every now and again, for him to take to Garrison. Mostly just hype for her latest album, like fake press releases that she wrote herself, full of phrases like 'What's more rock and roll than just a voice and a saucepan lid? Nothing, it turns out. *****.' But even so. Matilda's right. If Hush'd known, she would've found a way to tell. Then the McCluskeys would never have taken them in.

This is all true, but it still hurts to be told that her sister regards her as a silly little kid. As someone who talks too much, who trusts too much. Like Matilda's always said,

Hush has never seen things for what they really are. That letter to a sweetheart? It's actually a ticket into Garrison. That kid with amnesia? He's really a Carcosan spy. According to Matilda, nothing is just itself. Everything – love and kindness included – is just a road that you take to get to something else. And for the first time ever, Hush finds herself wondering if her sister might be right.

They fall back into silence as they search. Hush realises that if she closes her eyes and thinks blue, then more of those coloured waythreads seem to rise up into view. She finds navy routes, cyan ones, cerulean and sapphire and indigo and ultramarine. But no Blue Ruin. Not yet. How long is this going to take? No way of knowing. They search and they search. The muck bubbles and burps. The hot mist billows and the pipes splurt and groan. And they look for the waythread that will lead them to Nate.

But the undoers find them first.

• • •

In this world, they look like leeches. Bloated tubes of wriggling dark, each one as long as a forearm. Round mouths lined with needle teeth. Gurgling as they gorge like maggots on the garbage of a thousand worlds, rending it all to havoc.

It's just like Gram said: fear and Matilda's shotgun are what keeps Hush alive. She's wading knee deep in muck, still unable to find the blue waythread, when she suddenly yanks up a route that's bright red and flashing, like an alarm klaxon. And it's short. No more than an arm's reach long. Danger's here. Right in front of her.

Opening her eyes, she yelps and jumps back as something rises up from the swamp by her boot. A long and bloated horror with a mouth hissing like a wasp's nest. Matilda is already firing her shotgun. A stunnerbee whips past Hush's face, corkscrewing the mist with its wings. The undoer twists away from Hush and snatches the bug from the air. There's a crunch as it's sucked away to nothingness. Then the undoer swings its blind head back towards Hush as she points her thimble and closes her eyes and braces herself and fires.

At point blank range, even scant power is enough. The undoer pops like a blister. A spatter of foul black goop splashes into the swamp as its body crumbles like a burned matchstick and its terrible mouth closes up like a healing wound.

Hush knows the cold is coming but it still takes her breath away. Everything up to her elbow goes numb and every other part of her starts shivering. She has to pull her eyelids up with her fingers because they've frozen shut. The waythread to the undoer has vanished, but when she blinks she can see others, dozens of them, all red and all shortening towards her feet.

Matilda's hand takes her elbow and pulls. She's yelling something but Hush can't hear it over her chattering teeth and rising terror. Matilda shoots another stunnerbee behind her, aimed at nothing, just hoping it might draw away the undoers, might slow them down for a moment.

Another undoer lunges at them and Hush trips and loses her hat. As it falls, she sees that it has redecorated itself one last time. An image of a battered sheriff's poster is across the front. The poster is a sketch of a blue waythread underneath the word WANTED. She tries to snatch it midair but misses. The undoer squirms over it and slurps the hat into its mouth.

Matilda stamps on the undoer with her heel and points her thimble and fires. Its mouth knots up and darkness spills out of it like trash from a sack. But the hat's already havoc.

Ma bought that cap for Hush. Long time ago. It was the only thing she managed to carry out of Dustbowl. She wore it every day in the pocket world. Every day, for three long years. Now it's gone, just like Ma and just like Gram.

Matilda grunts and looks, blue-lipped, at her frozen thimblefinger. 'Come on,' she snarls, and drags Hush with her. They stumble on, then wheel around and stop. Red waythreads are every which way. Left and right and forward and back. There's nowhere to run. Not in this world, anyway.

'C-c-can you cross?' Matilda says over her chattering teeth.

Hush tries. But her head's aching. It's like her power's frozen solid. The thimble on the end of her finger is like a ten-tonne weight. She's too cold and too damn scant. She shakes her head.

'Can you take me?' she starts to ask, but she stops herself, because she knows Matilda can't, and won't be able to admit it. They're both too weak. If only they were strong with the power like Gram had been – like Gram *is*.

'You c-c-can do this. You h-have to do this.' Matilda wraps Hush up in a bear hug. Her own dungarees crackles from where they have frozen stiff. Undoers are closing in all around them.

'I'm s-s-spent, Mattie,' Hush says. 'You gotta cross without me.'

Matilda curses. Does it softly, the way you'd say a prayer. She picks a frozen tear beaded in the corner of her eye. Knots her hand in Hush's hand. And despite all the numbness and terror, Hush feels a warmth. They're sisters. Gram told them to remember that. And they have. To the very end.

Then Matilda turns and runs, dodges three undoers that grope at her heels, and shifts out of the slurry world and away to safety.

'WHAT?!' Hush yells. When she said to cross without her, she didn't actually mean Matilda should cross without her. 'Mattie?! MATTIE!'

But she's talking to no one. Matilda's not in this world to hear her. There's only Hush, and the undoers, wriggling slowly towards her.

Nearby there's a rotted telegram pole, sticking out of the swamp at an angle like a shipwrecked mast. Hush scrambles up it as far as she can go. Clings there with her legs whilst she rubs her frozen arm and blows into her icy fist. Looks out into the mist like a stranded sailor, seeing only sharks.

Matilda left. Just *left*. Just went. The thought lashes Hush again and again like a whip. What happened to them 'slower, surer powers'? If they ain't between two sisters, how can they be anywhere?

Below, the undoers have found her. Some of them start gnawing away at the pole. Hush throws her boots at them but they won't be distracted for long. The pole starts to wobble under her weight. Hush keeps closing her eyes and trying her power and each time she does, nothing happens. It's still frozen or depleted or something like that. The undoers chomp and grind away, their mouths hissing like vipers. There's a splintering sound. The pole wobbles. All Hush can do is wait to fall.

A green pickup truck comes out of the mist, engine roaring, wheels spinning, wipers smearing muck back and forth across the windshield. It skids to a stop. Someone kicks the sidedoor open.

'You getting in or getting eaten?' Matilda yells.

Hush is so furious and so grateful at the same time. She scrambles down the pole and leaps over the undoers and launches herself headfirst into the truck. Perched on the dashboard, Gobi peers at her.

'You mucky,' he says.

Matilda floors the accelerator and the wheels spin but don't move. Hush can hear the undoers hissing over the engine revving.

'Vroom,' urges Gobi. 'Vroom!'

Finally the tyres grip and the truck hurtles away, bucking wildly over the hills and dips and smashing through piles of trash, the side door still swinging with Hush's bare feet half out of it.

'Havoc's sake, Mattie,' she says, buckling herself in to her seat. 'Why didn't you say you were going to get a car?'

Matilda squints through the muck-splattered windshield. 'Explaining would've just wasted time.'

Hush gives Matilda something between a hug and a body slam. She calls her sister several bad curse words and then covers her with kisses.

'Ah,' coos Gobi. 'Lovey dovey.'

'Sisterly reunion later.' Matilda shoves her away. 'Maybe at a time when you ain't covered in slurry and don't stink like an outhouse.'

'You're so mean.'

'And you're so thankful.'

'I said thanks, didn't I?'

'Did you?'

'Thank you, Matilda.'

'Never quite the same when you have to ask for it, but there we go.'

'All right, all right, I'm sorry.'

Matilda shrugs, in a *didn't even care anyway* sort of way. Her eyes flick up to the top of Hush's head. 'Ah, havoc. You liked that cap.'

'I like being alive better.'

'Yeah.' Matilda slows the truck a little. It feels like they've outrun the undoers. 'She got it for you, didn't she?'

Hush nods. 'From that store world.' She clicks her fingers. 'What was it called?'

'Thingummy Bob's,' says Matilda quietly.

Hush claps her hands. 'Thingummy Bob's World of Everthang!' She thinks back to that day. They crossed over in a bright red coach, with all the other shoppers from Dustbowl. It was so exciting as they shifted over. Like going on holiday. The store world was full of shelves as tall as houses on aisles as wide as streets. All sorts of woven marvels stacked as far as a kid could see.

Ma told them they could choose one thing each. It wasn't even either of their birthdays. She'd often do stuff like that. Treat them, just because. Matilda used to say that Ma was bribing them. She said it was something called lovebombing. You lovebombed your kids with gifts so they'd never be naughty for you. But Hush always thought that Ma gave them gifts because she loved them. There didn't need to be any other reason. Not everything is a way to get something else.

'I bought my infinite cap,' Hush says fondly. 'And you chose Mr Bitey.'

'My pet T-rex!' Matilda laughs out loud. 'Ah, he was so cute.'

'And terrifying.'

'Yeah, that too. I should've got a cap like you, though. He only lasted a week.'

Hush remembers. Tyrannosaurs were expensive, and Ma could only afford the cheapest one, so Mr Bitey's pattern didn't hold for long at all. He turned back into a fossil pretty quick. She giggles. 'Ma warned you that he had a short lifespan. But you just had to have him.'

Matilda grins. 'Of course I had to have him. He was a pet T-rex! Who cares what she was telling me.'

Mathilda's grin fades suddenly and she turns her attention back to driving. She does this anytime talk starts on the subject of Ma. Matilda doesn't speak of her. Hasn't for a long time. Acts like Ma doesn't matter to her, the way she doesn't matter any more to Ma. Won't even use her name. Calls her she, or her.

'How's your power?' Matilda asks, changing the subject.

Hush puts on her thimble and closes her eyes. 'Better,' she says. 'You wanna try crossing?'

'In a bit. We can't stay in this world. Got to find a safer one. Who knows how long it'll take to find Nate's waythread?'

'Will it be faster with a car?'

'Doubt it. But it'll be comfier and safer.'

Hush nods and takes a look around the truck. She's green and boxy and old. 'Where'd you find this old girl, anyway?'

'Some crummy old world. Just thought *car* in my head as hard as I could, and ran to the first waythread I came across.'

'She needs a name.' Hush peers at the manufacturer's crest on the steering wheel, a circle with a T inside it. The model name's printed on the dashboard in chrome letters. 'Somehow I didn't think of her as a Roadster G9.'

'Let's call her something different then.'

Hush claps her hands. 'Yes, yes, yes. How about the Bang! Bang! One Dollar! Official Tour Bus?'

'Your names are always too long,' Matilda tells her.

'Vroom,' says Gobi on the dashboard.

Hush grins. 'I like it, Gobi. Vroom.'

'Yeah.' Matilda revs the engine and grins too. 'Vroom is good.'

Hush looks at her sister. Some shift seems to be happening between them, like they've just crossed over together into some secret sibling world, a place that they used to visit all the time, before the war happened and they both got so different. Maybe they will make it to Garrison without murdering each other. As long as Hush's power is OK. She puts on her thimble and closes her eyes and feels it dripping slowly back into her, gradual and steady as a leaky tap. Still a bit longer.

Vroom has a radio. Hush turns it on to pass the time. She wheels the dial but of course there's nothing but static in the slurry world. It sounds a bit too much like undoers, and she mutes it with a shiver. Then she finds some old tapes in the glove compartment and slides them into the deck until she finds one that soundtracks how she's feeling. Settles on a song with an epic drumbeat and a guitar solo that sounds like a dentist's drill. A singer's screaming a chorus but she can't make out the words. She turns up the volume. It sounds like he's yelling out, 'HER TOOTH IS A FISH.'

Hush starts singing along with him. And Gobi joins in too. Then finally even Matilda. 'Her tooth is a fish, her tooth is a fish.' Even when they realise in the second verse

121

that he's saying 'The truth is at risk', they keep yelling out their version, because it's so much funnier and better. Sometimes, Hush reckons, you need to see the world how you want it to be, and not how it is. Her tooth is a fish. Her sister is a hero. And them slow, sure powers will come to save you, if you just hold out and wait.

• • •

When Hush's power is strong enough, they thimble up and find the greenest waythread they can and track it out of the slurry world. Beyond the filthy windows, the world blurs as they start to shift to somewhere else. Shapes beyond the fog flicker and collapse. Then the mist draws away like a curtain, and when Hush opens her eyes, she's squinting in bright sunlight. They've crossed into a world of rolling prairie and wide blue skies. Beside them, herds of tri-horned buffalo are grazing with their heads bowed as if in prayer to the endless green land. As the truck shifts over, the buffalo lift their heads to see, then one by one they fall back down to continue their worship of the grass.

On the dashboard, Gobi lets out a low noise of admiration. 'Big moos,' he says.

'Massive moos,' Matilda agrees. She slows the truck right down and turns off the tape, leaving birdsong and wind swishing through the prairie and the faint noises of the herds. It's peaceful. Good. When Hush closes her eyes and feels for havoc, she can't find any.

'The pattern here's strong,' she says.

Matilda nods, feeling it too. 'It's like the war's not been here.'

'The war was everywhere though.'

'That was three years ago.' Matilda squints through the windshield. 'Maybe things have mended.'

That's a good thought. That scars can heal. That things can mend. That time can pull anything back from the brink of havoc. Hush sags back in her seat, exhausted and filthy, her arm still aching with a faint chill from the fight with the undoers.

'We'll probably need some gas soon,' Matilda tells her, pulling up the handbrake. She points at a dial on the dashboard, teetering towards empty. 'And food. And you need boots.'

'Uh huh,' Hush mumbles, eyes closed and chin on her chest.

'And also,' says Matilda, slapping her lightly on the arm, 'go do something about how badly you stink.'

Hush groans and puts the music back on, loud. 'Fine.'

With a lot of effort, she manages to dry out the muck from her clothes by patterning the water into steam. Most of the slurry flakes off. Then she gets out of the car and picks a bunch of tiny pink prairie flowers and stuffs them into her pocket and spends a while trying to weave their smell into her clothes. Hopefully it's enough to cover up the reek of slurry.

Boots are impossible for a scant to pattern from thin air. Hush doesn't bother trying. She just toughens up the soles of her socks until they're something resembling leather.

Back in the driver's seat, Matilda sits twirling and tugging her thimble, scowling with concentration as she looks for the waythread of Blue Ruin.

'It's here, we know it's here,' she grumbles. 'Some Tuesday afternoons I used to even see it, even though half the varnish would be scuffed off by then. How come this layer ain't as strong as all the others?'

Hush slaps her forehead. Suddenly she knows the answer. It's so simple. They're so stupid. She falls to her knees and starts scraping one thumbnail against the other with the focus and franticness of someone trying to start a fire with flints.

Matilda looks at her like she's gone cuckoo. Hush barely notices. She scrapes, scrapes, scrapes the edge of one thumbnail against the other, then moves on to her fingers.

'Love and Mercy,' says Matilda, finally getting what Hush is trying to do. 'Can't believe I didn't think of that.'

'It ain't worked yet,' Hush says as a reminder, but her heart is pounding because she knows it will. Just knows it. Time's only one part of the pattern. Colour's another. Also the sameness of the bottle, and the brush.

But there's also the need. By Tuesday afternoon the varnish would be chipped and scratched from a whole week of chores. Hush is hoping that maybe, just maybe, if she scuffs up her nails so they look a little more like they would on a Tuesday, that it might increase the connection and thicken the waythread . . .

'Don't go too crazy,' Matilda urges. 'Just get them to what they'd look like on Tuesday.'

'I know it, I know.' Hush stops to inspect her nails. They

look about the right level of scuffed and scratched. She slips her thimble on and closes her eyes and sees it at once, snagged on the end of her thimblefinger, dim but there, and unmistakably Blue Ruin. A waythread reaching across worlds and patterns, connecting varnish bottle to varnished nails.

Hush leaps up and whoops so loud, it startles away some nearby buffalo. Matilda comes rushing out of the truck and gives her something between a body slam and a hug. Gobi's clapping his antennae together and burbling, though Hush doubts he has any idea why they're celebrating.

They bundle back into Vroom. Matilda turns the key and revs the engine and lowers the handbrake. Hush turns up the music so loud she can see the speakers shake. Then Matilda floors the accelerator, and they go.

They pin the waythread beneath the truck, wire straight and electric blue, as worlds slide past the windows like sheets of rain in a storm.

They drive through a piston forest where rusted machines as tall as trees pump and wheel, and pump and wheel, slowly drowning themselves in dark lagoons of oil that no one comes to collect.

They cross a world of metal marshes where tin reeds sprout from quicksilver pools, and machine spiders spin webs in intricate silicon circuits.

They pass by abandoned fields of planted jewels, where emeralds sprout huge as cabbages, still in the rows they were sown in, and rubies hang in unpicked bunches upon their stems.

They motor down empty toll roads, past silent cities all gone dark, as distant undoers beat black wings across the skyline and burrow holes through the moon.

With each crossing, Hush sees the waythread clearer. It's leading them deep into raggedy country, skipping through places where the pattern's close to havoc. Hush's initial excitement has long since gone. Now there's only nerves. These worlds belong to the undoers. Venturing through them is by no means safe. Not even in Vroom. Hush wants the music back on to stave off her unease, but the truck's red fuel light is blinking now, so Matilda won't allow it. Maybe they should've stopped off in that piston forest to pattern some gasoline. Too late to turn back now.

They cross to a dark highway where the moon has shattered like a mirror and all the stars are dying, coming loose from their constellations and falling out of the night like neon snow. Their bodies are little sparkling flecks that dust the peaks of the sand dunes and catch in the twin beams of Vroom's headlights. When Matilda clears them off the windshield with the wipers they leave smears of gemstone-coloured light on the glass, like rainbows or comet trails, which gradually go dark.

'Pretty,' coos Gobi on the dashboard.

The dead stars falling, and the engine going, and the highway gravel rattling against the underside of the truck. The red fuel light shining, and the waythread brightening, and the silver shards of moon spinning their last waltz in the sky above. Gobi muttering, and Matilda's fingers drumming patterns on

126

the steering wheel. For a long time, that's all there is. Until ahead of the truck the stars begin to fall into shapes, that build up and collapse again like sandcastles on a shore. Fluorescent shop logos flicker on and off and on: a noodle bowl, a tall gas pump sign with a list of prices, the word TRAVLIN SALOON. In the sharp angles of the broken moonbeams, Hush can see the shadows of things that aren't there. Cars and buildings and wagons drawn by horses. Red tailgate lights and the smell of exhaust. The sights and sounds of a town.

Suddenly everything collapses as the waythread twists and buckles beneath the weight of the truck. Matilda curses and spins the wheel to keep them from falling off. Hush shuts both eyes, all her focus on the waythread as it struggles in her grip like something caught in a snare. This is the last stretch, when the pattern is at its most treacherous. They're close. So close. If they hold on just a little longer.

'Waaaaaeeeeee!' says Gobi, like they're on a fairground ride.

And then it's night-time on some other world, a world where there's no moon but the stars are still falling, and Hush and Matilda find themselves hurtling towards the bright lights of Travlin town.

• • •

Travlin town is moving. On feet, on tracks, on wheels. There must be a thousand different vehicles and animals, tracking their way together through the dark night of this fringe

127

world. A rambling ragtag rabble of vehicles and beasts that rattle over the tarmac, wheels and hooves flinging up fallen stars behind them like sparks from a welder.

Matilda floors the accelerator, heading for the outskirts at the backend of town. It's treacherous driving. Grit peppers the windshield glass and exhaust fumes roll over the car like dark clouds of fog. The wheels crunch and slip over all manner of trash left behind the town like slime behind a slug. Rotten food and used plastic and empty cans. Then at last they catch up to Travlin, and plunge into its noisy and jostling heart.

The clamour's the first thing that hits Hush. Engines roaring and spluttering and chugging, a thousand wheels turning on their axles, all kinds of feet plodding or bounding or scurrying. Then it's the motion that dizzies her. Everyone wobbling over potholes and swerving to avoid trash. Headlights criss-crossing back and forth like search beams. The wet and starlit tarmac rushing below them like a glittering dark sea. And all around them, vehicles weave back and forth, jockeying for position. Seems no one wants to be downtown in Travlin, on account of the fumes and the trash coming from the front. Looks like everyone takes their turn at the back, though. Just after Hush and Matilda arrive, there's an almighty honking of horns, and on that signal the whole town reshuffles itself, front to back. A new neighbourhood springs up around them, all in the space of a few minutes.

'This town is crazy,' Matilda mutters.

'I know,' says Hush. 'Ain't it wonderful?'

She stares out of the passenger window, eyes wide, scared to blink. She wants to see it all, all of it, everything. She looks out at double decker buses racing beside a horse-drawn carriage. She sees a truck carrying a watertower, another towing a pink caravan that sells bowls of noodles out of a side window, a third decked out in armour and spiked wheels. She watches motorbikes weaving swift as minnows beneath the plodding feet of a dinosaur that carries houses upon the sloped hill of its back.

These are worldless folk, Hush realises. Weavers who used to have a home and lost it on account of the war. But unlike Hush and Matilda, these people never had a Gram to save them, and no pocket world to flee to. So they've just kept running. Shifting from pattern to pattern, world to world, hoping to keep away from undoers and ahead of Carcosans.

Only these people ain't just fleeing. They've made themselves a life out here, a town, a home. There are balconies and bedrooms patterned on the backs of each vehicle, and almost every rooftop is festooned with washing lines where clothes flutter like semaphore flags. Numbers or names swing from side doors that have been woven into porches. Postboxes dangle from wing mirrors. A few car bonnets have even been converted into tiny gardens: covered with turf and lined with white picket fences. And in these extraordinary travelling homes, folk aren't just running but living.

Behind the windows of a long grey coach, Hush glimpses a man with his sleeves rolled up to his elbows, slapping tortillas from palm to palm and tossing them one by one onto a hot oiled skillet. His kids are all asleep in one long row of swinging hammocks, and his partner's got her feet up, sipping coffee and cradling a newborn in the crook of one arm and watching the stars fall. An older woman the same age as Gram is driving, and when she sees Hush staring, she smiles and tips her hat to say howdy. Hush nods in reply, a lump in her throat. There are families here. Families that are all together and whole. She watches that kid with its mama until the grey coach slips out of sight again.

Some of the vehicles they find themselves neighbouring aren't homes, but farms. A green double decker bus has been converted into a greenhouse, its top deck jungle-thick with plants and sunlamps. It moves away and is replaced by a locomotive that runs on self-patterning rails, towing flatbed wagons from which corn sprouts in a host of different colours. The train puffs out steam from its funnel that thickens into micro-clouds, which drizzle down on the crops trailing behind it.

And there are shops too. A herd of small sheds with legs patterned underneath them weave in and out of the paths of the other vehicles, nimble as ostriches, their riders hawking newspapers and gasoline and snacks pilfered from a dozen other worlds. Matilda hails down a nearby seller and explains that they're new to town, and asks what they take in Travlin for currency.

'Welcome, newbies!' says the seller, a woman riding an oversized trike and a miniature kiosk lit up with fairy lights wobbling on top of it. She has gold front teeth and sequins for eyebrows and topaz skin and as she talks to the sisters, she steers the trike with her feet. Her name is Urrivabatonga.

'Urri if you're in a hurry, or Urrivabatonga if you can stay a little longer,' she tells them with a laugh, even though she must have said this hundreds of times before. 'What can I get you?'

'Um, well, some fuel for starters,' says Matilda cautiously.

Hush leans across to Matilda's side and gives the seller her most charming grin. 'Also some snacks, please.'

'But we're a little cash light right now,' Matilda adds quickly.

Urri laughs again. 'Don't fret, newbies. Ain't no coin needed here. In Travlin, we trade in favours. I help you, and later you'll help me. Now let's get you and the truck filled up, shall we?'

With a pull of a lever, the fairy lights adorning her kiosk start to blink in code. Moments later, a gas tanker draws level beside them, and a slick crew in yellow boilersuits and goggles start refuelling Vroom whilst the truck is still moving.

'What snacks you want?' asks the seller. 'I got all kinds, from all worlds.'

'We ain't fussy,' says Matilda.

'Yummy ones, if possible,' says Hush.

The seller tilts her head as she rummages for snacks with one hand and all the trinkets in her hair clink and chime. 'Lemme see what I can find for you. Where've you come from, newbies?'

'A pocket world,' Hush tells her. 'Until it failed.'

'Sorry to hear that.' Urri gives them a concerned look. 'It's a rough thing. But you'll be OK.' She brings out a paper bag with an old logo printed on the side of it that says THINGUMMY BOB'S WORLD OF EVERYTHING. The bag gets tossed through the window and as it lands heavy in Hush's lap, she hears the unmistakeable rustle of snacks. Hush is desperate to tear it open and feast on the goodies within, but the seller is still talking at them, so she nods and listens politely.

'You did a good thing coming here,' Urri continues, 'instead of heading for one of the safe worlds. Some folk, when they first get worldless, go trying to worm their way into Yonder or Garrison or somesuch. Don't know how many of them make it, but I don't reckon it's many. Much better to join Travlin. We might not have a world of our own, but as long as we keep moving, we get along just fine.'

Seeing their doubtful looks, Urri throws her head back and laughs, loud above the engines.

'I looked just as skeptical as you two when I came here two years back,' she says. 'And you know what the sheriff I talked to told me? She said, "What's the point in owning a world when you've got no one to share it with? Ain't a place that makes a home. It's people."'

The seller grins and spreads her arms out wide, and says again: 'People.'

• • •

Before long, Vroom has been favoured with a full tank, and the sisters are feasting on ransacked road snacks. Hush rifles through Urri's bag, finding twists of jerky and dried fruit flakes and foil bags of paprika crisps and a packet of jet black gummies. Urri notes down their names and what they've taken in a leatherbound ledger. As she does this, Hush feels a guilty twist in her belly. By the time the seller comes to collect on the favour they owe her, the Quiets will be long gone.

Matilda's obviously thinking the same thing. Before the seller waves them off, she asks, 'What sort of favours will we owe you?'

'Most likely a supply run to a store world,' says Urri, pocketing her ledger away and taking hold of her trike with her hands again.

'But what if we won't help you, when you come?'

Urrivabatonga just shakes her head with a chuckle. 'You two need to trust more,' she yells over the roar of the town. 'In Travlin, trust is everything.'

Then the town reconfigures itself again, and Urri vanishes behind the gas tanker and into the rushing night.

For a while they just munch through the snacks, and watch the town, and ride the road.

'Can I have your gummies?' Hush asks after she gobbles up her share.

'No,' Matilda says, chewing hers slowly, one by one.

Hush does puppy dog eyes, which only makes Matilda eat her licorice gummies in an even slower and more exaggerated fashion.

'Aw, please, Mattie! You don't even like licorice flavour.'

'I like it when I'm starving.' Matilda squints over the wheel, left and right through the shifting town, as the rows of vehicles align into temporary streets and dissolve again. 'Where in havoc is Nate? Shut your eyes and search, will you, Hush? If I so much as even blink, I feel like we'll get pancaked by a bus.'

Hush keeps her eyes open and holds out her hand. She tries not to sound too smug as she reminds Matilda that Travlin is a town that runs on favours.

Matilda glances at her and then at the gummies and scowls, knowing she's beaten. 'Fine,' she says. 'One.'

Hush makes a gleeful sound and scoffs the sweet. Then she shuts her eyes and focuses her thimble, and eventually she manages to find the waythread again and track the line of Blue Ruin through Travlin's traffic, until it winds inside a fine-looking saloon that's carried on the back of chunky tractor-type wheels. Even over the roar of town, the sound of honky tonk and chatter comes clear through the saloon's swinging doors.

'He's in there!' Hush claps excitedly. She is about to tease her sister by saying that she can see Valentine Pink woven into the strands of Blue Ruin, but then she remembers. It was all an act. A way to get them into Garrison. And then Hush thinks something that she hasn't considered before.

'How long are you going to have to pretend that you like him?' she asks slowly, afraid of what the answer will be.

Matilda gives a long, weary sigh. 'Just long enough for it not to be suspicious when I break things off.'

Hush gulps. They've escaped undoers, found the waythread, reached Travlin, but there are still so many ways this could all end badly.

'Stop looking so panicked,' Matilda says as she steers them towards the saloon. 'It'll be fine. The only way it can go wrong is if you somehow tell him. So don't. And don't mention Garrison to anyone.'

Matilda pauses, obviously going through various other nightmare scenarios in her head.

'In fact,' she adds, 'it's probably better if you don't say anything. At all. From – now. You got it?'

'I got it,' says Hush.

Matilda scowls. 'That was a test and you failed it.'

'Oh! I mean . . .' And Hush mimes zipping her lips shut and locking one corner of her mouth and pocketing the key. She gives a thumbs up.

'Good. Just remember that Nate's probably lying about who he is, too. I doubt the McCluskeys are too popular in Travlin.'

Hush manages to ask why by raising her eyebrows and scratching her head.

'Think, Hush. The McCluskeys have themselves a world. They could let all these weavers in. But they don't.'

There are so many ways this could all go wrong, that Hush hasn't even thought of all of them. She shakes her head and forces herself to be calm. They'll be fine. It'll all be fine. This is Matilda's plan, and Matilda is smart. She'll sort it. All Hush has to do is not talk.

Even though, she thinks, *talking's my flaw*.

Trailing behind the saloon are dozens of tow cables, with cars and trucks tethered to them, all rattling together like the tin cans behind a wedding carriage. A nimble little person, all their features hidden under goggles, balaclava and coat, comes hopping over the bonnets towards them. They clip Vroom into place, secure some bouncy rubber things to the truck's sides, then give a gloved thumbs up through the windshield and go bounding off to secure another car that's just arriving.

Matilda turns off the engine and picks up her stunnerbee shotgun from the backseat.

'Wait here,' she tells Gobi.

'My there too,' the gobetween points out.

Matilda shrugs. 'I guess you are.' As he shrinks back inside his shell, she hides him in the glove box. Then she and Hush scramble out of the side windows and onto the bonnet. Grit and fumes whip past on the cold wind as they hop across the narrow gap between the truck's bumper and the back of the saloon, and make their way over to the entrance.

The bottom windows are shuttered up, so Hush can't see in, but she can hear a hectic kind of music playing inside. Music! Piano, and fiddle, and some twangly sort of guitar, all racing each other neck and neck through some folk song. No saucepan lid or singer, though. Maybe the band has an opening!

But no. Travlin ain't a new home, is it? Just another place they're passing through. Which sort of feels like a shame.

Garrison might well end up being safer than here, but Hush wonders if it'll feel as alive as this town does.

Just as they reach the swinging doors, the music stops. The saloon whoops and hollers. There's applause from more than a few hands. Must be crowded in there.

Suddenly, Hush is nervous. She does not look presentable and she still stinks faintly of the slurry world. She backs off a few steps and spits on her hand with the intention of patterning it to water so that she can give her face a wash, but her saliva's still all black from the licorice gummies that Urri favoured them, so she ends up just grimacing and wiping it on her jeans.

'What are you doing?' hisses Matilda, beckoning her towards the doors. Then she rolls her eyes when Hush tries to give an answer with makeshift sign language.

'Love and Mercy, just say it out loud.'

'Oh. OK. Well, I want to make a good first impression. Don't you?'

'Wasn't planning on it, no.'

'But what if Nate takes a look at you and decides he won't bring us back to Garrison?'

Matilda looks surprised, like she hasn't considered that. Then she scowls deeply and says, 'Fine.'

They spend a few minutes sprucing themselves up. Hush plaits Matilda's hair and inspects her teeth for bits of licorice and even manages to pattern some more perfume from some of the leftover petals from the prairie world that are still in her pocket. Then she steps back and looks at her fierce, strong, loyal sister, her face strewn with freckles and her hair garlanded with dying stars.

'The most beautiful kid in all the worlds,' Hush declares, stepping away.

'Shut up, Hush.' But before Matilda can turn on her heel, Hush sees the smile she's trying to hide.

• • •

They head through the swinging doors and into the saloon. Inside, it's packed. Standing room only. Everyone's outfitted in grubby, mismatched attire. Torn hats and oil-stained jeans and scuffed blazers and patched dungarees. The saloon smells like sawdust and spilled drinks and dancing. The lights are all down to a low golden glow, apart from the raised stage at the far end of the bar, where the band is starting up another song, even faster than the last one.

Except it's not a band at all. It's a creetie – a woven being. Hush has never seen anyone like them before. The music maker is made up of hundreds of pairs of pink-white human hands, all joined together in one wriggling ball, each finger like a petal on a chrysanthemum of flesh. Part of them is playing the honky tonk. Another part is working the fiddle. Several dozen other bits are clapping and finger-clicking a beat. The creetie beckons for their banjo and starts to pluck a wild jangle on the strings. And as Hush watches in awe, the rest of their fingers start to move in rippling dance patterns. The audience whoops and hollers and joins in, stomping their feet and slapping their tables. It's a real hoedown in here. Hardly anyone notices two newbie girls standing by the swinging doors.

Matilda pulls Hush reluctantly away from the performing creetie. 'Stop getting distracted. We gotta find Nate.'

Hush makes a grumbling noise and looks longingly at the crowd. 'Maybe he's in there dancing.'

Matilda snorts. 'As if. He'll be at the bar, trying to look tough.'

So they head for the drinks, squeezing sideways past the packed tables of oldtimers and goodtimers and card players. The few people that clock them are all broad smiles and tipped hats, all *Howdy* and *Howaya* and *Looky here, newbies!* Hush grins and waves back. It's so good to see people again, to be amongst people. And creeties too. There are woven folk everywhere: a blue lobster sitting in a chair, blowing bubbles from a conch that he holds pinched in one claw like a pipe; cute little doggy creatures that sit on the laps of their weavers and grin at the music, their pink tongues dangling sideways out of their mouths; a sour-faced turtle who sits alone playing backgammon and feeding a tin plate of what looks like marsh weed into his mouth in a series of miserly little pinches. Looks like everyone and all kinds are welcome here in Travlin, just as it should be.

This is a good place, thinks Hush. She feels it. She knows it. And when the thought comes, she's only surprised that it's taken so long. Because it's obvious. They should stay here. They should make a home, here. With the other worldless folk. With the people just like them.

She grabs Matilda's sleeve. 'Mattie. Mattie. Matilda.'

Matilda turns and gives her a look that says, *No talking, remember?*

But Hush pulls at her again. 'Yeah, I know that, but, I've been thinking—'

Matilda groans and runs a hand down her face. 'OK,' she yells over the music. 'From now on, no thinking either. You get? We are literally steps away from getting to – to where we need to go.'

'But that's my whole point!' Hush shouts back at her. 'We don't need to go to Garrison at all, we can stay right here—'

A heavy hand, big as a bear paw, falls on Hush's shoulders, and too late she realises that she's done the exact opposite of what Matilda told her to do.

She talked.

About Garrison.

And now there's a man right behind her, putting his hands upon her shoulders.

'You two girls are heading where now?' he says.

Hush looks up into the enormous, bearded face of the man towering over her. He's wearing tinted goggles that make his eyes two mirrored discs in which tiny saloon folk dance and laugh and drink.

'You *girls* ought to be careful, talking about that place here,' he says. His voice growls over the raucousness, but only loud enough for them to hear him. Hush doesn't like the way he says *girls*. She can't explain why, but it makes her insides turn.

She tries to twist away but his grip on her shoulders is scarily strong. His right hand has a branded letter *R* on the knuckle of his thumb, and it's missing its middle finger.

'I wouldn't do that,' the man says to Matilda, as she reaches for the stock of her shotgun. And his other hand presses a thimbled finger against Hush's hip like it's a pistol barrel.

Matilda gives Hush a furious, despairing look. 'You and your big mouth. You couldn't stay quiet, could you? You just had to—'

The man leans forward. He stinks of too much moonshine and not enough washing. Whatever he whispers in Matilda's ear makes her face go kind of slack with some emotion that Hush can't quite decipher. Whatever the man says, it must've been a threat, because Matilda stops haranguing Hush at once and hands over her thimble and shotgun.

A few folk around give them curious glances, but not for long. Soon their focus is back on their drinks or their cards or the hoedown.

Hush tenses up, readying herself to make one unholy scene. She will scream and bite and scratch. She will slam knees into the most painful of places. But Matilda senses what she's about to do, and puts a hand on her arm to stop her.

'Hush, don't. It's OK.'

Hush glances at the hairy, spectacled man. 'Why is it? What did he just say to you?'

'Hush. Please.' Matilda gives her a stare that says, *Trust me.* So Hush does. She trusts. Always has, always will.

She hands her own thimble over, and the man ushers them away from the bar and the crowd. Soon they're at a side door that's guarded none-too-subtly by another man, equally enormous and bearded. This guard is spectacled too.

'This them?' he grunts.

The first man nods. 'Reckon so.'

The man guarding the door puts his thimble to the handle and turns his finger like it's a key. Then he's pushing it open and the man behind Hush shoves her lightly into the side room.

Inside, there's a large octagonal table covered with green felt. Over the table hangs a lamp with a mother of pearl shade. A little woodburner crackles in the corner, and there's a mirrored shelf with a small selection of drinks and glasses. This is a place for folks to gamble at cards, away from the noise and the crowds in the main part of the saloon.

A boy is at the table. He's big and scowly and fur-clad, just like the two other men. But he's not wearing glasses, and his beard's nothing but gingery fluff under his chin and brown whiskers on his top lip. On the table next to him is a half-eaten punnet of gravy-smothered fries, a wilted red rose, a pinecone-shaped shell, and the bottle of Blue Ruin varnish.

So this is Nate McCluskey.

As Hush comes in with Matilda close behind, he looks up with his mouth full of mashed-up potato and lumbers to his feet.

'Tilly-Boo?' he says. His voice is tremoring with nerves and longing. 'Oh, Tils, finally, finally.'

Only he's speaking to Hush. He's got the wrong sister. Hush had been feeling relieved that the big scary spectacled men are McCluskeys, but that's instantly overshadowed by the terrible awkwardness of Nate's mistake.

Matilda barges Hush aside. 'That ain't me, that's my sister. And it's Matilda. Not Tils, not Tilly-Boo. Matilda.'

Just like a rose, Nate goes red and then wilts. It's not exactly love at first sight. The two men start snorting with laughter. Then Nate turns to them with a terrible wrath upon his face.

'Shut up,' he says coldly, and they instantly go quiet.

'Just stand there,' he orders, and they do. 'Don't smirk, don't laugh, don't even breathe,' he says, and they don't. They don't breathe. It's like Nate has suddenly patterned all the air from the room. Hush watches both men start to panic, their faces turning red beneath their beards, hands clutching and unclutching by their sides. Nate's watching them too, sitting back on his chair. He folds his arms like he's enjoying the show.

They're slavestoned. That's what their spectacles are hiding. Travlin has probably made parasitic gems illegal, like they were in most worlds before the war. Hush gets a sick feeling in the pit of her stomach. She knew that the McCluskeys slavestoned people. But actually seeing it is different. So much worse. It's vile and evil. It's the sort of thing they'd do in Carcosa.

'Nate,' Matilda says. Then again, louder: 'Nate.'

Nate's grin sours when he realises Matilda doesn't

approve of the entertainment he's putting on. 'It's not like I'm gonna let them fully suffocate,' he says, a little petulantly. 'McCluskeys don't treat our geminis like that.'

Gemini. That's the term slavestoners prefer to use. Sounds less cruel, more like a partnership. Parasitic gem and person, twinned together in a lifelong bond. Hush feels sick to her stomach.

'Anyway,' Nate is saying, as the two men continue to gape like fish, 'it's not like they're good people. Why d'you think we had to slavestone them? You want to know what they did?'

'For havoc's sake,' Matilda almost shouts. 'Just tell them they can breathe again.'

'Fine,' Nate grumbles. 'Proctor, Clint: you can breathe again.'

Both men double over, gulping all the air they can.

'But do it quietly,' Nate snaps, and the two men are quiet.

Hush gives Matilda a look that says, *I do not like your boyfriend at all*. And Matilda gives her one back that says, *Me neither*. Nate McCluskey is a slavestoner. He is cruel and controlling and vengeful. He is not the sort of boy you make your sweetheart. And definitely not the sort of boy that lets you break up with him with no drama or nastiness.

Suddenly it occurs to Hush that Matilda might not have been the only one putting fakery in her letters.

'Anyway,' Nate says, getting to his feet. 'Tilly-Boo.' He smooths his hair and his beard with his hand. 'Aren't you going to come say hi to your Natty-Cakes?'

Matilda sits at the table and gives him a cautious, cordial nod. 'Hi,' she says stiffly.

Nate pouts. His arms are wide. 'No hug?'

Matilda affects a grin but her jaw is clenched. 'Aint you gonna wine and dine a girl first?'

Nate drops his arms and gives a somewhat begrudging nod and clears the table in a hurry. He takes Gobi's shell and chucks it sideways like it's a piece of trash. Hush rushes over and picks up the little creetie and checks him over for cracks.

'You OK, Gobi?' she whispers.

His small voice comes back: 'My fine.'

'You stay in there,' Hush tells him, and slips him into the pocket of her coat. Things seem on the verge of getting ugly. Better for Gobi to stay hidden.

Nate, meanwhile, is waving his thimble across the table. The green felt goes all ruffly, then peaks upwards like a mountain range, and smooths itself out into a romantic candlelit dinner for two.

Moments later, there's a knock at the door to the room. A gruff voice from outside says, 'I better not have just felt you patterning in there.'

Nate scowls. 'Sorry,' he calls.

'Thimbles are for waythreadin' only. Especially in a world like this'n.'

'We're newbies, sir. Didn't know it wasn't allowed.'

Whoever's outside considers this. 'Well, don't do it again, OK? Or I'll have to fetch the sheriff.'

'OK, sir,' says Nate meekly.

'If you bring undoers down on us, you'll owe us one heck of a favour.'

'Yes, sir. Thanking you.' Whilst Nate speaks, he makes curse gestures at the door and grins at Hush and Matilda. Maybe he's the sort of boy that reckons it ladylike for girls to find anything he does utterly charming.

'Let's eat, my sweet,' he says, once the gruff voice is gone. He sits at the table and wipes his mouth with the back of his hand.

There are napkins and silverware and steaks and tall glasses full of fizzy elderflower and a chocolate fondue fountain. Only Nate's not quite so amazing at weaving as he thinks he is, and the steaks he's woven are blood-red and twitching. He insists on feeding Matilda some of the fondue, but she gags and almost spits it back in his face. Turns out the melted chocolate tastes like beef gravy. Some of the steak's flavour must've gotten mixed up with it during the patterning. Mercifully the fizzy elderflower drink is all fine, although it makes Matilda burp.

'Let me pattern out those bubbles for you,' Nate says, holding his hand out for her glass. 'Burping ain't exactly ladylike.'

'Uh-oh,' Hush says under her breath.

Matilda tilts her head just slightly, like a boxer accepting a challenge. Then she downs her elderflower and burps low and long like a foghorn. She dabs her napkin sarcastically at the corners of her mouth.

'What do you mean, it ain't ladylike?' she asks. 'What do all the girls of Garrison do when they're gassy, Nate? Giggle it out?'

Nate looks at her like she's said something completely stupid. 'I don't know,' he says. 'You'll be the first.'

Matilda does another burp, out of pure shock. 'What?'

'There ain't any girls in our world. That's the whole reason my dad let in your gobetween.'

In Hush's pocket, two little eyes come timidly out from their shell.

'My needed?' Gobi says in his little voice.

'Not now I got myself a sweetheart,' Nate says, grinning.

Hush needs to get Matilda out of here. Now. Right now. It's just like Urri said before. The McCluskeys have a whole world, but no one to share it with. Oh havoc, coming here was such a big mistake. Hush looks around at Clint and Proctor, the two slavestoned guards. They're standing by the door, quietly breathing, just like Nate told them to. She wonders what they'll do if she and Matilda try to leave. But she already knows the answer. They'll do whatever Nate orders.

'We've got all sorts of other stuff,' Nate is saying. 'You'll see. Plenty of space, a nice strong pattern, loads of geminis. But no girls. Which is good for you. Both of you.'

For the first time since she came in, Nate glances over at Hush. It's not a nice look. It's one of appraisal. Like she's a truck he's about to purchase, and he's checking her over for dents and scratches and signs of wear.

'So, I got this older cousin back in Garrison,' he tells her. 'Travis?'

That's when Matilda makes her move. She does it so quick and so subtley that it's done before anyone realises what's happened. Reaching out across the table, she takes Nate's hand. She laces his fingers with hers, just like a typical sweetheart would. Only it's the hand with his thimble, and she tugs it off his finger and onto her own before anyone else in the room has moved.

Nate opens his mouth. He just looks confused. As if he simply can't conceive of how unladylike this all is.

'Do something,' he says.

'Gladly,' says Matilda. But she only gets as far as closing her eyes. Because Nate was speaking to Clint and Proctor. Before Matilda can weave anything, there's a loud *pthhp* sound and a buzz, and she drops face first into her plate of uneaten steak and then slowly slides off her seat and onto the floor, open-eyed and slack as a ragdoll.

There's a pause as Nate bends down under the table to retrieve his thimble from the carpet. Hush can hear the muffled music of the saloon's hoedown through the walls. None of the Travlin folk know what's happening. They might as well be worlds away.

Proctor points Matilda's shotgun at Hush. 'Do I gotta stunnerbee you too?' he asks her. 'Or do you know how to behave?'

'I know how to behave,' Hush tells him. Then she boots Proctor between his legs and punches him hard as she can in the throat and tries to yank the gun from his grip. He takes all of Hush's violence with a look that says, *Aren't you just adorable?* Then he drops her with a slap so hard that her teeth cut her inside cheek. Hush lands on the floor next to Matilda and tastes her own blood. In her pocket, the point of Gobi's shell presses hard against her ribs. She starts to scream for help, because noise is the only weapon she has left. If she can get the Travlin folk to realise what's happening—

'Shut her up,' orders Nate, and Proctor shoots her with a stunnerbee, and for the first time in her life, Hush finds that she's a Quiet sister in every sense of the word.

• • •

Proctor picks her up and slings her over his shoulder like a sack of loot. Inside her head, Hush wails and rages and wills herself to move. But all she does is dangle upside down and stare at a patch of floor. Her arms dangle like a puppet's. She can see the stunnerbee sting still lodged in her left wrist like a dark splinter.

'What in havoc are you doing?' That's Nate talking, his voice lowered to a hiss. 'You think you can just carry them out of here like that? If folk outside find out what we're doing . . .' Nate lets out an irritated huff. 'Why am I even explaining this to you? Just put them down.'

At once the world spins and Hush finds herself propped up beside Matilda on a chair. She drools on herself and stares downwards at her hands, which are curled up on her lap like sleeping pets.

There's no sting in her left wrist any more.

It must have fallen out when Proctor put her onto the chair.

With every fibre of her being, Hush screams at her body to move.

'Hold up their heads,' Nate orders. He's flustered and sweating and rummaging around in his huge coat for something. He brings it out. A little silver box with a sliding hatch at one end. Thumbing it open, he shakes two pairs of pearl-white slavestones out, like they're after- dinner mints. They start scurrying around the table. He gathers them up in his huge paw of a hand.

Hush's fingers twitch. Just a little. Then a little bit more. The venom's not wearing off fast enough.

'Put these on them,' Nate says, holding the slavestones out to Clint and Proctor. 'I'll pattern them some glasses to wear. Then we all just walk out of the exit together, nice and calm. You get?'

'We get,' Clint says.

'Yes, Nate,' says Proctor.

Hush tries to scream. Tries to shut her eyes. Tries to do something, anything. She manages to tip her head to one side. That's all. It's not enough.

Proctor holds out the slavestones. Hush can see their millipede legs. And the tiny mouths filled with tiny teeth, beneath those pearl-white shells.

'Please,' she tries to say. The word gurgles in her throat.

Then a hand pummels on the door. 'Everything all right in there?' says the voice outside.

Hush tries screaming, waving, star-jumping. Her body jerks a little. Pins and needles are spreading outwards from her wrist. *Move!* She tells herself. For the love of havoc, move! If you have any desire at all not to marry Cousin Travis, move!

The door thumps again. 'Hello?'

Clint and Proctor pause and look at Nate, who was about to pattern two forks into spectacles. He stops what he's doing and runs a hand through his hair in barely controlled fury.

'We're fine, mister,' he says through his teeth. 'Don't you worry about us.'

But the bartender or concerned citizen or busybody or whoever it is won't be deterred that easy.

'We heard a ruckus,' he says. 'One of them girls your friend brought in?'

'She tripped over a chair,' Nate lies. 'She's fine.'

There's a pause. Then: 'Let's see her then.'

Nate looks at the ceiling with a look of exasperation. 'Havoc's sake,' he mutters. 'All for two girls who ain't even pretty. Travis is gonna owe me so big after this.'

'Hello?' says the person on the other side of the door. Then they try the locked handle. It rattles but doesn't open. 'You ain't supposed to lock doors here, you know that? What did you pattern in there, anyhow?'

Nate flounders for an answer. Doesn't find one in time.

'Don't make me fetch the sheriff on you. She won't appreciate you interrupting her card game.'

'Aint no need, no need,' yells Nate hurriedly. 'Just give us a second, OK?'

'Quit stalling and come out,' comes the curt reply. 'Naw, that's it. I'm fetching the Law.'

Nate jabs a finger at Clint and Proctor. 'New plan. Clint, you stay here. Once we're gone, open the door and start a brawl. Vicious as you like.'

Clint grins. 'Vicious. Sure.'

'Proctor, pick these two up. Forget about the slavestones, they take too long to bed in. We gotta go with them now.'

Nate turns and draws a rectangle on the outside wall with his thimble. A door patterns into the wood and Nate opens it up. Beyond it, the town rushes through the dark of this midnight world in a torrent of noise and light. Proctor leaves the slavestones crawling over the table and heaves Matilda onto his shoulders, then grunts as he bends down to get Hush. She manages to slap him feebly around the face. Her fingers tangle up in his beard. Over by the door there's commotion. More voices than just the first one now.

Someone says, 'They're patterning again!'

And someone else says, 'Get that door open!'

'Nate,' says Proctor as he picks Hush up. 'This one's moving.'

'Just come on.' Nate pulls Proctor out of the room as the locked handle on the door to the saloon melts into a hot molten puddle and Travlin's sheriff bursts in with two of her deputies. Hush has managed to lift herself up a little, so she sees the cavalry arrive. The deputies are heavies, just like Proctor and Clint, but the sheriff is just a kid, a full head shorter than Hush. She has a round face with a jet-black mushroom haircut and dark purple lipstick that matches the acne on her cheeks. A tin star is pinned to her faded pink sweater, and the sweater has *Larissa* on it, a worlds-famous singer that Hush used to love back in Dustbowl. She's just about the coolest-looking person Hush has ever seen, and if the infinite cap was still on her head, it'd be decorating itself with lovehearts right about now.

The sheriff and her deputy have their thimbles raised and ready, but Clint's fists are waiting for them. He swings and one deputy goes down and doesn't get back up. Then he stunnerbees the sheriff in the gut. Or tries to. But her power's lightning-quick, and with a casual flick of one finger, she patterns a bend into the shotgun barrel so that Clint shoots himself in the throat. He makes a surprised *gak* sound, and topples forwards like a tree.

As the sheriff skips around Clint, Nate pulls Proctor through the door he made and weaves it away behind him. Then they're outside, and Hush can see they're standing on a metal grid walkway around the edge of the saloon, and beneath that, rows of enormous wheels are turning and turning and turning over this world's endless tarmac.

'Come on!' Nate is screaming, and Proctor lumbers after him, wheezing for breath, a sister on either shoulder. Hush can see a thin line of light sketching itself on the wall of the saloon behind them in the shape of a rectangle. The sheriff is opening back up the door that Nate unpatterned. And from up ahead by the saloon doors comes the sound of commotion. Shouts of, 'Go round the side! Damn slavers!'

Hush watches Nate realise that he's surrounded. There are people flooding out of the saloon, and the tiny implacable sheriff will be coming through the wall in moments. He runs both his hands through his hair. His eyes are huge and wild and white in the rushing dark. It's a look of someone who's out of options. Or so Hush thinks. Because as the sheriff kicks open the new door she's patterned, Nate turns to Proctor and screams at him to jump over the side. And Proctor vaults, obedient as a dog, off the moving platform of the saloon.

Hush clenches every part of her that she can clench, and waits to hit the tarmac. Waits for her flesh to shred and her bones to snap and her skull to crack like an egg. Instead she feels a stinging wet slap. The cold is stunning. Like a thousand bee-stings, all over. Nate has patterned the tarmac into a pool of water to break their fall.

Hush flails around feebly. She can't see and she can't breathe and she can't move enough yet to swim. Then Proctor drags her up roughly by the hair. She comes up next to Matilda, both of them splashing and choking and retching. All around is deafening noise. All around is blinding light. Horns blare and tyres swerve and hazards flash and drivers yell. Then the last of downtown roars past and Travlin dwindles away to a swarm of red dotted lights.

It's very dark and so very cold and Hush is soaked to the skin. She staggers to her feet. Matilda slides back under with a look of panic. Her stinger must have only fallen out when they leaped off the side of the saloon. Hush drags her up and hauls her clumsily out of the water. The two of them crawl onto the freezing tarmac, dripping wet and shivering and hugging each other tight with no talking. The trash twirls round and round in the last of the town's tailwind. The dead stars fall like snow.

Nate's standing across from them. Slouching in the dark like a bear. His eyes are closed and fog is billowing off him as he patterns his dripping fur coat dry. Once he's done, he stands up without bothering to help anyone else, even though Proctor is still in the water, and Hush's jeans and hair have all frozen stiff. She's beyond cold now. She's almost beyond shivering. She clutches Matilda as tight as she can. But if Matilda's warm, Hush can't feel it. Can't feel much of anything.

'Can you run?' she asks in the barest whisper.

Matilda tries to stand up and can't and shakes her head with tears in her eyes. Hush looks around them. Nowhere to run to anyway. Not without thimbles. Now that Travlin's gone, this world is very still and very silent and very empty. If only Nate wasn't in it, it'd be almost beautiful.

'Get up,' he orders Proctor. The slavestoned guard is still sitting down in the icy water up to his chest. 'Pick up Tilly-Boo and the sister and take my hand. We're crossing.'

Proctor tries to stand and grunts and flops back down. 'M-m-my leg snapped,' he says. 'From the f-fall.'

'Havoc's sake.' Nate roars with frustration. He curses and turns away to kick furiously at a bag of trash that Travlin has discarded behind itself. Hush knows exactly what he's thinking. To shift from world to world, you either need a thimble, or you need to be holding onto someone that's wearing one. But Nate can't carry both sisters over to Garrison. Not on his own, not if they resist him. Could he slavestone them? A horrified second passes before Hush remembers that he left his little box of gems back in the saloon.

'Nate,' says Proctor in a voice like a child. 'I am very cold. Please help me. I don't want to stop seeing the colours.'

'Shut up, shut up, shut up. I'm trying to think.'

Nate paces back and forth. He looks around the highway. Hush watches his little black eyes darting around from thought to thought and plan to plan. It's only when he turns to look at the sisters, shivering and thimbleless, that he seems to have some sort of epiphany.

'You *have* to follow me,' Nate realises with a smug smile. 'Unless you want to freeze to death here, like Proctor.'

'Honestly gonna need a moment to weigh those choices up,' Matilda manages to say weakly.

Nate looks up at what's left of the heavens. 'Are you listening to what I'm saying? If I leave you here, you die.'

'As I just said,' Matilda murmurs, almost sleepily, 'it really is a heck of a quandary.'

'Don't be smart,' Nate snaps. 'Because you ain't. You're just a stupid girl who fell for my stupid love letters. And you ain't nearly pretty enough to be my sweetheart, so you oughta be grateful I'm taking you to Garrison at all. So come. Now. Right now.'

Hush's attention is starting to wander. She looks over at Proctor, still in the water. There's a warm sleepy fuzz to her thoughts now, so it takes her a moment to notice that there's no white puff of breath coming from his beard any more. His body's just sat up in the middle of the ice.

Nate hasn't even noticed. He's quickly realised that he can't order the sisters like he could his slavestoned bodyguards. So now's he's moved on to begging.

'Please,' he says. 'Please. Pa's gonna kill me if I don't bring you back.'

'Fantastic news.' Matilda leans against Hush and closes her eyes. 'Now I can die happy.'

Nate is trying his best not to cry. His voice is wobbly and whinging. 'Am I really that bad? I ain't that bad, am I?'

Hush ignores him. Suddenly he doesn't seem to matter any more. Not much does. Just Matilda. Only Matilda.

'Whatever happens,' Hush tells her drowsily, 'we're sisters. Don't forget that we're sisters.'

Matilda nods and smiles faintly. Her lips are dark blue in the almost-dark. A few specks of stardust drift onto her cheeks and sparkle there like tears.

'Love you, Celeste,' she says. 'Love you fierce as a flame.'

And she gives Hush something between a kiss and a

headbutt. And they hug and hug and hug, until they can't feel each other any more.

• • •

'Havoc damn,' Nate says, from somewhere very far away. 'That a train coming?' He lets out a low whistle. 'Nate McCluskey, you lucky son of a gun. Hey! Hey, over here!'

Train, thinks Hush. Though everything's gone dreamy now, and she no longer knows if this is all really happening. Is that bright yellow light really there? Is that chugging in her ears the sound of an engine approaching and slowing, or just her own heart coming to a stop? Whose footsteps are coming over the tarmac towards them? Where has this beautiful man come from, with his porcelain face and his perfect smile? And why is he kneeling down beside Hush and Matilda, telling them it's OK, telling them not to be scared, it's Daddy, it's Daddy, he's here?

PART THREE

MATILDA'S DIARY

ENTRY 1: NINE SLEEPS UNTIL THE OPERA (HOW LUCKY WE ARE!)

Two nights ago at dinner, Father told us about our treat. Next week, he is taking Celeste and I to the opera! We shall attend a performance of *The King in Yellow* at the grandest auditorium in all Carcosa.

This is how much he Loves his Daughters.

And to think, I used to doubt that he did!

'The final aria in Act Five is the most Beautiful song in all the worlds,' Father informed us. 'Almost as Beautiful as my two precious peachflowers.'

('Peachflower' is what he calls us both, instead of using our names. I can count on one hand the times that he has called me Matilda.)

A trip outside! To the opera! I felt such delight that I giggled. It came out of my throat all high and fluttery, like a trilling flute. Father gave me this new laugh not two weeks past, and at first I was not fond of it at all. Yet here was news so wonderful that I just had to use it.

As I giggled, I saw how it pleased Father so. He always maintained that my old laugh was much too sarcastic.

What does that word mean, I wonder? Sarcastic. I remember how to spell it well enough. S-A-R-C-A-S-T-I-C.

And yet its meaning has gone from my head, just like my laugh, and so much else.

Oh well. What else is there to do, but be patient? When one has been as Sick as Celeste and myself have been, getting better takes time. Father says that soon, we won't suffer any more Confusions, and eventually shan't even remember ever having them at all.

That is why I am resolved to write here, in this little book of diamond-wafer pages. The writing shall do the remembering for me.

And look how much I need it! I have already forgotten the story I was telling; the story of Father giving us the gift of the opera tickets.

Here is how it happened:

• • •

Celeste and I were dining with Father in the Jewelled Chamber, at the long silver table that sits in that room's centre. The walls of the chamber are painted with gem dust. In the dim light of the floating spheres, they sparkled blue and violet and emerald around us like a starry sky.

We ate quietly, the way Father likes us to. Under our heavy cutlery the porcelain plates shrieked and screeched, as if we were torturing them.

Then, Father spoke up: 'Peachflowers, how would you like to see *The King in Yellow*? I have three tickets. We'll go all together, like a family.'

(At the time I did not think upon it, but writing it down, is that not a strange thing to say? *Like* a family? We *are* a family!)

Anyhow, at Father's words I stopped eating my sugar mice at once. And after I was done gasping and giggling, I settled down to let Father explain, as he often has to. For in Truth, I had no idea what an opera was, nor why it is so special. And so I listened, rapt, as he told us all about the opera house in Carcosa, and how we will hear music there, and see sights, that will be more Beautiful than anything we have ever known in this House.

Of course, we remembered none of this. It must be so wearisome for him, to have two Daughters who have forgotten all about Carcosa. Father tries to hide his annoyance as best as he can. Sometimes I wonder if he ever wishes he could be rid of us.

But of course he does not. He Loves us far, far too much!

I have done it again. Lost the run of the story. I am new to this skill. And my mind is still so full of loose threads! Where even was I? Oh yes, the opera.

'You must wear your finest dresses,' Father ordered. 'The opera house is a mighty fine place. If you want me to take you, you better listen closely to the Boy. He'll tell you all about how to behave.'

'We shall,' I said, dancing about in my seat. 'We shall, we shall. Oh, Father, thank you!' I got down from the table and ran the long silver length of it, past all the food as it glittered and twitched and pleaded in little voices to be set free, and I hugged him.

Father ruffled my curls just a little with his hand, then Patterned them back to Perfect. 'You're welcome, peachflower. You will like it. The final song is so Beautiful, each singer can only perform it once.'

I giggled my new laugh, and set about dancing, already thinking about how I would adorn myself. Above my head, my sister's canaries flittered around the crown chandelier, singing the little melodies they had been woven with that morning.

But Celeste did not clap or dance or say thank you. She did not even glance up from her plate of toast. I could see Father looking at her, unable to hide his disappointment. Celeste is still mightily Confused, but she has always adored music. No doubt Father expected the opera tickets to delight her. But they did not. She chewed her toast and began muttering one of her little nonsense songs. Father has tried to cut them out of her, so many times. Yet they always grow back, like weeds.

'Hush, little baby, I love you, Grammy's gonna varnish your fingers blue,' she sang.

I tried ignoring her, like Father has instructed me to do. I did not want those songs and Words to plant themselves into my mind too. Not now I am so much Improved.

So I thought to myself: The opera! I am going outside, to the opera!

And I felt as happy as I could ever remember being.

It was only when I sat back at my place again that I grew fearful. Sometimes, Father subjects us to Tests, as a measure of our Condition. In the past, you see, there were times when we pretended to be better even though we were not. There was one instance, for example, when I appeared so greatly Improved that Father rewarded me with a present of a silver pistol in a box lined with red silk. (This was some weeks ago, when I was feeling far more murderous towards him.)

It was loaded with blanks, but he still Punished me greatly when I tried to shoot him with it.

I would never do something like that now, of course. Since then, Father has spent much time and effort on my Improvement, and I am so much less Confused. I try my best to think and speak and act in the way that he wants me to. My appearance is even starting to Improve as well.

It has not been easy. Yet look how Father rewards my hard work!

With a trip! Outside the House! To see the opera!

Unless, I reminded myself, this is a Test.

For one never does know with Father.

So I replaced my jubilation with caution. I went back to my seat for the serving of dessert, and sipped at my rose petal soup in a most Daughterly fashion, and when I spoke, I did so demurely.

'Are you quite sure that we are ready, Father?' I said. 'To venture outside, I mean? What of our Affliction?'

Father took a candied butterfly from the table's cage and fed it into his mouth, wing by wing. 'I believe we're over the worst of it,' he said to me. 'You are quite an Improvement from before.'

I nod. It is true. I have my new giggle, and I have my

new hair, and my thoughts are almost never Confused. But what of Celeste? What if she starts shouting during the performance about her mad delusions and conspiracies? If she embarrasses Father, perhaps he might never let us from the House again.

Celeste must not be a nuisance. She must not spoil things. We so desperately need to leave this place. Neither of us have been outside the House since before we became Unwell. And when was that? A long, long time ago, certainly.

A trip into the city shall do us both the world of good. After all, peachflowers do not bloom indoors. They need sunshine and air, as I have suggested to Father many times.

~~And now at last, it seems as if he is agreeing with me, which means I win!~~

I have crossed that last bit out. It is wrong to feel that. It is Shameful. After all, Father only wants us to be Well. I must stop seeing every decision he makes as a battle to be fought.

Perhaps this opera will be the start of a new peace between us. Though you would never know it now, there was a time when I was the most difficult Daughter. I remember the days that I screamed and spat at him. I remember clawing at his face like a wild she-cat. I dimly recall my cursing too; I could spew such vile language that Father had to take those Words out of my head altogether, for the sake of decency. There was one beginning with an F, I think? That one was the worst of all.

And, of course, there were all the times I tried to murder him.

But now just look at me! A model Daughter, almost (apart from my looks). When Father shows me off at the opera, he might almost be proud. That is how much I have Improved. I can barely even fathom why I was so vile to him in the first place.

ENTRY 2: EIGHT SLEEPS UNTIL THE OPERA (WE WERE NOT WELL)

We were not Well, my sister and I. Not Well at all. Through some Mishap, the details of which Father has not made all too clear, we became lost in one of the Midnight Worlds – that is a place where the sun has gone out, and the stars have all fallen like snow. Everything comes undone in worlds like that. Minds, most of all. When Father finally reached us, our heads had completely unravelled.

We didn't even remember we were his Daughters. In fact, we refused to believe it.

Such an Affliction is not easily cured, even for one as powerful as Father. It is months since our rescue (how many months, I am not sure), and Celeste and I still suffer bouts of Confusion.

During such periods, our behaviour becomes nothing less than shocking.

In particularly severe bouts, Celeste and I begin to believe ourselves not to be Carcosans. We refute that this House is in fact our home. Most appalling of all, we even deny that Father is our true and rightful parent. Instead, we come to consider him to be our Enemy! (I think that is why I still sometimes feel victorious when Father agrees to one of my requests.)

Our Confusion has made us exceedingly difficult Daughters. We have attempted escape and plotted his demise too many times to count. I have already told you of the silver pistol. There was also the time with the kitchen knife, and the incident with the poisoned coffee, and our extremely imaginative plan involving the electrified toilet seat.

Luckily, this Mischief did not succeed.

Father is too strong with the Power.

ENTRY 3: LATER THAT DAY
(I HAVE RESOLVED TO BECOME EXTREMELY PRETTY)

I am determined to become extremely pretty before our visit to the opera. This will be a challenge, of course. For I know that I am still Ugly. When Father first brought us here, I was positively hideous. My face was freckled and my nose was too round and my hair was too frizzy.

(Of course, back then I refused to consider that these things were Ugly at all. It took Father much patience and persuading to clear up my initial Confusion.)

I am so very lucky that he has the Power to Improve me. My front teeth might still be gappy, but I have gold ringlet hair now, and my freckles are mostly gone, along with all my scars. My speech has been refined, and I have my new laugh, the soft and giggly one that Father prefers so much.

Although, I am still not sure that I prefer it. I liked my old laugh, that would come up from my belly as loud as a gunshot, and startle the canaries to silence, and make Celeste smile.

I should not have written that. It is not True. My new laugh is better. Father says so. And Father is Right, always.

Although, sometimes I do wonder. After all, there have been times before when he has vowed to never let Celeste and I leave this House. Yet we go to the opera in only eight sleeps! If he has changed his mind about us going outside, perhaps he will change his mind about my laugh too, and go back to preferring my old one, as I do?

Not that it really matters how it sounds either way, for I almost never laugh. To laugh, you must feel joyful.

It is strange that, for all Father's Power, he cannot make me happy.

ENTRY 4: SEVEN SLEEPS UNTIL THE OPERA (A GREY DAY COMES)

Today I have had what Father calls one of my Grey Days. On a Grey Day, I do not do much, except lie in my bed. Everything seems Dismal. The most sumptuous food tastes of Ash. There is not a Wonder in the House that can amuse me. I feel weak and tired and heartsore. Sometimes I weep without knowing why.

Grey Days are deeply tedious. I despise our serving Boy, and his constant fussing. He feeds me vitamins and bathes my brow and strokes my cheeks to raise my spirits. Sometimes Father comes, to skulk at the doorway to my room and irritably ask if I have Improved yet. Other times he will storm in and subject me to one his Tests, to determine if I am Confused. Or else he will approach my bedside as meek as a child, with gifts intended to cheer me up.

This little book that I write in now was one such present. Father got it from the markets in Carcosa (he knows that I adore anything that comes from beyond the House). Other things he has brought Celeste and I include: cones of pomegranate sorbet, flocks of singing canaries, dresses made of flowers that unfurl or eyes that blink, and the tea called Bliss (which makes you feel as if you are Loved, but only for as long as you drink it).

None of the gifts ever help though. A Grey Day is grey, and no amount of presents can ever paint it a different colour.

When the feeling passes, as it always does, more or less, I am at a loss to explain why it was ever there at all. Father has provisioned this House with all a Daughter could want. The finest foods, delicious drinks, innumerable dresses and beautifications. I have a serving Boy to care for me, and Pets to amuse me, and a Father that Loves me dearly. It feels ungrateful to be unhappy in such a place.

And yet it is not Perfect. What is? Perfection does not exist, even in Carcosa. There are faults with the House, and my Life within it.

It has just occurred to me that I should list them. Perhaps in doing so, the reason for my Grey Days will appear upon the page.

REASONS I AM UNHAPPY

1. We cannot leave the House.
2. Nor enter many of the rooms.
3. Nor even look out of the windows.
4. I am fearful of becoming Confused again.
5. I am fearful of Father's Punishings.
6. I do not remember my Mother, nor many other things.
7. I am not Ladylike.
8. Father finds me Ugly.
9. It is so very lonely here.
10. And so deeply boring.
11. I barely see Celeste.
12. She is not Improving, like I am.
13. I miss my old laugh.

I think I will stop there. Not because there are no more reasons, but because this is only a small book. It does not have endless pages.

Of course, no one is to blame for this unhappiness. It all stems from my Affliction. If I were not Confused, it would be safe for me to leave the House. Thus Father would not have to Punish me. Thus I would Improve faster, and become Beautiful and Ladylike. Thus it would become acceptable for me to meet other girls, and make friends with them. Thus Life would become more fun. And so on and so on and such forth.

Everything rests on me becoming Well again. I must work for that. It must be my sole focus. Then all my Grey Days will surely disappear, and my unhappiness too.

Though I would still miss my old laugh. And Celeste, most of all. I wonder, does she have Grey Days, as I do? Is she happy, singing her songs over and over, defying Father again and again? Yesterday, the Boy's slavestones instructed him to tell me that Celeste has stolen a bag of chilli powder from the kitchens, and is secretly practising flinging handfuls of it, so as to blind Father with it at some point. Father is only letting her carry on because it keeps her from other Mischief.

Hearing that, I felt sad. There was a time not so long ago when she and I would both be trying to fling that chilli powder together. I do wish my sister would Improve herself soon, so that we can do things with each other again. Even speaking with her would be a tonic to me, but Father does not permit us much time together, saying we only encourage the other's Confusions. That is a frightening thought. I do not know the exact nature of mine and my sister's Affliction (that is what makes it so pernicious) but Father's comments lead me to believe that it might be contagious.

And yet, if that were true, then why doesn't Father himself ever seem to suffer its effects? If the Affliction can be caught like a virus, surely he would have it?

But no. He never remembers things that never happened, or recalls people that never existed, or accuses us of not really being his Daughters. Father is always sure. Father is always Right.

ENTRY 5: SIX SLEEPS UNTIL THE OPERA (I LIKE THIS DIARY)

This diary was a grand idea. It is so very soothing. Even when I write down bad thoughts, or record some of my earlier Shameful Deeds, still at the end of it all, I am comforted. I imagine that all the Sickness and Confusion is flowing out of me and onto the paper, and each time I put down my pen I feel lighter, cleaner, better. Like I have taken medicine.

That is all I wanted to say. I may write again later. It is early morning still. Father left before dawn for more of his Adventures. I don't remember much of what I dreamed last night. It must have been a nightmare. Something about a town on wheels. And a little table with a green top. Querazade swam into my head and gobbled most of it up.

ENTRY 6: LATER THAT DAY (I DESCRIBE THE BOY)

Whenever Father leaves the House, it is Boy's slavestones that care for us. They move him like a puppeteer moves a marionette, or dreams move a sleepwalker. They make the Boy clothe us, and feed us, and tell us how to be more Ladylike. Occasionally, when we misbehave, they make him summon Father so we can be Punished. They are Cruel, those slavestones, that glitter where the Boy's eyes once were. Because of this, I have always disliked the Boy himself, with his shaved head and his stiff, pleated, brown paper overalls.

I have mentioned him before in my entries, I know, but only in passing. Even when I write, it is so easy to forget that the Boy is even there at all. He lurks like a shadow might. I turn around, and he is there.

Apart from his name, and the way he looks and sounds, I know nothing else about him. Not one thing. That has never bothered me before, but now that I am recording things within this book, I know that I must include them within my writing. For they are a part of this House, and thus a part of its mystery. And unlike the pygmy bear, or the Hallway of Dancing Stone, the Boy has a voice. As long as the slavestones let him use it.

And so this morning, as he rustled into my room with my breakfast upon a silver tray, I decided to strike up conversation.

'Let us strike up a conversation,' I told him.

The slavestones replied through the Boy. They told me that a more Ladylike way of indicating you wish to talk with someone is to make some statement about the pleasantness of the weather.

'But we're inside,' I said. 'And the House does not let me look out of the windows. Besides, I do not want to talk about the weather. I want to talk about you. And by you, I mean the Boy.'

The Boy lay the silver tray on my bed and slid it up onto my lap. 'What I want is for you to eat your breakfast, as your Father commands.'

I looked down at the breakfast. There was a light pink froth of marrowfoam, with a tiny bone straw to suck it up with. There was a crisped sliver of flayed pig, covered with a sweet gold dusting. There was a little bowl of glistening jet black eggs, plump as olives. And finally there was rose tea, steeping in a crystal pot.

The Boy was made to lean across my bed and tuck a crisp white napkin into the neck of my pyjama top. For a moment, I could hear the gemstones chittering their commands to him from the hollow caves of his eyesockets. Then he bowed his head and backed away, and the hems of his long paper trousers scraped lightly across the floor as he went about fetching a new dress from my wardrobe – the one made entirely of tulips – and began to smooth the wrinkled petals.

I took up the bone straw and sucked a little of the marrowfoam. Then I cut a tiny strip of the flayed pig and chewed it.

'I am eating breakfast,' I informed the Boy. 'Now can we talk about you?'

'It is not Ladylike to talk with your mouth full,' the slavestones told the Boy to tell me.

He really is so very annoying. Though I know it is not his fault. I covered my mouth with the corner of my napkin, and said, 'Father likes it when I converse at the table.'

'But,' responded the Boy, coming over to pour me a cup of tea, 'Mr Rapture does not like it when you ask about Life outside of the House.'

'That was to stop me becoming Confused.' I pinched

the teacup in my fingers and blew on it in a Ladylike way. As I did, a thought occurred to me. 'Were you once Confused too? Is that why you have to wear eyestones? To stop you making Mischief?'

When I asked this, the Boy was laying my petalled dress upon the chair beside my bed, ready for me to wear. He went very still, as if my question had made a statue of him. Then, as fast as he could, the slavestones made him leave.

I waited. For a long time. Until I was sure they were not making the Boy come back. Then I reached beneath my pillow and took up my book and I wrote this entry. I wrote it slowly and carefully. I didn't rush. Because I wanted to be sure. I wanted to know that when I came to write these next few Words, that I hadn't been mistaken or Confused.

It could have just been the gemstones sparkling. But even now, after waiting and thinking, I still think that the Boy had tears in his eyes as he ran from my room.

ENTRY 7: STILL LATER (I DESCRIBE THE HOUSE)

Father's House is most grand. The parts that I have seen are, at least. Much of it remains forbidden to me, though. There are windows that, if I pass them, will close like eyes. There are doors that, if I approach them, seem to shrink down infinite corridors, so that even if I were to walk all day towards them, I would never be any closer. The door to Celeste's room is such a one. So is the door to the East Wing, which Father enters when he retires to bed, or leaves upon his travels.

However, since my gradual Improvement, Father has rewarded me with access to new rooms. I can go to six in all, which is a great deal more than Celeste (she is only trusted to visit three).

Besides my bedroom and its adjoining bathroom, I can choose to go into the Middle Hallway, which connects to all the other rooms, as well as joining East Wing with West. Then I might visit the Jewelled Chamber, where we dine when Father is home; or the Yellow Shrine; or the kitchens where the Boy sleeps (though I have only been to them once. It is so very wretched there.)

Most of these rooms are very splendid. They gleam and shimmer and dazzle. Or else they are remarkable in other ways. The Middle Hallway is one such example. Its main features are the two rows of columns that line each side of it, which, along with the floor, are made of the material known as Dancing Stone.

Dancing Stone is a liquid marble that moves with glacial slowness. To the naked eye, the hallway will appear still. To the touch, it will feel firm. Yet over time, an attentive and curious person will begin to notice subtle differences in both the columns and the floor.

I have seen the pillars flex and twist like giant braids of hair. I have seen long ribbons of white and lilac marble travel down the lengths of them and into the floor, where they swirl and disappear. I have seen small, fragile baubles gather at the base of each column like froth. And once, over the course of a week, I watched one corner of the hallway as the whiskered mouth of a pink marble fish broke the surface of the floor, and gaped once, and descended again.

It was only when I saw the fish that I understood: the House's hallway is actually a river, brought here by Father from a world beyond this one, a world where rock can move like water and like flesh. Its pillars are marble waterfalls, that tumble so slowly and plunge with barely a ripple. And beneath our feet, living things are swimming unseen through currents of stone.

In part, it was understanding the True Nature of the Middle Hallway that inspired me to begin writing this diary. For I knew then that much in this House, whilst appearing to be one thing, later reveals itself to be something else entirely.

That conclusion has led me to another thought: perhaps the Illusory Nature of the House is one of the reasons why Celeste and I are not getting better. Is it really any wonder that we continue to suffer in such a place? Surely Truth is remedy of all Confusion – and yet in this House, Truth moves out of sight like a fish in the Dancing Stone.

The Truth is a Fish.

I don't know why that phrase is in my head, swimming round and round and round.

Mysteries upon mysteries! That is why I keep this diary. I shall wait, and I shall watch, and I shall write down what I see. Until I glimpse another Truth stirring from the place where It lies hidden.

ENTRY 8: JUST BEFORE DINNER (I INTRODUCE THE PETS)

I should add something here, about the Pets. These are living creatures that Father has encountered during his Adventures in other worlds. Most of these creatures go to a place in the city called the Pattern Market, where they find new homes and owners, but Father always keeps a few that especially amuse or beguile him.

How many Pets live here, I do not know exactly. But currently there are at least three, although this number is often changing, for if they are sufficiently ungrateful at being rescued, then Father is sometimes forced to dispose of them.

I shall describe the current Pets of the House now, in case any suddenly appear or disappear in the future. Whenever that has happened in the past, my first worry has been that I am suffering a Confusion, and have imagined the existence of a Pet that never resided in the House at all. But by keeping this record, I need not think that, nor even ask the Boy (for the slavestones barely permit him to talk to me at all). All I need to do is consult these pages: then I shall be able to work out what is Real and what is Not Real.

I never realised before writing how Words themselves are quite the Power. Of course, they cannot compete with Father's ability to cut and Pattern. What can? But Words have a strength, all the same. They are one of those slower, surer powers, like Kindness, like Love, that we

ENTRY 9: JUST BEFORE SLEEP (I REMEMBER A WOMAN)

I had to put down my pen, before. Even now, it is shaking in my grip. I cannot steady my hand. My heart is racing. Those Words – the ones I just wrote down – I know them from somewhere.

If I stop writing and listen, I can hear a woman speaking them to me. She has a rough voice, like boots treading through gravel.

Sooner or later, you'll need them slow, sure powers. You know the ones I mean. I don't know what'll happen to you out there, but I know you'll need love and kindness to make it.

I should not have written that out. I should not listen to her at all. Whoever this woman is, she is wrong. Love is not a Power. It is a Grave Duty, which as Daughters we are obliged to perform for the benefit of our Father. His is the only Power. His is the only Truth.

The Confusion within me might try to say otherwise, but I shall not listen. I will win this War with myself.

I will Improve. I will.

ENTRY 10: FIVE SLEEPS UNTIL THE OPERA (I RESUME DESCRIBING THE PETS)

Now is another day, and I am much Improved from the previous entry. What follows is a list of the Pets of the

180

House, which I endeavoured to begin before being rudely interrupted by a slight bout of Confusion!

First, there is the pygmy bear, who is a little fellow about the height of my hip. He has rusty red fur and an all-pink nose and twitchy black whiskers and round white teeth. Once he had a voice too, but Father cut it out for our safety. That's what the Boy's slavestones told me, once, when I asked why.

Which seems a strange thing.

It is not like Words can be weapons, is it?

Though the pygmy bear cannot speak, he is certainly a clever creature. All day he sits in the Middle Hallway, crafting daggers for himself. He makes them from gnawed chicken bones, or broken shards of crockery. Then sets them with twine or wire into the broken ends of kitchen broom handles.

Outwardly, I pretend to find this process loathsome and imbecilic, as a girl should. But secretly (and I have told no one this, not the pygmy bear, and certainly not Father) I admire and respect this little creature. He is a fighter – a fighter who does not know he is beaten. I used to be like that, once. Before I Improved.

Father keeps the pygmy bear around because sometimes, after dinner, he will let the little thing try and murder him. To me, this seems an extremely ungrateful thing for the pygmy bear to try and do. Perhaps fighting is the way his kind show their affection. I do not know. It is not like he can tell me any more, though often he has tried to communicate a great deal to me in growls and whimpers and hand signals.

Whatever the reason for the violence he wishes on Father, Father himself doesn't seem to mind. In fact it amuses him. The pygmy bear is like his jester. He will duel with the little creature, usually in the Jewelled Chamber, often forcing the Boy to watch. During the fight, Father will allow the pygmy bear's newest makeshift dagger to within inches of his throat. Until suddenly, with a flick of his thimble, he will Pattern its blade into something else. An ice-cream, for instance, that he will then eat it in front of his dismayed adversary; or else some other such teasing transformation.

This causes the pygmy bear much anguish, and my father will double over and slap his thighs and laugh his songbird laugh. Then the pygmy bear will skulk away in shame and defeat, to cobble together another dagger, and in another few weeks, the duel will repeat itself again.

(I asked Father once why the pygmy bear does not ever try and hurt Celeste and I, or the Boy, and Father replied that we are all quite safe, which is good to remember. Yet in its own way, that is quite curious too. If the little creature had a little more wit, it would realise that hurting us would hurt Father like a dagger through the heart.)

Apart from the pygmy bear, there are Querazade and J'lzacoatl, the dreamfish. Unlike him, these creatures speak, being much smarter and much smaller, each being about the length of my little finger. Their bodies are like little twists of coloured silk that ripple in the air. In truth, I do not see much of either of them, even though Querazade lives in a conch shell beside my bed, for dreamfish only come out at night, to swim into the heads of those near to them, and nibble up any bad dreams.

Father keeps them for our sake. Bouts of the Confusion often begin when I am asleep. For example, I will dream I am walking in a peach orchard, perhaps, or climbing up the sides of a great bowl of dust, or stinging my own shadow with bees. And then, before I can stop it, the thought will come that I am not the eldest Daughter of James Décollage Rapture. And from there, it is only a short while until the inevitable Mischief begins.

And so I am grateful for Querazade. Even if she is somewhat annoying.

Father has no other Pets, unless you count the plates of things that the Boy serves us from the kitchens, like the sugar mice, or the candied butterflies, or the miserable Squid-Thing which bleeds an ink that Father drinks like it is coffee. Although, I suppose the House itself is a kind of Pet to him, since its windows and doors are like eyes that only open on Father's whims. Sometimes I wish that this place would let me gaze upon a sunset or a dawn again. Perhaps I could ask Father for a painting of one to be hung in my room, perhaps by a master artist like Hogan

I do not know where I heard that name, Hogan. Not in this House. And as it came to me, I had a most frightening Confusion. I saw in my mind Celeste and I, standing amongst a peach orchard in blossom, and there was a woman with us, a grey-haired woman with one hand. And then in my mind, that image swung open like a door, and a little voice spoke in my ear, so clear that I turned around in fright.

'Tilly-Boo,' the little voice said to me. Though that is not my name.

Oh, when will I be delivered from this Affliction?

ENTRY 11: FOUR SLEEPS UNTIL THE OPERA (I DO NOT WANT TO TELL FATHER)

I am in bed now, wondering if I should tell Father about the minor Confusions I have had these past two days.

He would be able to remove them from my mind very easily. He has done it before: to my curses, and my sarcastic laugh, and my many other imperfections and delusions.

All it would take is a few minutes, then out each Confusion would come like a rotted tooth, and soon I would be feeling better again.

But I do not want to tell Father. I do not want to admit that I might not be as Improved as he thinks I am. It is only four sleeps until the opera. What if he does not take me? That would be most hideous. I must go. I simply must. Sometimes I feel that if I do not get out of this House soon, I will scream and scream and never stop.

ENTRY 12: THREE SLEEPS UNTIL THE OPERA
(THIS DIARY IS A DANGER)

It has occurred to me, after writing yesterday, that this book is now a Danger to me. If Father read it, he would discover not just the small (and inconsequential!) Confusions I have suffered – but (and this would be far worse!) he would know that I have kept knowledge of them from him.

He would cut this book into atoms. And I would be Punished for certain. It is somewhat vague to me what that means exactly, because as part of my Punishing, Father cuts away any of my memories that have become Confused in anyway. Some of these return afterward, but in a hazy and half-remembered way, a little like a dream. The first thing I truly recall clearly, is waking in my bed last month, with Father beside me, patiently explaining (for what must have been the tenth time!) that I am his Beloved Daughter.

I must make sure he never reads this. Not ever. The thought of having this book taken from me makes me feel quite Grey. For I Love this private world that I am Patterning, letter by letter, upon these pages. I have never really considered myself to be overly keen on Words. Now I cannot imagine being without them.

ENTRY 13: TWO SLEEPS UNTIL THE OPERA
(CELESTE HAS BEEN VERY AWFUL)

I do not know why Celeste has done it! Why must she upset Father so? And so close to our opera trip?

It is not Right, it is not Daughterly, for her to treat him as she does. He might not be the warmest of Fathers, but no one can say that he is not Dutiful. Not only has he provided the Boy to tend to us with the strictest care, but he endeavours to give us each the little luxuries that make life tolerable.

So why then does she spurn or spoil them all? (By 'them', I mean his gifts.) It is the very Height of Ingratitude. Why, Father more than showers her with presents. She is positively deluged. The singing canaries that he procured for her last week are just the latest such example. I imagine they were greatly expensive, too, for they travel about in little choirs of six or seven birds, and sing all manner of tunes in three-part harmony.

Such a splendid gift! And so thoughtful. (Celeste Loves music.) Yet she has to go and ruin everything.

You see, she has taught them murder-ballads. The most frightful musical numbers imaginable! Full of Death, and dismemberment, and other Unladylike things. I spent the entirety of today chasing little hosts of them away from me. But they would not stop their chirruping! I began feeling positively murdersome towards them.

In the end, it got too much. Father had to go around, clipping the wings of the canaries with little swipes of his thimble. Then the slavestones made the Boy brush them up into fluttering, helpless little piles, and took them off to the kitchens to bake them in a pie with pomegranates and saffron.

When we ate it at dinner, Celeste didn't seem upset at all. She just kept asking me which murder-ballad was my favourite. Whenever I answered that none of them were, she seemed annoyed, as if that were the wrong answer! It felt as if she were trying to provoke me into some outburst. But I did not. I remained Ladylike and demure.

She is so very annoying, though. I wanted to shout at her to ~~Hush~~

~~be Quiet~~

not talk.

My own thoughts will not cease, either. One of the murder-ballads, 'Janey's Lying Still', keeps repeating in my head, no matter how many times I try not to think of it.

It is doing it again, right now!

Curse Celeste and her canaries!

I shall write the hideous lyrics below. Perhaps by doing so, I can expel them from my thoughts.

> *Upon the ragged highway,*
> *Janey met a ragged man*
> *and together they did weave themselves*
> *a wicked ragged plan.*
>
> *Janey lay down in the dust*
> *where the road meets marshy grass,*

and wore herself a face of tears
as if it were a mask.

The ragged man he hid himself
within the reeds, just like a toad
Until a stranger came a-wandering
where the marshy grass meets road.

The stranger's clothes were silk
and his hair was darkly curled.
He walked a golden waythread
from noble world to world.

He stopped by weeping Janey
upon the rotten bank.
Her cheeks both wet from weeping,
her eyes both red and blank.

The stranger said, 'Why do you cry?
Oh maiden, tell me true.'
So Janey smiled and told him,
'To stop someone like you.'

Then came the ragged man,
with power sharp as any blade
and cut until the stranger
lay in pieces by the way.

He took whate'er he wanted:
the stranger's suit and shoes and face
and wove it o'er himself,
'til he was adorned in stolen grace.

There are other verses too, where Janey and the man continue their murderous deceit, but to make the trick more convincing, the man begins to change Janey as well, cutting parts of her away, making her something more and more pitiable and wretched, so that further wayfarers will stop to assist her.

The final verse, which I have included below, is meant to be ambiguous – are Janey and the man still practising their deception? Or has the ragged man simply killed her?

> *Then he turned to Janey lying,*
> *with her single weeping eye.*
> *And Janey's lying still today.*
> *Yes, still does Janey lie.*

I believe it to be a commentary on how Men like the Ragged Man use Women like Janey as Tools.

I do not know why it is lodged in my head. Nor why it torments me so. I suppose I am just lucky that my father is not a Man like that. Though he does alter me, he does so to make me more Beautiful, not more Ugly. And that is a very different thing, is it not? I think it surely is.

ENTRY 14: ONE SLEEP UNTIL THE OPERA (THE SONG IS GONE)

When I awoke this morning, the song was gone. I could not remember a single one of the lyrics, nor even what it was called.

Querazade must have eaten up the words and melody, even though she is only supposed to eat my nightmares.

I am not cross. On the contrary, I am glad of the mistake! Hopefully my (slight) Confusions of the past few days are behind me now. It is but one single sleep until the night of the opera. I intend to be as Perfect as my limited looks allow.

ENTRY 15: LATER THAT AFTERNOON (I PREVENT A MURDER)

I had lessons this afternoon, but I could not concentrate at all. The slavestones were making the Boy tutor me on the Fifteen Greetings.

In Carcosa, I am told, there are different curtseys that girls must give, depending on whomsoever is in front of them. There is a curtsey for family, one for friends, another for strangers, a fourth for other girls who are prettier than you, and so on, and so forth.

'I'm sorry,' I said to the Boy as I mixed up my curtseys for the tenth time. 'I cannot focus. However will I go to the opera if I cannot master my manners?'

The Boy's paper sleeves rustled as he laid a rough hand across my brow.

'No, I don't feel Grey,' I lied. 'Not very Grey, anyway.'

The Boy stood aside and gave me the Bow of Servitude. He motioned at the door, as if to say, *Perhaps a walk will refresh you?*

And that is how I came to be wandering down the Middle

Hallway to the Yellow Shrine (where I go daily to pray for deliverance from all Confusion), and discovered Father, sitting in the sickly light of the candles, staring miserably at the golden altar of the Sign.

He looked wretched, though his face was as Perfect as ever. But his eyes were dark pits, and he held a cup in his hands with the barest dregs of tea.

At once I knew that Father has begun drinking Bliss again.

Bliss is a popular tea from Carcosa, purple in colour and bittersweet in taste. Drinking it brings about the warm, giddy sensation of being Loved. But this feeling lasts only as long as the tea itself. After the last sip of Bliss, the drinker feels an intense and forlorn heartsickness. It is not uncommon for people to cry into their Bliss whilst drinking it, so that their tears might replenish the cup a little and so stave off their sorrow for a few moments more.

That is what Father was doing, as I entered the Yellow Shrine. He was weeping silently but powerfully, his shoulders jerking as tears rolled off his nose. Poor Father! He gets like this whenever Celeste or I cause Mischief. The melancholy our disobedience stirs in him becomes too much, and he seeks solace in Bliss.

I hesitated by the door to the Shrine, and luckily Father was so subsumed in his sorrow that he did not notice me there. So it was that I heard him muttering to himself, whilst wracked with sobs.

'Pathetic,' I heard him say. 'Stupid, stupid fool. At war

with yourself. With the bit of her you put in you. And you can't cut her out, because the idea of not loving them is . . .'

His voice broke, and he cried for a little longer, before gathering himself again and taking another tiny sip of his cup of Bliss and tears.

I slipped back out into the hallway, filled with guilt and pity. But also (and it shames me even more to admit this) I felt some faint sense of triumph, too. Why does seeing Father that way evoke some twisted pleasure within me? What wicked Daughters we are! I mean myself, as much as Celeste. For though I might be more Ladylike and Obedient than she is, I still somehow cannot bring myself to Love him, as I should. All the other Daughterly virtues, I exhibit to Perfection. I Respect him, and Defer to him, and Please him with what prettiness I have.

And yet there is no Love for Father. Not in me, not in Celeste, not anywhere in this House, except in those fleeting teacups of bittersweet Bliss.

As I began to edge back into the hallway, I noticed a shadow detach itself from the walls of the Shrine, which lie curtained with darkness, and begin to creep towards Father. It was the pygmy bear: I could see a new dagger in his paw, like a long and vicious claw.

The duel! My heart leaped up into my throat, and I cried out, 'Father!'

He turned just as the pygmy bear struck. The Bliss had made him slow, made him distracted, but even then he could still draw his thimble with rattlesnake speed. Though the pygmy bear was faster. The dagger flashed in the gloom of the shrine as it drove downwards and buried into Father's throat, right up to the hilt.

A gout of red spilled itself down his suit. I let out a shriek. My legs buckled beneath me. I heaved once, turned, and vomited my lunch of sugar mice onto the Hallway floor.

Father just laughed his songbird laugh. Then he stood and took hold of the dagger's handle and let it fall to the floor of the shrine. It was a crumpled paper cup of dark red wine. He had Patterned the knife in time. He had won, as he always does.

The pygmy bear let out a howl and slunk away into the corner. I sat in the doorframe with the bitter taste of my own bile in my throat. And Father laughed and laughed and laughed, until the tears fell from his eyes.

ENTRY 16: THE MORNING OF THE OPERA (I RECEIVE A GIFT)

Tonight!

We go tonight!

To the opera, to Carcosa!

We breakfasted this morning in the Jewelled Chamber. Just a light rose soup that wouldn't make us look 'heavy' in our ballgowns. I babbled on to Celeste about how good this trip would be for her, and how Improved she would be at the end of it, but she just looked sad and hummed her own songs to herself.

Then Father entered, wearing a green silk bathrobe, tied tight at the waist. On his bare neck, the Yellow Sign glowed and throbbed like a cattle brand. He looked younger. His face was pink as a cherub's, and he had cut off his moustache, and added dimples in his cheeks. Perhaps he did not want anyone at the opera to see him with his Daughters and consider him Old.

And yet he does look Tired. There's a slight stoop to his shoulders that not even the cut of his clothes can fully hide. Like he's shouldering some invisible burden.

That's the Bliss, I think. And us. My sister and I. How dearly Father needs this. The opera, I mean. Perhaps even more than Celeste and I do. There's only so long you can Love without being Loved back, before it starts eating away at you, like an undoer inside your heart.

I don't know how I know that, but I do, deep down. I Loved someone once too, someone who wouldn't – or couldn't – Love me back.

Who was it?

'I bought you a gift for tonight,' Father said to me.

I was so caught up in my own thoughts, that I almost didn't hear him. But luckily some part of me that was on autopilot said, 'Thank you, Father.'

He took out a black velvet case from his bathrobe pocket and motioned lazily for the Boy, who was made to shuffle up and take the case and bring it down the long length of the silver table so I could see inside.

There were twenty-eight dazzling teeth, all arrayed in a

perfect crescent across a black velvet cushion. They were long and white, like mint lozenges.

I tried to look overjoyed. Or at least grateful.

'Shall I change them over now, peachflower?' Father asked me.

I tried not to look at his hands, as he slipped on his thimble. I tried not to swallow, though my throat had gone suddenly dry. I knew this was one of his Tests. I knew that if I refused, he would Punish me, then put the teeth in anyway.

Father inclined his head very slightly. He was staring at me. He was not blinking.

'Peachflower?' he said again.

I forced out my giggle – the one that pleases him. And in as Ladylike a fashion as I could muster, I said: 'Will it hurt? I'm not strong and tough like you.'

Father tapped his finger on the table, then lifted it up like a conductor of an orchestra.

'It will pain you hardly at all,' he said.

But that was not True.

ENTRY 17: MOMENTS BEFORE THE OPERA (I WRITE A LAST FEW THOUGHTS)

Three hours I have just spent in the bathtub!

Three!

I have undergone shampoos and lotions and face peels and tinctures and all manner of other prettifications. Now

195

the crack of sky beyond the curtained windows is dark. It's not long before we leave. I am sitting at the vanity table in my room, scribbling these last few thoughts.

My new teeth are still tingling, although that might just be the peppermint wash that the Boy just made me swill around my mouth and spit out into a silver cup. He's just left to dispose of it, along with the trolley with the rolling irons and the empty lotion bottles and the cotton buds and the steel pins and whatever else I've just been prodded and slathered and stuck with.

Just now I looked into the mirror. Someone almost Beautiful stared back. My new smile flashed at me, brighter and whiter than a truck's headlamps. I had to wince and look away and go over to the bed. My dress for the opera was laid out atop the covers. When I slipped it on, it reached down to my ankles.

The dress is very heavy. The fabric is interwoven with veins of red wire, and strung on the wire like pearls on a string are thousands of pairs of moving eyes. Their thickly-lashed lids are blinking lazily, like a swarm of butterflies sunning themselves, and the porcelain eyeballs stare at me inscrutably.

At least, I believe they are porcelain.

But enough writing for now. The opera beckons, and so does Father! I have my new dress and my new smile, and at last I am ready.

To be the Daughter that he deserves.

To go to Carcosa.

I cannot wait to tell all about it.

ENTRY 18: ONE SLEEP SINCE THE OPERA (HELLO DIARY)

Hello, diary.

It is a full day now since the opera.

It was

Carcosa is a place that

It still haunts me to think of her

No. I must just treat this like any other story, and start at the start.

I just need a little time, to prepare myself.

ENTRY 19: ONE SLEEP SINCE THE OPERA (I RECOUNT AN INCIDENT IN THE HALLWAY)

When I left my room last night, wearing my dress of eyes, I met Father in the hallway. He wore a coat of white fox fur, and a tuxedo of black silk, and his new boyish face.

'Now here comes a truly splendid Daughter,' he announced, as I slowly approached.

My dress closed its eyes bashfully, and I did my best to curtsey within it. Father smiled and gave me his hand to kiss. I came close enough to smell his lavender perfume, and see the line beneath his chin where the pale skin of his face met the even paler flesh of his neck.

'Are you excited for the opera?' he asked.

'So excited, Father.'

He smiled. 'I'm excited too. I can hardly wait for them all to see you. I know it's been a long time, peachflower. I know it hasn't been easy. But look how Improved you are!'

I showed him my dazzling new smile. Behind me, I could hear the Boy trying to coax Celeste from her room. For a few moments, Father and I were alone. We looked down the hallway towards Celeste's door. Father checked his cufflinks, and slipped his thimble off and then on again, and I realised he was trying to think of something else to say to me. But he could think of nothing. Neither could I. It was hurtful. We were supposed to be Father and Daughter. And yet we were like strangers.

'What is taking so long?' Father called down the hallway in irritation.

The Boy's glitter-eyed face turned to us. Even in the gloom I could see how fearful he looked.

'She has—' The slavestones paused him in order to choose his words more carefully. 'Your Daughter is not wearing the outfit you picked for her.'

Celeste's voice echoed defiantly from her room: 'Because I'm already dressed!'

Father hissed with annoyance, and beside me his thimblefinger began twitching dangerously. I went to cover my face, not wanting to witness what was surely about to happen. But then I realised that in doing so, my fingers would smudge all the prettifications around my eyes. And so I was forced to watch as Celeste barged past the Boy and emerged from her room, performing a vulgar cartwheel with her face painted like a carnival clown.

'It's tiiiime,' she announced, 'to face the muuuusic!'

Her dress was made from a silken pillowcase. She had slashed holes in the sides for her arms and her legs, and with eyeliner, she had scrawled across her outfit in big block letters:

MATTIE, GRAB HIS THIMBLE!

It was a message to me. It was an instruction.

But I did not do as my sister ordered. Instead, I just felt a deep sadness. Until then, I still fully believed that Celeste would come with us to the opera. What a capacity for self-delusion I possess! How could I believe such a thing, when the Truth was so obviously otherwise?

'Mattie?' Celeste said, in a foul and uncouth accent. Then she punched her thigh in annoyance. 'Damn and Havoc, I really thought I'd got to you with the murder-ballad.'

'You are Confused,' I told her sorrowfully. 'So very, very Confused.'

'Remember Gram,' Celeste said to me urgently. 'Remember when we—'

But Father had had enough of her insolence, and with a slice of his hand, he Patterned a wooden box around Celeste. She disappeared within it. It started to rock a little as she beat fists against the insides.

'I'll deal with her later tonight,' Father told the Boy wearily. 'If I Punish her now, we'll miss the opera.'

At once, I realised what my sister had tried to do. In trying to provoke Father now, mere moments before our departure, she had sought to ruin the opera for me as well as her! My sorrow was now fury. It is one thing to be Sick – but to try and sabotage the Improvement of your own sister? That is altogether more detestable.

Beside me, Father looked like he had in the Yellow Shrine that time, when I spied him drinking Bliss and weeping. I suppose I have always known that he finds our continued defiance of him a kind of agony. But until then it did not hit home how easily we can hurt him. In a Pattern duel, he is invincible. Even the sharpest dagger is useless. Yet what Celeste had just done was like a blade through his heart.

'Come, peachflower,' he muttered, taking hold of me. His hand in mine felt cold and brittle as glass.

'Father?'

'We're going,' he said. 'Just you and me. I won't let her spoil this. We're going, do you hear? Hold tight to me, and close your eyes.'

I did so.

The Pattern of the House lifted up and away: gone were the pink pillars of Dancing Stone, the unreachable doorways, the dark and watchful silhouette of the Boy, the box with Celeste inside it like a corpse inside a coffin. All of it was carried away, piece by piece, like the scenery upon a stage.

Then Carcosa rose around us, and we fell into it like a fever dream.

ENTRY 20: LATER ON (I RECALL THE CITY OF CARCOSA)

In Carcosa, it is always dusk.

Carcosa. Dim Carcosa.

Ancient, it is. Old beyond all reckoning. Black stars shine there and the sun is a dim fire in the west. The flags all hang dead on their masts and no wind blows to stir them. Lily flowers rot in the dark waters of the canals.

We walked, Father and I, through the silence and the stillness. Glitter-eyed servants drifted past us like phantoms. The rustling of their paper robes made a sound like a whispering crowd. I drew close to Father. I clung to his arm. In my shoes I was wobbly as a foal.

'Is it always so empty?' I asked.

'Why, peachflower, no. Everyone is attending the opera, of course. We must hurry. Come, be quick.'

Onwards we went; down lamplit alleys; under crumbled arches; past gardens where marble fountains trickled and paradise birds sang; over canals filled with sunken gondolas whose prows jutted up like the snouts of crocodiles; up shadowed stairways and doors that Father opened with whispered words.

At last we came to a wide square lined with yellow banners, and before me I saw a great building of curved stone. Its shape was at once both elegant and sinister. It looked like an enormous human ear, that had been severed from some colossal face and laid sideways upon the ground.

I knew from its splendour, and from the faint sounds of an orchestra tuning itself, that we had come to the opera house, and the show was about to start.

I had thought I would be more excited. To come here, I had learned more than a dozen curtseys; even sacrificed my own smile. For nine sleeps now, I had been counting down to this very moment. Yet now it had come, I felt only a growing dread. Perhaps if Celeste had been with us, I might have felt braver.

At the doors to the opera house stood servants with emerald eyes and uniforms of yellow paper. They took our tickets, and let us through. We came into an empty foyer draped in black velvet, and hurried through another set of doors. There, a second servant directed us up a spiralling staircase. At the very top, a third and final servant stood waiting, and drawing back a curtain, they revealed a small viewing box, with three seats, that looked out upon the curtained stage and the dim auditorium.

Three seats, not two. I missed Celeste even more. I thought of her back in the House, in another Pattern entirely, and suddenly I felt more alone than I had ever felt.

Which was nonsense.

I was with Father.

And in the dim auditorium, and the other viewing boxes all around us, were the Carcosans.

So few of them for such a vast city. Perhaps a few hundred at most. Yet it was more people than I ever remembered seeing before, and I was overwhelmed. There an architecture to each one of them – a sense of exquisite design. There was a woman wearing, somehow, an actual waterfall that tumbled from her shoulders like a cloak. There was a man with blue antlers that looked like vivid forks of lightning. Robed in golden sparks and diamond auras, they seemed to me like Gods. But Cruel ones, and ancient. Gods you worshipped only out of fear.

As we entered, the Yellow Sign on Father's neck opened. It shone like a brand. There was a slight lull in their murmuring chatter, and beneath the orchestra tuning itself, all manner of eyes – golden and tattooed and luminous and neon and cat-like – turned to gaze upon me.

'Show them your smile,' Father murmured as we sat, and Obediently I displayed my bright new teeth to the auditorium.

Then the dim lights faded out completely, and the glow of the audiences' Yellow Signs shone in the dark, as the orchestra fell to silence, and the stage curtains rose, and the opera began.

I did not understand the story. The songs were all performed in the language of High Carcosan; the singers all wore masks. Their voices swelled and wove together with the orchestra, sometimes in exquisite Patterns, sometimes in discordant Havoc. Father spent most of the show leaning into my ear and saying things to me like, 'The First Act is about to end: gentle applause is appropriate.' Or, 'This next moment is amusing: make sure you laugh, but not too much.'

More often than not, though, his comments were about the Carcosans in the audience.

'Look down to your left, peachflower. Do you see him? That is the Duke of Moonshatter. He cracks the moons of other worlds like they are eggs, and bathes in the stuff that bleeds out.'

I saw the man Father was talking about: a thin, bald man with alabaster skin and eyes like pools of silver.

Then he pointed across the auditorium and said, 'Look opposite us – there is Lady Caress.'

I glanced at a young girl who sat in a box all of her own. Her long hair was garlanded with fallen stars and she wore a necklace of agate stones and a dress of woven flames. I felt envious to look at her: not just because she was far, far prettier and Ladylike than I, but because her own father had allowed her to visit the opera all by herself.

I remarked to Father how she was all alone, and that, perhaps one day she might visit our House, and be friends with Celeste and me.

At my suggestion, Father smirked and asked if we wouldn't rather play with someone our own age. And glancing back at Lady Caress, I noticed the frail hunch of her shoulders, and the cane of polished ivory resting beside her chair, and with a shudder I realised that she was not a young girl at all – she just wore the face of one.

ENTRY 21: STILL LATER (I HEAR CATELIN SING)

At the interval, a gaunt man with long teeth came to our box to sell us tears. He held them up on long strings, like necklaces of pearls, and let the drops sparkle in the auditorium lights.

'Catelin's Death, the final song in Act Five, is famously moving,' Father told me. 'When it ends, we ought to cry.'

'Those accentuate Sir's profile most exquisitely,' the pattern-seller remarked, as Father dabbed a few tears to his eyes and let them trace wet paths down his jawline.

'I'll take them,' Father said. 'And those smaller ones there, too.' He pointed. 'For the girl.'

'Excellent choice,' said the seller. He shook the tears from the string they were hung upon, and with a tap of his thimble, he Patterned them into yellow silk handkerchiefs for Father and I to dab at our eyes when the time came.

After a time, the lights dimmed and the show began again. I tried my best to follow what was happening, to appreciate the music that I had waited so long to hear, but it was so difficult for me, and so strange, and Father kept whispering in my ear about the Carcosans around us. 'Miss Vatsenov is looking at you, peachflower: give her a smile! Ah, I see Dunsany has brought along a Daughter too. Curses, she's prettier than you. Wherever did he get her from?'

'From her Mother, I imagine,' I whispered back. 'Just like most other children.'

At my comment, Father gave me the strangest look: startled, almost frightened. He opened his mouth to say something, but at that moment upon the stage, the scenery lifted away abruptly and the orchestra fell down to a low drone. Father scrambled in his pocket for the handkerchiefs of tears as a masked performer came forward, spoke in High Carcosan, and unmasked herself. In the spotlight, I saw that she was slavestoned. She shrugged off her robe. Her bare arms were covered in crude, purple tattoos. Some of them were moving in little Patterned loops.

'I found her,' Father whispered to me in a boastful tone. 'Before that, I was only rarely permitted into the city – a Carcosan is something you become. Perhaps one day, you might be one of us too.'

The singer on the stage took a deep breath. Her emerald eyes sparkled as if filled with tears. Though I was high above her, I could see her hands trembling. She was terrified. Or was it all part of the performance? I was Confused. I could not tell.

'She might not look like much,' Father said, 'but she's got the most Beautiful voice in all the worlds. And now she'll sing the finest song. Get your tears ready, peachflower.'

An expectant hush fell over the audience. The orchestra droned on, low and buzzing, like cicadas from a desert world. The singer breathed in deeper. The tension, the sense of waiting, wound tighter, stretched out longer, until suddenly it snapped.

She sang.

She sang a single note, high and soaring above the orchestra, pure and unreachable as a bird in flight. Her voice was very Beautiful, just as Father had said.

But the song, I did not understand. It was only the one note, single and endless. I kept waiting for something else to come, but nothing did.

Gradually I came to realise that this note *was* the song. There were no verses, no chorus, just this interminable wail.

'Catelin's Death', it was called. And it could only be sung the once. That was what Father had told me.

'No,' I could not help myself from whispering. 'No, you mustn't. You have to stop.'

But the singer did not stop. The stones in her eyes would not let her. They made her sing on, sing on and on and on. Even as her voice began to falter, even as her lungs emptied, as her face reddened and then paled and her knees buckled beneath her, still she didn't draw a breath.

Father took his handkerchief of tears, held it poised and ready. On the stage, the singer's voice dwindled like a guttering candle, until it was a strangled gasp, then a noiseless scream. And all at once the spotlight turned off, plunging us into blackness, and in that long and terrible silence, I heard the sighs and sniffs of the Carcosans in the auditorium all around me.

Then the lights came up slowly, to the sound of scattered applause. The Lady Caress was smiling. The Duke of Moonshatter stood up in ovation. Beside me Father was weeping artful tears that were not his own. The applause grew and grew. The orchestra put down their instruments and made the Curtsey of Obedient Thanks. But the singer did not rise from where she lay upon the stage. Her jewelled stare looked out beyond the dark auditorium at some place beyond all Patterns. The tattoos upon her arms, some of them, were still moving. Her mouth was still open, as if the song had still not finished. I dabbed my handkerchief to my eyes, until the tears blurred out all sight of her.

. . .

I have not seen Celeste since returning from the opera. The Boy says she is still in her box, whilst Father decides what to do with her.

Still in her box? Like some doll that he doesn't know whether to keep or return to the shop! My anger is the colour of steel, my shame is an overcast sky. Whenever I close my eyes, I see the dark circle of the singer's mouth, there in my mind like an undoer's, sending all my thoughts to Havoc.

I was supposed to find it Beautiful. But all I saw was Cruelty and Death. I do not just mean the song. I mean all of it. I mean Carcosa.

I dare not say this to Father. Whenever he comes in to see me, I pretend to have adored our little trip. He believes me, too. He is already planning a visit next month, to something called the Torture Pageant. I nod and grin brightly. I can fool him much better now that my smile is not my own. It is like something from my wardrobe that I can slip on and off.

ENTRY 22: TWO DAYS SINCE THE OPERA (AN ACCOUNT OF CELESTE'S MISCHIEF)

Last night, the room around me shook. Some of my perfumes and vanities fell and rolled off my mirrored table, as from somewhere inside the House there came a muffled boom.

Celeste was making Mischief.

By my bedside, the slavestones stopped the Boy from helping me into my nightdress, and hurried him quickly from my room. As he opened the door to leave, I heard Father shouting distantly, and drifting in from the hallway was a faint smell of smoke.

Celeste had made her Mischief far away from here indeed. Perhaps even in the East Wing. How had she managed to escape the box Father had put her in? And then to cause an explosion so far from where she was permitted to be? I almost felt proud of my sister and her deviousness. And yet, of course, I knew I was required to behave where she could not, and so I put on my nightdress all by myself, then waited Obediently for quite some time. Beside me, my dreamfish Querazade peeked her head from her conch.

'He'll Punish her mighty severe for this,' she said.

That worried me. I hate to think of Celeste being Punished, even when her Mischief warrants it. I got out of bed and went to my door and shrank back and wrung my hands together and listened. The House's usual silence had descended again like thick velvet drapes.

'Why didn't she wait?' Querazade hovered by her conch shell, tutting. 'He is departing in a few days. Surely she would've had more chance of escape if only the Boy was here?'

'She is not trying to escape,' I snapped at my dreamfish. 'She is trying to kill him.'

Without a thimble I could feel nothing of what might be happening. There was only a vague sense of the House shifting around me, probably as Father repaired whatever parts of it my sister had just destroyed. Suddenly, I heard footsteps, and my door opened. It was the Boy. His paper trousers were blackened with soot and his sleeve was badly singed.

'All is well now,' he said.

'What happened?'

He led me away from the door. 'A slight Confusion, that's all.'

I lay back down in my bed and the slavestones made the Boy draw my covers up to my chin. 'Is Celeste OK? I mean – is my sister's condition Improved?'

'It will be, very soon,' said the Boy somewhat mournfully. 'Your Father is just administering the Punishing now.'

ENTRY 23: LATER THAT DAY (I DO NOT FULLY REMEMBER WHAT PUNISHINGS ARE LIKE)

I do not fully remember what Punishings are like. Or how many Celeste and I have endured. Father cuts the memory of them out, along with everything else that is Wrong about us.

It is one cutting for which I am grateful. I do not want to remember more than I already know.

Punishings are painful. They are frightening. They are hideous beyond measure. Of that much I am sure. Just the word itself is enough to send a shudder through me. It wells up from the black depths of my mind where Father's Power cannot go. In those deepest of places, which are out of reach to even me – in the subconscious caves from which our dreams rise – the terror of the Punishings remains.

Knowing it is there makes me more anxious than ever. For if I can retain fear of Father's Punishings, might I not hold other things within me too? Might old Confusions return to Afflict me once again? Mighty as he is, Father's Power is yet to make perfect Daughters of us. He cuts and he cuts and he cuts and he cuts. Still the Patterns of the past lie within us, like scars. Mapping out our old selves, the ones that he sought to annul.

ENTRY 24: THREE DAYS SINCE THE OPERA (I DIDN'T SEE CELESTE TODAY)

I didn't see Celeste this morning at breakfast. But I saw Father, and though the silver table is very long, and we are seated at separate ends, still I could not help but stare at the raw pink burns on his hands, and the underside of his chin. He sat down and got up from the table very slowly too, as if he were in pain.

Celeste's explosion had come very close to doing what she had wanted it to do. At the very least, it has killed the good mood Father has been in ever since our return from the opera.

I am anxious to see my sister. How extensive was Father's Punishing? The question has troubled me all day. It might have been very severe. Perhaps even (and I can only write this, not say it) too severe. He Patterned her inside what was little more than a coffin, and left her in there for two days! Is it any wonder that she came out like a revenant, to put him a box of his own?

ENTRY 25:

I just saw Celeste and she ~~striked~~ ~~scribbled~~
How could he ~~scribbled~~ *There*
are not the words to ~~scribbled~~
~~scribbled~~
~~scribbled~~
~~scribbled~~
~~scribbled~~ *My thoughts are not ordered, I cannot* ~~scribbled~~
~~scribbled~~
~~scribbled~~ *My poor*
Afflicted sister ~~scribbled~~
~~scribbled~~
~~scribbled~~ *the Confusion* ~~scribbled~~
~~scribbled~~ *No Father would do such a thing* ~~scribbled~~
~~scribbled~~

ENTRY 26: FOUR DAYS SINCE THE OPERA (ARE ALL FAMILIES THIS CRUEL?)

It is late now. Some hours have passed since my last entry. I am calm enough to write, though a part of me does not want to. Yet at this hour, what else is there to do but sleep? And if I sleep, I am afraid of what I will dream tonight. I am afraid of seeing her face again.

When I finally saw Celeste again at dinner, my fears from the day were all confirmed. She has been hideously Punished. Father has cut up her mind so badly that she can barely hold a spoon. The Boy was having to feed her porridge, as if she were a baby. Her eyes were blank and fixed on nothing. Tears ran out of them constantly, the way blood runs from wounds. She was still humming her music, but the tunes were wordless and her voice was no louder than a whisper.

I could not listen. I could not watch. It was more monstrous than even the opera. As fast as I could, I ate my rose petal soup, then ran back to my room and vomited it all back up into my washbasin. I gripped the porcelain hard as I retched and wept. Do all families fight like mine does? Are all families this Cruel? The horror of it. The horror. Father Loves us, this I know. But what he does with his Power? That is not Love. It is not.

Greyness sweeps over me again in a wave. My hand aches with all this writing. So many words, and all of them useless. What good are they against such Power? What use is anything at all?

ENTRY 27: FIVE DAYS SINCE THE OPERA (LAST NIGHT I HEARD HOWLING)

When at last I fell asleep last night, I was woken by Father howling. There was great anguish in his cries. As if he were

terribly wounded. All around, in the dark, my room
tremored and twisted. It seemed as if the Pattern of the
House itself was in danger of coming undone. And in the
world beyond it, I heard a thousand things hissing, like
hives filled with wasps.

I don't recall anything more than that. Querazade ate up
whatever happened next. Perhaps it was nothing more than
a nightmare.

ENTRY 28: SIX DAYS SINCE THE OPERA
(FATHER DEVISES A NEW STRATEGY FOR CELESTE)

Punishing Celeste is not enough. Father has decided that a
stricter programme of discipline is required to curb her
constant rebellion. He told me so at breakfast this morning,
as the two of us ate bowls of sugar mice at the long silver table.

'I've been spoiling her,' he told me darkly, hunched over
his morning cup of Bliss. 'Flocks of canaries and trips to the
opera? No. Time for some Tough Love instead.'

'Yes, Father,' I said, though I did not understand what he
meant.

Father finished his Bliss with a suppressed shudder,
wiped away his tears quickly, and pushed his chair from the
table. I ate my last sugar mouse quickly and stood up too.

'Come, peachflower,' Father said, holding out his hand.
It was new, I noticed suddenly. He must have tired of waiting
for his old ones to heal from the burns sustained during

214

Celeste's Mischief. His fingers now were more slender, and his nails were small and white as milk teeth. The skin, as I took hold of it, was as soft as a baby's.

I wondered for a moment whether this man was less my father than before. For if he had changed his hands, discarded them like an old pair of gloves, did that not make him fractionally someone else, someone distinct from who he had once been? Does our essence not reside in even the smallest portion of us? Even in our scars? Our Ugliness?

Perhaps that is why I do not like my Improvements. In taking away my smile and my laugh and my hair and my freckles and more, Father has lessened who I am. And if that is Truth, then what else might I have lost? Who might I once have been?

The old Matilda must have been a very terrible Daughter indeed, for Father to have to destroy her.

I wonder what it was she did, to be so undeserving of his Love.

Father led me from the Jewelled Chamber and into the Middle Hallway. We walked past the Yellow Shrine, and the pygmy bear perched by a pillar, silently sharpening his newest dagger. As we came to Celeste's door, Father waved it open.

'Remember,' he told me outside her room. 'Sometimes we must be Cruel to those we Love.'

Inside, it was dark, and freezing cold, and damp like a cave. I clasped my collar with one hand as my breath plumed in the air. Not even the Boy lived in a place as wretched. The kitchens, though crowded with pans and foodstuffs, are at least warmed by the ovens. In Celeste's room, the walls have been stripped to bare plaster and the floor is wooden planks. There is one window. It is small and filmed over with frost, like an eye blinded by a cataract. The bed is a mattress on the floor and the covers are raggedy blankets. The only vaguely pretty thing in the whole room is the dreamfish conch where J'lzacoatl lives. Celeste had blocked the entrance to that shell by jamming it with straw from her mattress.

Upon our entry into the room, we found my sister engaged in some petty graffitiing. With a fingernail, she was scratching the word ꟻꞱƎH into the ice upon the window. As much as I was horrified by the condition of her room, I was relieved to see that she has recovered from the Punishing enough to know how to write again. And if she can write, I thought to myself, that means she can probably think and speak again, too. Though she is evidently yet to recall that this House is its own world, separate from all others, and that there exists no one outside the window who will read her message. I did not know whether to pity or envy her ignorance.

Hearing us come in, Celeste turned insolently. Her movements were still clumsy on account of the Punishing. She moved like a marionette, and her joints even made a rustling scraping sound. I saw then that she wore a dress of roughest paper, just as slavestoned servants do. Her wrists and ankles were red raw from the chafing.

The sight of her was so pitiable, I wanted to cry. I wished to snatch Father's thimble from his grip and Pattern her warm and pretty again. But I did not. I just stood there. By Father's side. Like a good Daughter should.

Father pointed at J'lzacoatl's conch, and with a flick of his thimblefinger, the mattress straw disintegrated into dust. The dreamfish swished out sullenly into the air, then let out a little squeak at the cold, and darted back inside.

Father took his hand from mine and held it out to Celeste. Slowly – shivering – wincing – she gave him an awkward curtsey, took his hand and kissed the top of it, like he was some King.

'Good,' Father told her. 'Much, much better.'

With a blink and a wave of his thimble, a plate of hot toast Patterned itself upon the floor by her feet.

'You see how things Improve when you are Obedient?' he asked.

Celeste didn't answer. Instead she struggled down to the floor in her stiff, unbending clothes. Her pale thin hands clutched for the toast. Father let out a disappointed tut. His thimblefinger twitched. He cut the toast from the plate.

'What a shame,' he said with a pout. 'You forgot to say, "Thank you, Father."'

Celeste looked down at the empty plate. She was shivering, which made her dress make a noise against itself that reminded me of the whispering in the opera auditorium. With hands clumsy from the cold and the Punishing, she picked up the plate from the floor. Then she took it back to her bed to lick up the crumbs with her tongue, like she was a dog.

Oh, Celeste. I am sorry. I am so sorry. I should have run to

217

you then. I know it is no excuse, but I was afraid. I am always so afraid now, that he will think I am a bad Daughter. And so I was a bad sister. Why should it be like that? Why should I have to choose between one or the other? Can I not be both?

'You always remember your manners, don't you, peachflower?' Father said, turning to me.

'Yes, Father,' I said.

'You are always Obedient, aren't you?'

'Always, Father. Always.'

He shrugged. 'And that is why you have a pretty room, and pretty dresses, and nice food, and a new laugh. That is why you get to go to the opera.'

I shuddered, but I am lucky: I think he believed it was on account of the room's cold.

ENTRY 29: LATER ON (HOW STUBBORN CELESTE MUST BE!)

I cannot imagine how stubborn Celeste must be, to still be fighting Father, even after he has reduced her to such a wretched state. Especially after she witnessed with her own eyes the benefits of Obedience. Did she not see how splendid my own dress was? Did she not mark how well-fed and warm I seemed? Surely that is why Father took me to her: so that she could note the many discrepancies between us?

Though it occurs to me now: perhaps she did note them, but drew an alternative conclusion to Father and I.

Maybe Celeste believes that, out of the two of us, she is

not the one who is wretched. Maybe she would rather fight, than surrender as I have done.

ENTRY 30: STILL LATER (I TALK WITH THE PYGMY BEAR)

I keep picturing Celeste in her room, shivering and defiant. Or else I see the singer of 'Catelin's Death', open-mouthed and silent. I can't stop thinking how we are Punished for our Sickness; how Father hurts us because of Love; how we must be made to Forget so that we can Remember.

None of it makes sense.

To quiet my mind, I took a walk to the Yellow Shrine. Outside it sat the pygmy bear, at the base of one of the hallway's pillars. He was working on his latest dagger, as usual. This new one is nearly finished. He has crafted it out of an old bottle cork and a piece of broken glass. He looked up at me as I passed, his dark eyes blinking in the dim light.

I never normally make small talk with the pygmy bear, on account of him being unable to speak, and also on account of him being dedicated to the destruction of my father. But I needed, just for a moment, to do something else except worry about my sister and dwell upon the opera. Maybe that is why I began a conversation.

'Hello,' I said, and gave him what I hoped was the Curtsey of Friends. 'How is your weapon coming along?'

The pygmy bear held up his dagger for me to see. He tilted it back and forth in his paws, letting the candlelight ripple over the glass blade in swirling patterns. I found it very Beautiful. Why am I drawn to weapons so? They are not Ladylike. And besides, I am safe in this House, I have no need of one.

'It is splendid,' I told the little creature. 'It looks exceedingly lethal.'

He made a gruff little noise, which I took to be a thank you. Then his eyes dropped down to the dagger again, and he was back to work, his stubby claws winding some old string around the hilt.

'Aren't you tired of fighting him?' I asked. 'I found it so very tiring. But you don't seem to. Even though you never win.'

At this, the pygmy bear looked at me, and though he cannot talk, his eyes said many things. I saw pity in them. Great pity. Not for himself, but for me. It was a look that said, *I may never win, but you have already lost.*

I felt a lump rise into my throat, along with something else hot and uncontainable and scalding, like steam from a lidded pot.

'I will not be looked down on by you,' I told him with all the venom I could muster. 'You are a Pet. I am a Daughter. I have left this House and seen the opera, but you shall always be here, forever sharpening your stupid knives. You think the sharpness of a knife matters when you fight a man like my father? You pathetic, beaten little plaything. That is what you are. And if it hurts you to hear that, I don't care. The Truth can hurt when you lie to yourself.'

My words flew out like wasps from a nest, to sting and sting and sting. In the silence after my tirade, the pygmy bear stood. He is as high as my waist, or thereabouts, but there is something in him that stands taller. And though I know he has sworn not to harm me, I would be lying if I did not write that I trembled a little at his gaze.

Because it was like he suddenly recognised me again.

Then he smiled and nodded, in a kind of greeting, as if to say, *Hello again, Matilda.*

And then he said, 'You are being grumpy again. That is always a good sign.'

I was astounded. Several times, I opened my mouth and closed it again, trying to think of something to say.

In the end, all I could manage was: 'You are not supposed to talk!'

'I know,' said the pygmy bear with a grin. 'But I am. Because I am very cheeky.'

I shook my head and backed away. Was this happening? Was I Confused? My heart was thudding and full of fear. It wasn't just that the pygmy bear was talking; it was that I had been told that he couldn't.

Either I was being lied to, or Father was being fooled. I did not know which possibility frightened me more.

'Your words were all cut out,' I managed to say, though at that moment it was I who was struggling to talk.

'Yes,' agreed the pygmy bear. 'Lots and lots of times. But one of you always teaches me again.'

'One of us . . . ?' At once, I knew who he meant. 'You mean, Celeste and me?'

The little creature nodded cheerfully. 'Last time it was

her, but I think I like it most when it is you, because you always taught me the really naughty words.'

I took another step backwards. Now I understood. Celeste was behind this. This creature's words were a part of her Mischief. Just like those canaries, singing their murder-ballads, this pygmy bear was trying to sow Confusion within me. Well, I would not listen. I could not. I gathered my dress up and gave him the Curtsey of Final Farewell. Then I turned and fled. As I reached the door to my room, I heard him call down the hallway.

'Are you sure you don't want to talk to the snail?' he asked.

ENTRY 31: SEVEN DAYS SINCE THE OPERA (I DREAM ABOUT A TYRANNOSAUR)

Last night, I had the loveliest dream. I was in a world where there was Everything, and All of it was For Sale. We went shopping down aisles that were as high as Always and as long as Forever. Every shelf was stacked with Wonders. Wonders upon Wonders.

I could choose one thing. I wanted a pet tyrannosaur. *Please*, I begged. *Oh please, oh please buy it for me.*

And someone said, *Yes.*

On its shelf, the tyrannosaur roared, and I woke up. It was dark outside my window, but Querazade's conch lit up my room with its rainbow glow.

'Go back to sleep, peachflower,' said my dreamfish. Her

sleek silvery shape came darting from my ear like it was a sea cove, and she rippled through the air until she was floating in front of my eyes.

It was still so very early that I almost did as Querazade asked. But as I sank back down into my dreams, something snagged in my mind.

'Where did my tyrannosaur dream go?' I asked her, yawning.

Querazade shivered in the air, and her pink eyes blinked. 'I ate it,' she said.

'Why did you do that?' I said crossly. 'You are supposed to nibble away at my bad dreams, but instead you eat my good ones.'

Querazade paled. 'I did not eat all of it,' she insisted. 'Just a piece.'

'Who was I with in the dream?' I demanded, trying to remember its particulars. 'Who bought me the dinosaur?'

'Father,' said Querazade. 'It was Father.'

But she was lying. I knew she was. I could tell from the way her pink eyes blinked, and her top fin quivered.

'No,' I said. 'It was – it was . . .'

But the dream had drawn away from me like a sea at low tide, and though I could see its outline, distant and shimmering, I could not dive back into its waters.

I lay back in my bed, but I could not sleep. The tyrannosaur dream had not seemed bad. There had been nothing Confusing about it. Yet Querazade ate a little piece of it, then lied to me afterwards. And I do not know why.

ENTRY 32: LATER ON (FATHER LEAVES FOR HIS ADVENTURES)

Just now Father came in to my room, to tell me that he would be leaving tonight. Off on more of his Adventures.

Sitting at my vanity mirror, I did not react to his news. I simply carried on untying the silk ribbons from my hair, and readying myself for bed. Ever since the opera, I have been practising my face in the mirror, making my expression pleasant and my eyes demure. But still whenever I look at him, the anger rises up in me like bile, and I have to look away before my mask slips.

'You are angry,' Father noted, which sent panic fluttering through me. 'Is this about Celeste's new regimen of discipline?'

'No, Father,' I lied.

'Then what?'

'I'm angry because I don't want you to leave,' I lied, willing myself to mean it.

Father is not easily fooled, though. Somehow, he picked up that something was amiss, because his reflection tipped his head to one side and regarded me.

'Is there anything you need to tell me?' he asked.

The pygmy bear can talk, I thought. And Querazade is eating my good dreams. And I hate Carcosa and everyone in it. And I wish you ill for what you've done to Celeste.

'No, Father,' I answered.

He narrowed his eyes, as if something in my reply hadn't convinced him. I felt a little tremor of fear run through me.

224

'And you don't feel Confused in any way?' he said slowly.
I shook my head. 'No,' I lied.

'No, *Father*,' he corrected.

'No, Father.'

'Hmm.' He caught sight of himself in my vanity mirror, and licked his fingers to smooth the tips of his newest moustache, and wipe the purple stains of Bliss from the corners of his mouth. 'So if I told you your Gram is still alive, and I'm going away now to kill her, how would that make you feel?'

Sometimes, Father's Tests are like this. He will say a name, or a phrase, and observe me for my response. If I react in a way that displeases him, he will enact a Punishing upon me. But luckily, I did not fail this Test. Since I don't know anyone called Gram, I just looked back at him blankly. Thankfully, that seemed to be exactly the reaction he wanted, and he smiled and kissed my two cheeks and straightened and turned to leave.

'Father?' I said before he went.

He turned on his heel at the door. 'Yes, peachflower?'

'Why do you have to kill someone?' I asked him.

His eyes widened a little, and I knew then that he had let slip something he did not intend me to know about: Father is, in fact, a Murderer. (Though I knew this from the opera. That singer would not have died if Father had not found her.)

I could see him weighing up whether to cut away my memory of him saying that. If he used his Power on me, it would be like he had never said it.

Instead, he sighed and came back beside my vanity mirror to crouch down beside me.

'I have to kill them because they're dangerous, peachflower.' He spoke very softly, and I could tell that he was speaking the Truth. 'They want to destroy our Family. They want to Confuse you and Celeste. And take you both away from me. I just Love you too much to ever let that happen. Does that make sense?'

I nodded. It did. Father was just defending us. He was keeping his family safe, whatever it took. I would do the same, if I had to. Even if it meant murder.

'Good luck, Father.'

When he stood, so did I, and gave him the Curtsey of Obedience. He smiled at that and poked my nose with his finger.

'That's my girl. And watch Celeste for me. See if you can Improve her. Someone has to.'

Then he left. I heard his long strides leave my room and echo down the Middle Hallway and back to the East Wing. And the slavestones rustled the Boy into the room to ready me for bed.

ENTRY 33: EIGHT DAYS SINCE THE OPERA (I HEAR MY SISTER WALK IN THE MIDDLE HALLWAY)

Early this morning when the sun had still not risen, I heard Celeste walking in the hallway. In the silence, her bare feet went *pat-pat-pat*, just past my room.

I remember first thinking: *She is allowed outside her room again*, and feeling very glad. But then I immediately became anxious. It was before sunrise. Father does not allow us to be up before it gets light. It is very easy for us to get Confused, you see, in the dark. And then there is the way that darkness can hide Secrets, and facilitate Mischief.

I lay in my bed. I lay there listening. And I thought: This means trouble. This means Celeste doing something foolish again. If she is caught, Father will be furious. There will be another Punishing upon his return. He will hack at her mind until all its disobedience is rooted out. He will leave her slumped and blank eyed again. He will throw her in that wretched room, and Pattern away all the doors and windows, and leave her in there, hungry and shivering.

That is what I thought, lying there in my bed, listening to Celeste walk the hall. And that is why I did not go back to sleep, though Querazade tried to make me.

'Close your eyes,' my dreamfish said, quickly shimmying back towards my ear. 'Close your eyes, sink back down upon your pillow—'

'Get off.' I waved at her like she was a gnat. Ever since she ate my tyrannosaur dream, I have been annoyed at her. She has been a little too greedy of late, I think. She has been nibbling on dreams that she ought to have left alone.

'Close your eyes, peachflower,' she said. 'Let's doze a little longer.'

'Stop trying to wriggle back into my ear.' I got up onto my elbow. 'I am awake now.'

'But you must not be,' said Querazade, sounding frightened. 'It is not yet dawn.'

She tried to soothe me with a lullaby, but I gave her a flick and she darted off, whimpering, into her conch. I sat up and kicked off the silk sheets. Then I swung my feet off the mattress and into my slippers and tiptoed across the room towards the door.

Around me, the House was quiet. The plum-coloured sky beyond my window was turning peach-pink. I saw that much before the window realised I was looking through it, and closed its curtains.

I had to hurry. The slavestones would wake the Boy soon. If I did not find Celeste and convince her to go back to her room, she would be caught by him for sure.

My bedroom door opened silently as I slipped out. My room cast a wedge of purple dark into the pitch black of the hallway. There are no windows there, and the Boy had not yet been forced awake to light the candles on their bronze gilt sconces. The dark marble pillars curved left and right until they dissolved into shadow.

Somewhere up ahead, I heard Celeste's wandering steps. I hurried towards the sound of her. But even as I went, I began to have doubts. How exactly was I going to compel my sister back to her bed? What was I going to say? After her Punishing, did she even remember who I was?

I went across the hallway in the same faltering way as I am writing across this page: stumbling from one thought to the next. Many times, I almost went back to my bed. I

228

bolstered my courage by telling myself that Father had asked me to see if I could Improve Celeste. In putting a stop to her Mischief, was I not doing as he asked? Surely I was being a dutiful Daughter?

And yet, I also knew that the truly dutiful thing would be to alert the Boy at once. This I did not do. Because in Truth, I went to Celeste not because of Father, but because she is my sister and I was worried for her.

So I went on, the stone beneath my slippered feet dipping and rising ever so slightly as it flowed slowly towards the East Wing. It was pitch dark, but I was sure now that Celeste was very close by. I could hear her shuffling around behind one of the pillars, as if searching for something. She was in a foul mood, and under her breath, she was singing what I thought might possibly be curses. I was glad I could not quite hear such Unbecoming Talk. And yet, I felt relief to know she could speak again. How terrible it must be, to find yourself suddenly bereft of all Words.

'Celeste,' I said, very softly. 'Celeste?'

At once, her singing stopped. The shuffling did too. I stood very still, listening and looking into the cool dark around me. Somewhere within it was my sister; a stillness within the stillness. We could not have been more than a few steps away from each other. Yet suddenly I felt like there were worlds and worlds between us.

'It's Matilda,' I told her. 'Why are you hiding from me?'

No reply came. Just the cool, hard silence of the hallway's Dancing Stone. I felt something welling within me that I could not name, a feeling more terrible than any I could remember. I think now that it was Grief. For I have suffered great Confusions; I have thought Father was not my father; I have wondered if this House was truly my home. But not once – not ever – not in the deepest depths of my Affliction – did I ever doubt for a moment what Celeste and I were to each other. It is the one Truth I have clung to, when all around me has been shifting. The two of us are sisters.

But there in the hallway, that silence seemed to be saying that we were not.

I turned and fled for my room, and in doing so I ran closer to one of the pillars than I was intending, and with my right slipper, I managed to kick something across the floor. It went bouncing away from me over the stone, then skittered to a stop in the lilac light fanning from my doorway. Some sort of shell, about the shape and size of the wafer cones of pomegranate sorbet that Father sometimes brings us from the city.

As I went towards it, I felt a sharp shove in my back. I stumbled forwards and Celeste ran past me, her bare feet slapping on the floor. Though I did not fully understand what was happening, I knew enough. This shell was precious to my sister; was important to her delusions; was part of some foolish Plot of hers to Escape the House, or bring about Father's Demise.

Many things happened quickly. I made a wild lunge for Celeste, and caught the trailing hem of her nightgown. She was running at full pelt, but I am much the stronger sister (Father has talked about one day procuring me a more

Ladylike frame, but for now I remain as I am). I pulled her, she span back into my arms, so that for a moment we were almost embracing.

And then we were fighting.

Celeste's knee came up to wind my belly; her hand struck at my face. I fell back, but I did not let go of her. I pulled my sister with me and then I took her by her hair and twisted at the roots until she let out the littlest shriek that she muffled with one hand. I was breathing very hard, not from the exertion, but from the adrenaline and anger. I am ashamed of it now, but I wanted to hurt her then. I wanted to show her that she meant nothing to me, the way I meant nothing to her. Before he left for his Adventures, Father told me that we must be Cruel to those we Love. How like him I was then, with Celeste completely at my mercy.

'Hurts,' she said beneath me, in a high little voice, like she was a simpering Pet. 'Hurting me, stop—'

'No, you stop,' I hissed at her. 'Whatever you're plotting, it won't work. It will just ruin everything for both of us. Do you want to be Punished again? Do you want to stay in your horrible room forever? I'm sorry I didn't help you before. He was Cruel, and I just watched, and I'm sorry. But you just keep fighting him and it's only hurting you and I can't bear it any more.'

'Ow,' Celeste said over me. 'Ow ow ouchy—'

But I silenced her by almost shouting, 'Will you just *Hush!*'

I jerked away like I had just been stung. The last word I

had spoken echoed back at me, bouncing off the hallway stone.

I flinched again. Something was happening in my head. All my thoughts began to writhe and turn on each other, as if my mind held two Truths, which each despised the other, the way that Pattern and Havoc do. Father was not my father, and the House was not my home, and a great Horror yawned within me like an undoer's mouth.

Then a light grew from far down the hallway, and I became aware of one thing that could not be disputed. It was dawn, and the Boy had risen to light the candles on their sconces and rouse us from our beds.

I hauled Celeste to her feet and flung her away from me and then I ran and reached the shell by my door before she could get to it. The Boy was still far towards the East Wing but coming slowly towards us and the glow of the candles would soon reveal us both. Yet I stood for a moment in the sliver of dawn cast by my doorway, making sure my sister could see as I raised my slippered foot and brought it down to crush the shell that was so precious to her.

In the dim and growing light, I saw her fling out her hands to stop me. And I did stop. I let my slipper hover just above the shell, and I told her to go back to her room right away, before we were discovered, or I would stamp down and grind my heel.

And she obeyed me. Wordlessly, she turned and shut herself inside her bedroom.

I bent down and picked up the shell. More Confusion

blew through me like a sudden gust of wind, and I almost fell over with the force of it, but I managed to pick the thing up and dart back into my own room. I closed the door with the barest click and slipped back under my bedsheets with the shell still in my hands.

'What is that?' said Querazade, aghast.

I stopped pretending to be asleep and turned my head sideways. My dreamfish was hovering at the edge of her conch, her body rippling with fright. Very soon, the slavestones would send the Boy into my room to wake me and ready me for the day. I just knew that Querazade would tell on me. That is just the sort of creature she was.

As quick as I could, I pulled open the drawer of my bedside cabinet, and pulled out a pair of socks, and stuffed them into the opening of the conch. Querazade let out a little shriek, and (because she is a small and somewhat cowardly Pet) darted further into her home, instead of out.

Now I had her trapped. If I turned the conch just so, the socks jammed into its entrance were barely even visible.

'That'll teach you to nibble up my nice dreams,' I told her.

Moments later, when the slavestones sent the Boy to wake me, I had managed to slow my breathing down to almost normal, and the Confusion skirmishing in my head had settled down to an uneasy truce.

The Boy said nothing as he opened my curtains and set about laying out a dress for me. Had he not heard the commotion? Surely he must have at least seen the light from my open doorway. But then, perhaps not. After all, his eyes are not like mine. I know that the gems the servants wear allow them to see the 'colours' that the Boy occasionally speaks of. Maybe these colours distracted him.

Whatever the reason, neither Celéste nor I were scolded. When I saw her at breakfast, she kept trying to seek out eye contact with me, presumably to try and negotiate some sort of return of her shell. It gave me great satisfaction to ignore her completely, just like she had done to me in the hallway.

ENTRY 34: LATER ON (I EXAMINE THE SHELL)

It is afternoon now, and I have stayed all day in my room to write the last account, and now this one. The shell I took from Celeste is sitting beside me now, upon my pillow. Whenever the Boy comes with cups of medicinal tea, I quickly hide it beneath the sheets, along with my book.

'You feel sickly,' he said just now, with the back of his hand to my forehead. 'Did you not sleep well?'

'Not very well,' I answered with a sigh.

(Querazade could not say anything, because she is still trapped in her conch.)

When the Boy left, I took out Celeste's shell again to stare at it, trying to discover why it is so precious to my sister. I thought perhaps at first that it was the home of another dreamfish, but I have peeked inside, and as far as I can tell, the shell is empty. Besides, dreamfish like to live in pretty shells, at least Querazade and J'lzacoatl do, and this one is a rather Ugly thing. It is rough and brown and there is moss growing upon it.

I cannot stare at it for long. If I do, the Confusion in my head stirs itself again, very strong. It is as if the shell exudes some sort of Malicious Power. Putting down my pen, I can almost *hear* it. It is said that other shells, if you listen to them closely, hold the sound of the sea. This one seems to whisper Evil Truths that seek to undo all my certainties.

I should not listen to it, just like I did not listen to the pygmy bear. I ought to hide the shell and never look at it again. No doubt it is the reason for Celeste's continued bouts of Confusion. Now I have relieved her of its burden, she will no doubt make wonderful Improvements. Yet in possessing it myself, I worry that my own Affliction will begin to worsen.

I could destroy the shell. But I do not want to. Perhaps this shows I am already falling under its Evil Influence! And yet I began this journal seeking to unravel the mysteries of this House, and the shell is undeniably a very great Mystery. I cannot solve it if I simply destroy it.

There is another option. I can hide the shell. If I put it away and do not look at it or think of it, surely it cannot harm me. Then, when Celeste has sufficiently Improved, the two of us could study it together, as sisters again, the way we used to be.

Where could it be hidden? Not in my room. The Boy is constantly rifling through my things; I would be too tempted to look at it; and besides Querazade is in here. Granted she is trapped for now, but I cannot keep her in her conch forever. Sooner or later, I will need to let her out, and somehow convince her not to tell Father what she has already seen.

Where else then, if not my room? The Jewelled Chamber is not suitable either, as Father frequents there too much. The shell would be quite well disguised in the kitchens where the Boy is made to sleep, for I could conceal it quite easily amongst all the rubbish and filth. But it would be easily lost, too. The pygmy bear dwells in the Yellow Shrine almost constantly, and as I am avoiding him, that is not an option either.

Ah!

But of course!

The only viable place is the hallway! That is why Celeste was wandering about there last night: she kept the shell hidden behind one of the pillars. No doubt it had become slightly enmeshed within that shifting braid of Dancing Stone, and she was endeavouring to retrieve it. Or else Father's Punishing had made her forget where it had been placed.

Keeping it in the hallway is risky. There is the danger of detection, but there is also the chance that the shell might sink inside a pillar if it is left beside one for too long. Or it might be swallowed by a stone fish.

And yet what if I managed to balance it on the candle sconces, which line the Hallway walls? They do not sink. They are always there. The Boy does light them, each dawn, as he did yesterday. But I could tuck the shell behind the candles, and besides, I have already surmised that his eyesight is poor on account of his stones . . .

I am decided! I shall put the shell in the hallway, on the candle sconce to the left of my door. That way, if I ever need it, I can retrieve it very quickly. And furthermore, if Celeste ever thinks to search for it, I am likely to hear her.

. . . Done! I have just gone and hidden it. The shell is balancing at the base of the three bronzed curves that bend like swans' necks from the wall, and hold dripping candles at the end. There it shall wait. Until Celeste has a chance to Improve.

ENTRY 35: STILL LATER (WHAT TO DO WITH QUERAZADE?)

Only one small problem left to solve, and then all will be well.

Querazade is still trapped in her conch. I cannot keep her there forever. Sooner or later, I will have to let her out. Not only will the Boy grow suspicious if she does not swim into my ear tonight, but it is exceedingly Cruel to confine someone within their home. I know how that feels. I shall not do it. I won't.

And yet, once I free her, how can I be sure Querazade will not tell the Boy about the shell, and that I left my room last night?

I cannot be sure. That is the honest answer. I shall just have to believe in her. It is funny that my future has come down to so small and slight a Power as Trust.

ENTRY 36: MOMENTS AFTER (QUERAZADE IS DEAD)

Havoc and disaster!

I let Querazade out, and it could not have gone more terribly.

I still cannot believe what has just occurred. Did it Truly happen? Or am I dreaming?

No, if I were dreaming then Querazade would be with me, nibbling up this nightmare until it was gone from my head.

She is dead. My poor little dreamfish is no more.

I want to write more of what happened, but I cannot. The slavestones keep hurrying the Boy in and out of my room, to question me and comfort me. And though he tries not to appear too obvious, I know he is being made to watch me too, for any signs that I am Confused.

I will write later. Now I must put this book away, and pretend that I do not know how Querazade was killed.

ENTRY 37: EVENING (THE PYGMY BEAR DID IT)

Querazade's conch is still beside my bed, empty. I keep looking at it, wondering if it could have gone differently. If I had said something, done something else, perhaps she might still be alive now.

Was I wrong to trust her?

What else could I have done?

I don't know. I don't know. Everything is so Confused right now.

It began when I picked up the conch and spoke to Querazade. I said several things.

I told her that I was going to let her out. (This was True.)

I told her that she had to promise me first not to tell the Boy anything about what happened last night, or the object I found. (This was also True.)

I told her that if she broke her promise, she would be killed. (This was a lie, although it turned out True.)

Inside her shell, I could sense Querazade listening quietly to everything that I had to say.

'Do you promise me?' I asked her. 'If you agree to promise, glow red.'

I waited, until finally in my hands the conch emitted a dull reddish glow.

'Good,' I said, satisfied. 'Now I shall be letting you out. Remember your promise. Remember what will happen to you if you break it.'

I put the conch down on my bedside table and paused a little before I released Querazade. Maybe I sensed the Havoc that was about to come. Although perhaps that is just hindsight. Because in the end, I reached into the conch and withdrew the socks and let Querazade go free.

She fluttered out into the air, stretching out all her fins and fronds, so that she looked like an orchid unfurling its petals. Her eyes blinked and squinted in the morning light. Then they darted to the open door, and I knew in that instance that whatever vow she had made me was worthless. I should not have trusted her. She was about to tell the Boy, who would then be made to tell Father.

I made a wild grab with my hands to stop her, but she darted out of reach, avoiding me easily. She floated in the air above my head, and looking up I saw Vengeance in her tiny flashing eyes.

'You will be Punished so terribly for this,' she said.

'Querazade!' I tried to sound threatening, but I could not control the panic in my voice. 'If you do this, then I will—'

'No,' she chirped at me. 'No you will not. After he's done with you, you won't even remember this happening. And if you do, I will just eat the memories up, as is my purpose.'

Then she swam through the air, fast as an arrow, heading for the door. I broke forward, but I was too late. I was never getting there in time. With a swish, she was gone. I kept running even though it was hopeless, even though I would not catch her before she reached the Boy. My thoughts were like a sea in a storm. The Confusion came in waves. And from the blackest oblivion of my mind, a half-forgotten terror was rising up. Father was going to Punish me. I was going to be Punished.

I started to sob. I began to call out. I yelled for help, even though there was no one to save me. As I said, I was Confused. I half fell out of my room and into the candlelit hallway to see Querazade glimmering through the air at speed. Already she was past Celeste's room and at the Yellow Shrine.

That is when the pygmy bear pounced from behind one of the hallway pillars. He moved so quick. In one leap and

240

one quick sweep of his arm, it was done. Querazade made not a sound as the glass blade flashed in the gloom. She simply fell apart into two pieces, which fluttered to the ground as slowly as a severed ribbon.

The sharpness of a knife, I told the pygmy bear when last we talked, matters not when fighting a man like my Father. But for a dreamfish, sharpness is enough.

I was in such a Confusion and Panic that it took me some time to comprehend what had just happened. Somewhere I could hear the Boy calling from down the hallway, drawn by my shouts and my crying. But for now there was only the pygmy bear and myself, and the poor thing that had once been Querazade.

'Love and Mercy,' I said. My voice trembled. I didn't recognise the way it sounded. It seemed rougher than before. Less Ladylike. Witnessing Querazade die had shaken me to my core, and parts of me that have long been buried had somehow been unearthed.

'Why did you do that?' I asked the pygmy bear. 'You should not have . . . why did you do that?'

'I will tell them it is because you were a big meanie,' said the pygmy bear. 'Because of your nasty words.'

By then the Boy had arrived, his paper slippers rustling across the undulations on the floor of Dancing Stone.

'Oh, Crockett,' he sobbed, both gemstones weeping. 'Oh, Crockett, oh, what did you do?'

'What I do best,' said the little creature proudly. 'Chopping baddies!'

'But he'll kill you,' the Boy cried out, as if he were the one dying.

I had never seen him like this. He raised his hands up to his eyes, as if to tear away the slavestones. Then slowly, his trembling arms lowered again, until the Boy was back under their control.

'You wicked little thing,' he was made to say coldly. 'Come with me at once.'

And the slavestones made the Boy lead the pygmy bear away down the hallway, into a part of the House that I cannot reach. He disappeared through the entrance to the East Wing. I have not seen him since. Nor am I expecting to ever again. Father expects the Pets of this House to be amusing and Obedient. Just as the Daughters are.

I remember, when the two of us spoke outside the Yellow Shrine, and I was Cruel with my words. I told him he was pathetic. I said he was beaten. I called him a plaything. But when I remember him walking away into the East Wing, he looked none of those things.

He looked like a warrior.

Like a warrior who was still fighting.

I did not think that I would miss him, but I will. I do.

ENTRY 38: BEFORE BED (I DISCOVER I AM LOVED)

Before bed I took a lit candle from the Middle Hallway and placed it on my bedside table, where Querazade's conch used to sit. When the slavestones brought the Boy to me just now with some rose petal tea to calm my nerves, he looked at the candle and touched my shoulder soothingly.

'A nice way to remember your dreamfish,' he said.

I did not tell the Boy that it is the pygmy bear that I am mourning. Strangely, I do not miss Querazade at all. I am even somewhat excited to dream tonight without her. For of all the mysteries in this House, my own mind is the most puzzling, and before her Demise my dreamfish revealed that she has been nibbling up my memories, not my Confusion.

The Boy was told to take my cup and lay me down, and bring the quilt up to my shoulders. 'You are very quiet tonight,' the slavestones told him to say.

'I am wondering when Father will return,' I said. 'Perhaps this Gram he has gone to murder is proving especially hard to kill?'

'Oh, definitely. She's a tough nut, your Gram.'

'You know her?' I asked the Boy, intrigued.

But his slavestones flashed, as they do sometimes when he does something disobedient, and he winced and did not answer me.

'Boy?' I said. 'What will happen to the pygmy bear?'

The slavestones allowed him a reply. But they could not stop the grief from wobbling his voice. 'Your Father will deal with Crockett when he returns.'

'I see,' I said. 'I see.'

And then my own voice shook and I found that I was crying. For Crockett, for Celeste, for all of us, for everything. I hung my head and sobbed into my hands as the Boy came rustling over to hug me, and he was crying too. He put his arms around me as my tears blotted onto his paper sleeves. And we stayed that way until all the tears left me and I felt empty and ruined but less alone.

'It's OK, Matilda. It's going to be OK.' I was so close to the Boy that I could feel his voice against the back of my head. It was him speaking, not the slavestones. I don't know how I knew, but I did.

What happened next was most unexpected. I am still not entirely sure whether it truly happened, or if, in my increasing Confusion, I imagined it.

After he bid me goodnight, the Boy bowed, and left my room. There is nothing unusual in this: he always bows to me whenever he leaves my presence, as is only proper for a servant to do.

But I have explained here before how there are numerous curtseys and bows: ones given between servant and master; between strangers; between friends; between Daughters and Fathers; and so on, and so forth. I studiously learned these many forms of greeting and goodbye, in order to be as Ladylike as possible for the opera.

Departing my room, the Boy did not give me the customary servant's farewell, but performed instead the goodbye known as The Beloved. His head dipped and the fingertips of his right hand touched to his heart and then to his lips, then made a circle shape with his thumb

244

and forefinger. *With love and caresses, always* – that is what those actions signify.

I could do nothing but stare dumbly as he departed. My first reaction, as I have already written, was to dismiss the farewell as a trick played upon my mind by my mounting Confusion. But then I remembered all the times that the Boy has spoken to me with tenderness, and all the pots of rose petal tea that he brings to me, and how he sits and strokes my arm whenever my days are Grey. Father never does these things. Only the Boy. And it is not the slavestones that make him do them. Not all of them. It is something else. Some higher Power.

Love.

The Boy Loves me.

Not in Father's way, but in his own fashion, that is devoted and kind.

I did not realise before now that there is more than one way that you can Love and be Loved. Like all other things, Love comes in infinite Patterns. It does not have to be Cruel. And it can emerge, too, as slowly as a fish from Dancing Stone, and change how you see things forever.

ENTRY 39: NINE DAYS SINCE THE OPERA (I DREAM OF MA)

Last night I dreamed the tyrannosaur dream again. And this time, I knew who else was there, with me and with Hush.

It was our mother.

Our mother, who loved us both so fiercely; who was so slight in her Power, but so mighty in her love.

Our mother, who taught me how to clean a shotgun, and win at *Triumvirate*, and drive a truck, and keep a T-Rex in the backyard.

I dreamed about her big bearhug cuddles. And the way she kissed my freckles. How I would push her away and tell her how embarrassing she was, but I would be smiling when I said it. And my smile would make her smile too.

I loved her so very, very dearly.

Her name was Cora. I have not said nor written nor thought that name in a very, very long time.

When I woke up, I started to cry. Because it was like she'd gone away, all over again. Why did you leave us, Mother? Where did you go? If you were here now, you'd stop him. Don't ask me how, but you would. Yes, Father is mighty, but all his Power dwindles to nothing when it comes up against Love.

ENTRY 40: LATER ON (I RE-READ MY EARLIER DIARY ENTRIES)

I began this diary in the days before Father took Celeste and me to the opera. I remember when he first told us of this trip. How excited I was to go! Reading back those first entries, that girl seems like a stranger to me. I suppose in a way she is. I am not the same Matilda as the one who started this diary, all those many nights and pages ago. The Matilda

246

who writes these words is much less Obedient, and far more deceitful, and very, very angry.

I think I much prefer her.

She feels much more me.

ENTRY 41: TEN DAYS SINCE THE OPERA (I FREE THE SUGAR MICE)

Just before breakfast this morning, Father returned to the House in the foulest temper. Presumably, his Adventure in the Worlds beyond here did not go as he hoped. The 'Gram' he is so keen on murdering must continue to elude him.

Celeste eats alone in her room now, attended by no one, so it was just Father and I at the table, with the Boy waiting upon us. I chattered away in the silence, about dresses and curtseys and nonsense, trying to brighten Father's mood.

'Quiet,' Father snapped.

'What is it, Father?' I asked.

'I told you to be quiet,' he said, louder.

And I dropped my eyes to hide my Confusion, for I was sure that he had just said my name.

'What happened with the pygmy bear whilst I was gone?' he asked suddenly. 'I hear he went berserk in the Middle Hallway. Killed your dreamfish?'

I nodded.

'So I must get you a new one,' Father muttered, half to himself. 'Yet another expense. And I hear he spoke, too?'

'Yes, Father. It was Celeste who taught him.'

'I see. And did he say why he killed the dreamfish?'

I remembered what Crockett had told me, and so I did not need to lie. 'He said it was because I was mean to him. A few days before, I called him a pathetic little plaything.'

Father's scowl became a grin, and his little songbird laugh burst suddenly from his lips. 'You said that?' He clapped his hands in delight. 'Oh, peachflower! That really has tickled me.' He laughed again and shook his head and wiped at the corner of one eye. I had no idea what was so funny, but I smiled too.

'Vicious,' he said admiringly. 'Just vicious. My peachflower has a few thorns to her still! Just as well. You are a Rapture, after all. Can't be all sweetness and light.'

'Father,' I said, and gave him the Curtsey of Parental Honour. 'What will you do with . . . with that horrid creature?'

'With the pygmy bear?' Father sounded surprised. 'I dealt with it already. It'll be much better behaved now that it's a rock, again.'

I swallowed down the lump in my throat. 'But much less fun to tease,' I managed to say.

Father began laughing all over again and even stood up to applaud me, as if I had just performed an opera for him. Then he poured himself more Bliss, and began pulling all the tails off the sugar mice that were heaped in his bowl. I could hear their little chorusing squeaks even from all the way over in my seat, so high and sweet and pain-filled, that

248

I winced and clenched my teeth. Poor sugar mice. Poor Crockett. Poor all of us who are trapped here.

'Now tell me,' Father said casually. 'How has your sister behaved these last few days?'

'She keeps to her own regimen,' I said carefully.

'And will do a little longer. She's insolent and conniving. The Boy tells me she snuck in to the kitchens one breakfast and made herself toast. And then there is the matter of teaching the pygmy bear to talk again. She may need another Punishing to fully straighten her out.'

That darkened his mood again, and mine. We fell back to silence. I looked down at my own bowl of sugar mice, trembling and staring up at me with their poppy seed eyes. They filled me with a sudden revulsion and pity. It was as if I were Truly seeing them for the very first time. How many breakfasts have I have eaten sugar mice, and enjoyed doing so? Yet suddenly the notion of pinching one up by the tail, popping it into my mouth, and crunching down with my teeth to stop its panicked wriggles . . .

I pushed my bowl away. Everything in this House was becoming Cruel and Hideous to me – even the breakfasts. *Do not let your disgust show*, I told myself.

There was a rustle behind my chair as the Boy approached me. 'Are you finished, Matilda?'

I nodded mutely, afraid that if I spoke, I might vomit.

'Pass me your bowl.' He held out his hands, but I hesitated.

'Where will you take them?' I kept my voice just a murmur, so as not to disturb Father.

'Only to the kitchens, to be boiled down to caramel.'

I shouldn't have asked. Knowing that, what could I do? I no longer wanted to eat the sugar mice, but the thought of them being tipped into a hot pan and melted into caramel was just as horrible.

There was only one other course of action: in picking up the bowl and passing it to the Boy, I feigned to have it slip from my fingers. It tipped onto the gemstone floor.

All at once, there was Bedlam. The bowl smashed into big triangle-shaped pieces, and the sugar mice were freed. Some of the more fragile ones broke in half from the fall, but the others scattered and ran. They went under the table and towards the door. Some of them hid beneath the Boy's trouser legs. He let out a yell and tripped over his own slippers and I bolted from my chair and caught his hand to stop him from falling.

'WHAT IN HAVOC,' Father hollered from the head of the table. He slammed his hands on the table as he stood and aimed his thimblefinger at the fleeing mice. Any who came under the focus of his Power unpatterned at once into granules of sugar. But he had been so startled that he could not get them all, and more than a few managed to escape into the hallway. I tried not to look triumphant as I watched them vanish, but it was too hard. As I helped the Boy back to his feet, I had to look downwards in order to hide my smile.

'Forgive me, Master Rapture,' the Boy said, giving him the Bow of Supplication.

'Clear up this damn mess.'

'I will, Master Rapture.' The Boy bowed again.

'And lay down some toffee traps in the hallway to catch the sugar mice.'

I was no longer smiling. I felt wretched with guilt. The Boy was trembling so badly that his paper apron rustled and scraped in the silence.

'It was not the Boy's fault, Father—' I began.

'You shut your mouth,' he said, jabbing his thimblefinger at me.

And I did.

Like a good Daughter.

I am lucky though, that the Jewelled Chamber is so dim, and that the silver table is so long, else he would have felt my hatred coming off me like heat from a flame.

The Boy was already on his knees, collecting up the broken plate pieces and little piles of sugar. I bent down to help, but Father barked again, making us both jump.

'THAT'S HIS JOB. YOU DON'T HELP.'

I made the Curtsey of Beseeching Forgiveness. 'Yes, Father. Of course, Father.'

He shook his head at me, appalled. Then turned and muttered a curse. Perhaps he thought he did it soft enough that I could not hear it, but I did. It was one of the middle-to-worst ones – the one that starts with 'S'. Then he spat sideways and stomped out of the Jewelled Chamber. I listened to his steps fade away before I spoke.

'Boy—'

'It's OK,' the Boy hissed at me, hurrying to the kitchens for a broom and the toffee traps. 'Go to your room. Keep out of his way until he calms. I don't want you getting Punished on account of his temper.'

And so I returned to my room. By the Yellow Shrine, a sugar mouse darted across the floor between two pillars. I barely noticed. I was too busy thinking thoughts that were both Unladylike and foul. All manner of curses were remembering themselves in my mind, not just the one that Father had let slip. They ran round and round my head like sugar mice in a bowl, until at last I whispered some aloud in an attempt to be rid of them.

I said the 'B' one, and the 'S' one, and the one which begins with 'F', which is the worst curse of all.

It was wrong of me to do that. Cursing is Vulgar and Awful. I know this to be Truth. Yet it felt so good to say them. Like hugging old friends that I had not seen for a long, long time.

It is as Father says. What good is a peachflower without a few thorns?

ENTRY 42: LATER ON (I RESOLVE TO TRUTHEN MY WORDS)

I've been thinking a bit about curses this morning.

Saying them made me realise how fancy I talk and write. All these long-winded words and highfalutin' phrases! Well, to Havoc with them. I'm done. Got far too much to write to waste time on all that ornamentation. (Very well, fine: some long words are useful, but only when there's no smaller one that comes to mind.)

Anyway, somehow it just feels good, writing things plain and writing them quick. Havoc knows that whenever I put my pen down, I still have to act like some Ladylike peachflower. So from now on, this book is gonna be a space where I can be something else. Something True.

ENTRY 43: LATE THAT NIGHT (I FIND GOBI)

Late at night I wake. Not from any dreams. Not even from memories.

I wake because of a little voice calling, just outside my door.

'My stuck,' it says in the hallway. 'Oh deary.'

I sit up straight in my bed, in the dark and the quiet, listening.

'Hushy?' says the voice. 'Hushy help?'

It isn't Celeste, or the Boy, or Father. For a moment I wonder if it's Celeste's dreamfish, J'lzacoatl. As far as I know, she's the only other living creature now residing in the House (apart from a few sugar mice, which cannot talk.)

But it doesn't sound like a dreamfish. At least, it doesn't sound like how Querazade had sounded.

'Helloo? Uh-oh, no no.'

Perhaps this is one of Father's Tests, I think with a shudder. Perhaps he's waiting outside in the hallway, to see if Celeste or I are disobedient enough to go out there.

And yet the voice doesn't feel like a trick. Instead, it feels somehow familiar.

I get out of bed and tiptoe to my door. Take the handle and open it, silent as I can. Out in the hallway, the dark is deep and cold. No candles lit at all. I blink. I steady my nerves. I stare into the blackness.

'Who's there?' I whisper.

And down by my feet, a happy voice says, 'Tilly-Boo?'

ENTRY 44: VERY LATE THAT NIGHT (I RECEIVE THE NOTE)

He calls himself Gobi, and according to him, we're old friends. Which is all kinds of awkward, because I've no idea who he even is, or what for that matter.

'Stop sliming up my bedsheets,' I tell him.

'My sorry,' he says back.

I'm sat on my bed. Gobi's on my pillow. This book is on my lap. I'm taking notes as we talk. It's still the middle of the night, but something tells me this can't wait until morning. This little snailcritter knows me, though his name for me is strange.

It seems I liked to be called Tilly-Boo, once, back when I was someone else – a Matilda who didn't mind ridiculous nicknames.

What else does this critter remember? I have to find out. This whole diary began as a way to try and solve some of the House's mysteries. Well, it feels like I'm about to finally get some answers for the first time since I don't even know when.

I can't believe I thought his shell was empty at first. Why did I think that? Was I Confused? Or maybe he was camouflaged?

'Hey!' I tell him suddenly. 'Don't eat that.'

Gobi swivels his little eyes at me, then back at the toffee strip that he's determinedly heading for. 'But it tasty, so tasty.'

'You'll get stuck again. You know that toffee strips are traps, not treats?'

The eyes roll on their stalks. 'My know that now.'

The toffee strip was where I found him, trapped. It was stuck down behind the pillar to the left of my door. The Boy must have put it there to catch the runaway sugar mice. Instead, he caught a Gobi. The toffee strip's sweet butterscotch smell lured the snailcritter out of his shell and coaxed him down from the sconce where I hid him a few days past.

'It's a good job I rescued you before morning came, Gobi.'

'Good jobby,' he agrees.

I nod.

I hesitate.

What's the best way to say this?

I decide on: 'Gobi, if it's OK with you, I'd like to talk.'

He nods. 'Me see if they can.'

This throws me. What does he mean? Before I can ask, the snailcritter shrinks back inside his shell until I can't see him no more.

'Gobi?' I say. 'Gobi?'

When I pick the shell up, it's empty. I don't know how. It just is. Just as empty as it was before. Where'd he go? I say a bunch of curses out loud.

I'm using my pen to dig around inside the shell when suddenly I hear him say, 'No jabby!' His voice sounds very faint and far away, like we're at opposite ends of a long tunnel.

'Gobetween,' I murmur.

I haven't said that word, *known* that word, for the longest time. But it comes back to me now. From some deep-down place within me that Father's Power couldn't touch. I remember it.

'Tilly-Boo?' Gobi's snaily body emerges from the shell with something gripped in his eyestalks. It's a little strip of paper, rolled-up tight, so that it's about the size of a matchstick. Gobi offers it up to me.

'There go. Talky.' He bobs his head. 'Little quicky scribbly wibbly.'

I don't understand. Not until I take the paper and unscroll it and see the writing.

'Who—?' My heart's beating so fast I can barely speak. 'Who is this from?'

'Gram,' says Gobi.

ENTRY 45: ELEVEN DAYS SINCE THE OPERA
(I DECIDE WHETHER TO REPLY)

MATILDA? THAT YOU?

That's what the spidery black handwriting on the note says. I'm holding it in my palm now. I'm reading it for the fiftieth time. Trying to decide whether to reply.

I have to make a choice quickly. It'll be dawn soon. The Boy will be coming to wake me and lay out my dress for the day.

MATILDA? THAT YOU?

I close my eyes and imagine another Pattern, another world, where right now, someone called Gram is sitting beside a shell like I am, waiting for an answer.

Father told me she was dangerous. Said Gram wants to destroy our family. That's why he went away last time. He tried to kill her but he failed. Which means this Gram is real powerful. I don't know of anyone else, ever, who has managed to stop him doing what he wants.

Actually, that's not True. I know one other person. I know my sister. Celeste hasn't let him change her into something Ladylike, something Daughterly, something proper.

The way that I did.

I look at the note again.

MATILDA? THAT YOU?

I shouldn't write back.

If I write back, there's no undoing it.

But before I can stop myself, I get this pen and scribble beneath it: MAYBE. Then I scrunch it up into a little ball and thrust it at Gobi. The little critter takes it into his shell, and vanishes again.

I chew my nails for maybe half a minute before an answer comes back. I snatch at it. A fresh little sheet.

It says:

WHAT DO YOU REMEMBER? ARE YOU STILL IN HIS HOUSE? ALONE? SAFE? WHERE'S HUSH? SHE STOPPED WRITING AND GOBI CAN ONLY TELL US SO MUCH.

She has written on both sides, which is very thoughtless, because now there's no room for me to answer. I have to waste a whole bunch of time ripping a little corner from my notebook to write my reply, and twice as I try to tear them, the diamond-wafer pages shatter into pieces. I sweep all the shards off my covers and under my bed to hide them. Slice one of my fingers in the process. Now there's blood on one of my pillows. I turn it over so no one will notice. But the amount of evidence that I'm needing to cover up is growing with every second: a ruined toffee strip, Gobi's slime trails on my bedsheets, shards of diamond-wafer under my bed, blood upon my pillow, forbidden messages in my palm.

I write back to Gram:

YOU WILL ANSWER MY QUESTIONS FIRST.
ALSO, STOP WRITING MORE THAN ONE SIDE.
I DON'T HAVE MUCH PAPER.

Then I draw a cross face that looks like this:

So she will know that I am pissed.

Whilst I wait for Gram's reply, I suck at my bloody thumb, and write these words, and glance every few seconds at the night outside my window as it lightens. I'm almost out of time, and so far, I don't seem to have found out anything new from this Gram.

Love and Mercy, why can't anyone just give me answers?

The next note comes on a much larger sheet. It just says,

OH, MATILDA. IT IS YOU!

WHAT DO YOU WANT TO KNOW?

I'LL TELL YOU ANYTHING.

That's thrown me. For so long now I've been like a dog beneath a dinner table, waiting on tiny scraps of Truth to get tossed my way: a knowing glimpse, a coded curtsey, a half-remembered dream.

Now, Gram's telling me to pull up a seat and tuck in.

I tear off a small strip from the sheet Gram sent and write a flurry of stuff down:

HOW DID YOU STOP FATHER FROM KILLING YOU? ARE

YOU MORE POWERFUL THAN HE IS? WHY DO YOU WANT

TO CONFUSE ME AND DESTROY OUR FAMILY?

I have more, so much more, that I want to say, but I run out of space to write. And when I put down my pen and read it all back, it's like the ramblings of a loon. I've barely talked with this Gram for five minutes, and already she's sent me half-crazy with Confusion. Just like Father warned.

I scrunch up the paper and stuff it under my mattress. Tear off another precious bit of paper.

HOW CAN I TRUST YOU? I ask.

I scrunch that one up too.

'Quit being wasteful,' I mutter at myself.

I've got to be smart. I've got to think. I need to Test her somehow. Like Father does. So I can be sure that she'll tell me the actual Truth, and not just what she wants me to hear.

I end up sending her this:

TELL ME ABOUT MY PET STEGOSAURUS. THE ONE I
GOT FROM THE WORLD THAT WAS ALL
AISLES AND SHELVES.

Gram's answer comes back, on one side, just like I've asked.

IT WASN'T NO STEGOSAURUS, she says.

IT WAS A T-REX. YOU CALLED IT MR CHOMPY OR
SOMETHING. AIN'T TOO SURE. IT WAS YOUR MOTHER
WHO BOUGHT IT FOR YOU. BACK BEFORE THE WORLDS-
WAR. PROBABLY FROM THINGUMMY BOB'S? THINK
HUSH GOT HER INFINITE CAP FROM THERE.
SO YOU DONE TESTING ME FOR NOW? OR DO YOU STILL
GOT QUESTIONS?

I write: I GOT QUESTIONS.

And I ask them all. I surely do. Every single one.

ENTRY 46: JUST BEFORE DAWN (I KNOW WHO I AM NOW)

Imagine flowers, right? Flowers, after the longest, coldest winter. Poking their heads up above ground and spreading their petals in the spring sun.

Now think of someone moving through a darkened house, round all the unlit rooms, and turning all the lamps on, one by one. Until everything's illuminated and that house is a home again.

Just one more, OK? Try to feel what it's like to get suckerpunched in the belly at point blank range. How that knocks the wind right out of you, and sends you to your knees, and makes you want to hurl.

Like a punch in the gut, like a light turning on, like life coming alive. That's how it felt just now, to finally read Gram's Truth. That's what it was like to be remembering who I am. It was wonderful and scary and joyous and sickening, all at the very same time. Because as Gobi passed messages thick and fast from Gram to me and back again, one version of Matilda kind of died, the same time as another, older Matilda sprung back to life.

Because I am not some demure little dress-wearing, curtsey-performing peachflower. No sir. That ain't me. Begging your pardon, Mr Rapture, but I curse and I spit and I listen to murder-ballads. I keep pet tyrannosaurs and I take my coffee black. I shoot people who piss me off with a shotgun full of bees. You get me?

I'm not your daughter.

I am Matilda Quiet.

And I know what you did to my ma.

ENTRY 47: A LITTLE LATER ON
(I WRITE WHAT MAY BE MY FINAL ENTRY)

It's morning now. The Boy just came in with a bow. Asked me if I was awake and I told him yes. Yes I surely am. Got a weird look for the way I spoke. Reckon my old Dustbowl accent is already creeping back into my voice. Ah well. It hardly matters now.

This might well be the last time I write in you, diary. Didn't think I'd be welling up at that fact, but I am. I'll never forget what you've done for me. You've shown me not just who I am but who I want to be.

It's funny: I don't remember ever having much of a fondness for words before Rapture brought me here. Always reckoned them to be Hush's domain. I was the practical sister. The one who prioritised doing. That's where I thought my power was. Driving a car, shooting a shotgun. The one time I actually tried using words to get somewhere, I got myself in all kinds of trouble.

But those letters to Nate weren't Truth, were they? That's why they led to no good. Because I wove a web of lies with them, and found myself trapped in it.

You got to aim for Truth. That's what I didn't know

before. Aim for Truth and words'll lead you there, as sure as a silver waythread will. And the Truth is the only thing that my father, James Décollage Rapture, is afraid of.

I know that I've fought him before. I know that I've never won. Not ever. But this time, it'll be different. I know a way to beat him. I think I've known for a long time. Ever since I first spoke to Crockett.

Truth can hurt, I told him. And I was right. Truth's a blade that'll cut deeper than any knife. Maybe that's why Crockett saved me from Querazade. Because he knew that I could win with words. Words that wield the Truth.

I've told all this to Gram, too. Written it down and given it to Gobi to pass to her. She didn't say anything to try and stop me. I think she could tell that there wasn't any point in even trying. Guess she really does know the real me.

I'M ROOTING FOR YOU, MATILDA, she wrote back.

LOVE AND TRUTH ARE MIGHTY WEAPONS.

BUT JUST IN CASE, TAKE THIS TOO.

And alongside the note, she sent a thimble.

I slip it on and close my eyes. Feel the Pattern around me. See the waythreads spiralling out from my feet. The sleepy grey route to my bed, and the candy pink line to my vanity table, and the fresh blue one that leads to my bath. I let them fall from my mind. Focus on the waythread that leads out of my door, red as a trail of blood. There's danger in that colour. Hatred and violence too. But ain't red also the colour of love, the colour of living?

I'm gonna walk it, diary. See where it leads.

Wish me all the luck in all the worlds.

ENTRY 48: UPON THE RED WAYTHREAD

Upon the red waythread, still in my nightdress, I walk the Middle Hallway of Dancing Stone. I go past all the rooms that I am allowed to go: Hush's room, the Jewelled Chamber and the Yellow Shrine.

I could go back and get Hush. Maybe even take off Kid's slavestones and rescue him too. We could all cross to another world.

No. There's no point. He'll only find us. He will.

And besides, I'm not leaving here without what he took from Ma.

My slippers make no sound against the marble floor. Or if they do, I do not hear. On this waythread, I am half in this Pattern and half out of it. Havoc faintly hisses, somewhere beyond the dark. The House shifts around me like jewelled smoke. I am crossing beyond the hallway. I am passing through the East Wing. I am in a part of the House that I have never visited before. The waythread wobbles beneath me but I pin it in place until it ends and the world suddenly comes into full focus and—

I find myself on a long platform, lit with dim lamps and built from yellow stone in the Carcosan style. Ahead of me sits a steam train, facing a dark tunnel. The train's not moving. The engine's not chugging.

All's still.

I am trembling. I know this dark locomotive. I've seen it before, many worlds ago. This is what he used to hunt us down. This is what he used to bring us back to the House. This is where he is.

I step up into the first carriage. It smells of oiled wood and lavender cologne and something else that I can't quite place, but which turns out to be the scent of flesh.

The carriage is filled with different parts of people, all hung up like costumes, ready for wearing. Racks of hands, slender and limp, hang upon brass pegs. Eyes, arrayed like cufflinks or earrings, sparkle inside glass cabinets on beds of black velvet. Glass jars on shelves rattle with the laughs trapped within them. And pinned onto squares of red backing are Rapture's neat moustaches, all laid out in a row like specimens of moths.

This is his dressing chamber.

This is where he Improves himself.

I walk past the neat arrangements of other people's Patterns, that Rapture has stolen to weave into his own hideous tapestry. I cross into the next carriage. I see a glass door with a golden handle. What's beyond the door is hidden by a pink ruffled curtain.

I'm so scared because I know that he's in there. And he knows that I'm out here. And he's just waiting.

I grip the handle and pull and step into Rapture's cabin. He's sitting by his bed at a little round table, filling his cup from a pot of Bliss. Everything about him is as immaculate as ever. Not a wrinkle to his skin, not a crease to his suit. I remind myself that that's all just surface. It's not the Truth.

'Morning, peachflower,' Rapture says between sips. 'You're up early. Come to kill me?'

I shake my head. 'Come to talk.'

He doesn't let it show, but I know from the way he pauses to sip at his tea that I've surprised him. That's good. This needs to be fun for him. He has to toy with me, the way he used to do with Crockett. If he feels threatened, he'll just cut out my words before I have a chance to say them.

'Well, go on then.' He gestures for me to sit. 'What do you want to say to me?'

I just shake my head again. 'I'm not here to talk to you.'

His songbird laugh flutters. 'No?'

'Not exactly.'

He looks at me, amused. 'This is different from all your previous Mischief, you know.'

'I know it. All that stuff was stupid. Knives and explosions ain't gonna beat you. That ain't where you're weak. That ain't how she beats you.'

'She?' Rapture's look of bemusement remains on his face like a mask, but his eyes narrow. 'Who are you talking about?'

I've annoyed him. But he's also intrigued. That's good. I've got a chance. I go to reach into the pocket of my nightdress, but his thimblefinger raises up.

'Nuh-ah-ah,' Rapture says. 'Not so fast.'

The sharp edge of his power dangles above like a guillotine. All he has to do is bring it down on me. I wait. His eyes flicker as he feels the Pattern.

'Paper?' He sounds somewhat disappointed. 'That's it?'

'It's a letter,' I say.

'Strange choice of weapon.' Rapture chuckles. 'Haven't letters gotten you into trouble before?'

'I guess they have. But I was writing to the wrong person then.'

Rapture claps his thigh delightedly. 'I think I've guessed your tactic: be as mysterious as possible for as long as possible, so I'm too intrigued to punish you.'

I shrug. Bring out the letter slowly. 'It's all in here.'

'What is?'

'How you lose.' I'm betting everything on the assumption that he doesn't reckon words to be much of a power. My bet comes off. He just smirks. He's not afraid of a few words. But he should be.

Rapture rolls his eyes and pats the table. 'Go on then. Put it here. I admit, part of me *is* intrigued.'

I lay the letter down and slide it across to him. He Patterns himself some ivory-rimmed reading spectacles and puts them on. Not that he needs them. They're just for show. He puts down his Bliss and takes it up and unfolds it and reads. And I watch.

He doesn't realise at first. Because it isn't until the very last paragraph that I even mention Ma's name. By the time he figures out that I'm actually writing to *her*, it's too late. The words are already in him, a part of his Pattern, just like she is.

He slams the letter down. I reckoned on him doing this. But I'm ready for it. I've been watching him all the while, and I reckon I know roughly where Rapture's refused to read any further. It's the very last bit. And I speak it aloud.

'Cora,' I recite. 'Ma. You are by far the biggest part of him now. He's nothing at all compared to you. That's why he wove you into himself in the first place. To try and fill his heart up. Because it was so empty, he couldn't bear it.'

There's panic in his stare now. Because I see him. The real Rapture. I know how little of him there really is, behind that perfect stolen face. He has whittled himself away, piece by piece. He has despised and discarded almost every part of his own Pattern, until there's almost nothing left. It's just like I thought, back when I saw his new hands. Each time he changes himself, he lessens who he is. Rapture's nothing but greed and power now, and what he took from Ma.

And my words just woke her up.

'Cora,' I say, talking to the part of her that's in him. 'Cora. Ma. It's me, it's your little Mattie-Pats. That's what you used to call me, right? I never liked no one nicknaming me, except you. Remember?'

And I see it happening in his mind, just like it happened in mine. Like flowers in the spring, like a house lighting up, like a suckerpunch in the gut. The Truth blooms, it lights up, it floors him.

Rapture stands, or tries to stand. But Ma stops him. The cup of Bliss spills across the table. He raises his thimble-finger. Ma slams his hand down. He bares his teeth and snarls but I see terror in his eyes. Within him are two warring Patterns, each trying to annul the other. Rapture's love for himself, and Ma's love for me and Hush.

He weaves a gun and fires it into my face. Ma cuts the bullets from the air and the gun from his hand. Rapture shrieks and runs at me and stops. His face is hideously riven. He claws at the Yellow Sign on his neck. He spins and howls like a beast. It sounds like he's being pulled apart. He is. He's tearing in two.

'Go Ma!' I shout. 'Go Cora!'

I keep talking, keep waking her up. I tell her every memory I can muster from back when we lived in Dustbowl. The time she fried us cornbread and the pan caught on fire. Taking us down to Deeker to watch the man who blew sugar bubbles. How she would pretend to play a tiny violin whenever me or Hush gave her puppy dog eyes. That lullaby she'd sing to us to the tune of 'Janey's Lying Still', replacing the lyrics with nonsense ones about a zany frog called Bill. And each thing I say is like a waythread, reaching into Rapture and drawing her out from where he's trying to bury her.

He covers his ears. I shout. He tries to cut away my voice. I feel the edge of his power flash like thunder. But Ma twists it like a blade, and sends it at Rapture's own throat. He lets out a ragged scream that suddenly cuts to a terrible silence.

His eyes go strangely blank, and I realise he's no longer

looking at me. His gaze is turned fully inward now, to the fight within himself. I watch his mouth working in mute spasms as he aims his thimble at his own head, and closes his eyes and patterns. He's trying to cut her out, to hack her away, but she won't let him. I can feel his power skewing sideways every time it slices. He gags and cuts again. Again, again, again. No precision to any of it, just terror, just frenzy.

With each strike, another part of him falls away. His flawless porcelain skin cracks and falls in broken shards. He spits out his perfect teeth, tears off his immacualte hair, one of his slender hands drops out of his sleeves and onto the floor. All the parts of other people that Rapture has spent his whole life assembling – he cuts them away one by one.

Until at last, she falls away from him. I look into his ruin of a face and see a ruin of a man. He's hideous and wretched. A body in shreds, a mind in tatters. His mouth hangs open in a silent scream, just like that singer he brought to the opera house.

Staggering sideways, he disappears. I close my eyes to see if I can feel him, but he's not in this Pattern. Maybe he crossed upon a waythread. Maybe he fell into havoc. I don't know. I don't care. I just raise up my thimbled hand and feel the part of her that's lying there, amongst the wreckage of everything Rapture cut out of himself.

She beat him. Of course she beat him.

She's there. She was always there.

She loves us. She never stopped loving us.

'Ma,' I whisper. 'Ma.'

And I take her love, pick it up like a sleeping bird, and carry it with me out of that awful place. Away from the train and the platform, back to the dim hallways of the House. I'm crying and I'm smiling and I'm loved and I'm free. I'm stumbling and I'm still terrified but I'm with Ma and she's with me.

ENTRY 49: I SET EVERYONE FREE

After that, I free the Boy. I find him in the hallway, picking up a toffee strip full of sugar mice. As soon as the slavestones see me, they know. They get that this is Mischief of the very highest kind. They force their Boy to turn and try to run, but he's never been fast in that servant outfit. His slippers slide on the floor, heading for the kitchens, but he's not even to the door when I grab him. The slavestones make him swing his fists at me. I take the punches and just focus on the stones. My fingers are already prising them loose. The Boy claws at me, but feebly, as the slavestones lose their grip on him. I can hear their tiny screams as I shuck them from his eye sockets like stones out of a peach.

There's a wet sucking sound that makes me shudder. Then the Boy goes limp and collapses, as the two slavestones skitter like pebbles over the floor and try to crawl away on their beetle legs. I press down on each one, grinding my heel until I feel them shatter. Then I go over to the Boy that the slavestones used to own. He's slumped on the floor, face down. When I turn him over he gives a weak little moan and his hands probe at the air like an insect's feelers. I wince at the sight of his face. The stones have eaten his eyes away and left him blind.

'Love and Mercy.' I look away.

'Matilda,' the Boy mumbles. 'Is it you? Really you?'

'It's really me. More or less. We know each other, right? From before? In the peach orchard? We didn't have a name for you then, either, did we? You were just Kid?'

The Boy called Kid nods. He keeps blinking, as if his eyes are gonna suddenly regrow themselves. He starts babbling that he's sorry, that everything is his fault, that Rapture had him Patterned from my shadow so that he could track me and Hush down.

I shush him. 'Never mind all that. We're leaving, OK?'

Kid looks desolate. 'Heard you say that before. So many times . . . But he never lets you . . . I wanted to help, but the stones . . .'

'That was before. This is now. And I'm telling you that we're going. Stay here whilst I go get Hush.'

I leave him resting by a pillar and go to Hush's door. I Pattern away the hinges and kick it in and watch it slam down like a giant domino. It falls so hard it makes the walls shake. Hush is lying on her straw mattress, hugging her knees to keep herself warm. We haven't seen each other since we fought over Gobi in the hallway. And haven't spoken – *really* spoken – since way before then.

I go up to her with Ma's love and tip it gently into her hands. I don't say anything at all. I just slip my thimble over

Hush's finger and let her feel it. Then I come forward and hug her, so Ma's love is between us, and together we weep into its warmth, and we stay that way for a long time. And just in case she's still Confused, I tell Hush that we're sisters. Always have been, always will be.

And then I take her by the hands and lead her and Kid into the kitchens and sit Hush down by the stoves to warm her up. I don't know what else to do whilst we wait, so I end up making toast.

ENTRY 50: I REMEMBER HOW COFFEE HELPS TALKING

Hush butters and eats eight whole slices, one after the other. That's how I know that she's in a bad way. I've only ever seen her eat that much toast once before, right after Ma left us for Yonder. That time she ate so much, she was sick.

I reach across the kitchens' marble countertop to gently pull the loaf and the butter dish out of her reach. Hush shrinks back from me, so fast that she nearly falls off her stool. Terror crosses over her face like the shadow of a passing train. Love and Mercy, it's like she thinks I'm going to punish her!

'Relax,' I say, softly as I can. Which is not really that soft at all. And Hush doesn't look relaxed. Anxiously, she shuts her eyes, and I watch her as she feels the Pattern for Ma's love again. It's still lying there on her lap, though I can't see or feel it any more, not since I gave Hush my thimble.

'You're going to be OK,' I tell her, but she doesn't look like she's heard me. Just sits there, not saying a word. And it isn't just because she's still got a mouth full of crusts. She hasn't said anything to me or Kid since I brought her from her room. Kid reckons she's in shock. I'm hoping that he's right, that it ain't nothing deeper, that Rapture's last punishing didn't cut out some essential part of my sister that we'll never get back.

No, I tell myself. She'll mend.

I will myself to believe it. I'd find it a lot easier if I could just hear her talk. There shouldn't be this much hush around Hush. It ain't right.

'Hey, say something, will you?' I try and make my tone playful, but it comes out as pleading.

Hush gets that deer-in-headlights look again. She swallows and says, 'Something.'

I wince. 'No, that ain't what I meant.'

Hush dips her head. 'Sorry,' she whispers.

'No, no.' I shake my head. 'No, you don't have to be sorry. That's not what I . . . Never mind.'

I have to be patient. It's going to be a long, slow process, to undo what Rapture has done. He cut away all her words, all her fire. Left her silent and meek. But it's OK, because I remember the real Hush. The one who bashes a saucepan lid and sings. The one who can fill up any silence, no matter how deep. That girl's still in there, somewhere. It's just going to take time to find her again.

I back away for now, and give her some space. Which isn't easy, because there's barely any at all down here. The kitchens are stuffed to bursting with filthy stoves and sink basins filled with rancid ponds of dishwater and blown-out water boilers and mouldering food crates. Seems like whenever something down here needed fixing, Rapture would just pattern a new kitchen onto the front of the old one. That's why they're called the *kitchens,* plural. The whole thing is as long and twisty as a corridor in a labyrinth, and Kid is all the way at the end of it, standing at the only working stove.

I pick my way over the clutter, trying not to slip on cracked tiles or puddles or startled sugar mice that dart across the floor. The walls and floors and ceilings are all covered with the same green tiles, which are all covered with a thin film of yellowy grease. No wonder I hardly ever came down here. It's hot and filthy and cramped. Everything about it makes me feel vaguely queasy. The fact that Hush just put away eight slices of toast in this place only affirms how checked-out she currently is.

When I finally reach Kid, I see he's fixing coffee. Or trying his very best to. His paper sleeve is brown and soggy from where he's accidentally dipped it in the mug, and there are granules spilled all over the floor. As I come close, I startle him. He turns and knocks the milk pot over.

'Woah,' I tell him, putting my hands on him like he's a spooked horse. 'Easy, Kid. Easy.'

'I thought I'd fix coffee,' he says anxiously, trying to mop up the milk as it drips off the countertop. 'It's not going so well.'

'So stop,' I tell him firmly. 'You're standing next to a lit stove in a suit made of paper. Havoc's sake, Kid!'

He opens his mouth to say something, but just hangs his head. Now I feel bad. He's just lost his eyes, and how am I helping? Now's not the time for harsh words.

'It's OK,' I say, trying to be soft. 'You don't have to be our servant any more, you get me?'

'I know. But I thought it might help Hush.' He fumbles for the mug, and I guide him to the handle. 'I heard somewhere that coffee helps talking.'

I squint as a memory comes back to me. 'You heard it from Hush. On Gram's stoop, back in the pocket world.'

'That's right!' Kid's face lights up, and he snaps his fingers. 'Just after you shot me!'

I wince. 'Oh yeah. Sorry about that.'

Kid waves my apology away. 'I probably deserved it.'

I consider that for a moment. 'No, you *definitely* deserved it.'

His laugh sounds hollow, hollow as the spaces where his eyes used to be. I'm glad he can't see the way I must be looking at him. Coffee and buttered toast and love and time might help Hush in the end, but Love and Mercy, what about Kid? What can I do for him?

If only Crockett was still here. He'd know what to do.

'I miss that little chinchilla of yours,' I tell him.

Kid goes quiet and still and then he says, 'Me too.'

'Excuse me?' Hush says from right behind us.

Me and Kid both just about jump out of our skins. The milk pot goes over again. And the sugar jar. A particularly brazen little sugar mouse darts out from behind the coffee tin and gets its paws on a couple of granules.

'Love and Mercy!' I shout at my sister. 'How long have you been standing behind us like that?'

Hush shrinks away a little at the loudness of my voice. But only a little. She bows her head and then her right hand thrusts the thimble at Kid. Firmly. Urgently. I can see her mouth working silently, like she's trying to find the words to say.

'Excuse me?' she says again. 'Use this?'

I'm struggling to understand what Hush is trying to say, until another memory comes back to me: a little brown boulder jutting up like a gravestone, in the middle of Gram's peach orchard.

And I realise that Crockett's come back from the dead before.

'Kid,' I say slowly. 'Can you still pattern?'

'I don't know,' he says. 'I don't have a thimble, so I—'

I don't wait for him to finish, I just take the one that Hush is offering, and slip it onto his finger.

Kid straightens up. His head lifts. He laughs again, and this time I can't hear no hollowness in it. He looks straight at me and Hush, not with eyes, but with his power.

He's going to be OK. All of us are.

ENTRY 51: I WRITE THE END

When Crockett first opens his eyes and looks at us, the first thing he does is pump his fist like it's a shotgun and yell out, 'Booya! Just can't stop this *ROCK* from *ROLLING!*'

Then he looks at our stunned faces and nibbles his lip nervously. 'Just before the last time I got killed, I thought *really* hard to think of something brilliant to say if I ever came back alive again. That was what I came up with.' He slumps his shoulders. 'I guess this version of me is just not that hilarious.'

That's when we all laugh. Even Hush. And after that come the hugs, and after that, the cake. Crockett insists on it. It is, he keeps saying, technically his birthday.

• • •

That's it. That's everything that happened. So far, at least. We're still in the House, but I've written a message to Gram through Gobi, and she's tracking a waythread to find us. She'll be here any moment.

And once she gets here, she'll lead the four of us back to Travlin. We're going to live there with her. Maybe we can find our place in that town's Pattern. Maybe we can weave our hearts with theirs. At the very least, my sister and I will repay all the favours we owe.

Hush says that when we arrive, she's going to do one of her songs in the saloon. And if all them folk give us a cheer, then we'll definitely stay, because that'll be a ready-made fanbase for her music.

I'm suspecting that they'll cheer her, no matter how out of tune she sings, because it's a town that runs on kindness.

We're gonna need that kindness sorely. Rapture cut us up so bad. We're all of us bearing his scars. I lost my smile and my laugh and my freckles, and Kid lost his sight, and who knows if all of Hush's memories will come back after how awful that last Punishing was.

But I reckon we'll be OK now. Nothing stays lost forever. Just look at Crockett, just look at me. And if we can get back to what we once were, maybe Kid and Hush will too. Heck, maybe the worlds will all mend as well. Perhaps one day Carcosa will crumble and the terrible people there will Pattern themselves into oblivion, in the same way that Rapture did. Then the war can finally end and there'll be no more cutting ever again. And who knows? Perhaps Ma might come back from Yonder and find how to love us again.

Won't happen overnight. Be a long time before any of that comes to pass. I have to keep reminding myself that love's a *slow* power, not a fast one. And so I'm fine to wait and let it work.

In the meantime, I'll keep writing. Of all the ways to weave the worlds, words are mine. Once we get to Travlin, I might put it all down: everything that's happened to me and

Hush, and Kid. Because if love is our highest power, maybe words are our highest waythreads. The right words in the right order can lead you off to anywhere. I'm proof of that. Words led me to the Truth. They told me who I am. They saved my life. All our lives.

And now they've led me here, to these last two words that I have to write. Out of everything you've read, these are the only words that don't aim True. Ain't no finish to anything. Crockett's the proof of that, and Ma's love, and all of us. Life goes on, the worlds go on, the Pattern goes on and so too does the havoc. But you got to find your way through it, I guess, and all ways, whether made of words or threads, must come eventually to the place we call

THE END

Acknowledgements

A long time ago, ten years ago or more, back when I first started sending out my writing to people whom I hoped would publish it, I kept hearing the same bit of advice:

They might not want THIS book, but they might want ANOTHER one. So get a second idea ready to pitch them, just in case!

Now, that's hard to do when you're pouring everything you have into the book you're already writing, and rewriting, so that it's as perfect as you can possibly make it. But I knew that it was good advice, all the same. Getting a first book published is HARD. Sometimes, I'd heard, it could take years. And for lots of writers, it took more than one go.

So I tried to think of another idea. Something I could say I was working on, if anybody asked. It needed to be a good idea, I decided. No use having a second idea if it was about something really boring, like the construction of a roundabout in, oh, I don't know, Maidstone. No. If they didn't like my FIRST book, my second idea had to grab them from the very first sentence. With that in mind, I scribbled down the opening line to a story, and tried to put as much danger and excitement into it that I could.

This is what I came up with:

He can't outrun the horses.

Not bad, I said to myself. As a first line, I thought it was kind of cool. It made me wonder all sorts of stuff. Who is 'he'? Why is he being chased? What's going to happen when 'the horses' catch up to him?

There was only one problem, which was I had ABSOLUTELY NO IDEA what the answers were to those questions.

Now luckily for me, it turns out that someone DID want my first book. And so I never had to pitch that second idea, and have that awkward moment where someone said, 'Ooh, that story about someone running away from horses sounds cool! Tell me more!'

But I couldn't shake my curiosity about that opening line for a second idea that I'd never really had. And so, periodically, I would start to write, to see if I could find some answers.

I wrote not knowing where I was going or would end up. There was no grand design in my head. But when I found something that felt right – like the moment this boy, running for his life, stumbles on two bickering sisters – I kept it. And gradually, bit by bit, the story took shape.

I couldn't tell you all the things that I found and lost along the way. There was a foul-mouthed baby who drove a cockroach the size of a stagecoach (a roachcoach, if you will). There was a blue moustachioed lobster called Mr Deeps, who blew bubbles from a coral pipe. There was a whale that sang to itself through a sea of stone. Worlds that were woven and unpatterned again as my story warped and shifted, and teetered perilously close to havoc. I even lost that first line, you'll notice. It's a shame, but it needed to go.

Some things, however, stay constant.

Like my editor, Eloise Wilson, who ALWAYS – and I mean ALWAYS – reminds me what my stories need to be.

And my agent, Becky Bagnell, who just never, ever stops cheering me on. Like, for years now.

And then there are all the other people in my life who helped me find the waythread that led to this book: my kids, Buffy and Poe, whose toddlerisms made it into this story in the form of much of Crockett's talk; my wife, Erin, who takes on heavy burdens so that I have the time to write; Marine Studios, of Margate, where I wrote those first early drafts; the work of Ursula Kroeber Le Guin, and Susanna Clarke, and Charlotte Perkins Gilman, for inspiring much of this book; the imaginations of Ambrose Bierce, and Robert W. Chambers, who both haunted my mind with visions of Carcosa; Chloe Sackur and the team at Andersen Press, for their amazing ability to debug manuscripts and then make them infinitely better; and of course, two sisters I know called Matilda and Celeste, whose names I took for my own Pattern.

Thanks, all of you.

The final acknowledgement, though, has to go to whoever it might've been, all those years and books ago, who kept giving me that advice to come up with a second idea. It took a while, but it's here now. Hope you like it. Here's to the next great weaving.